Praise for *Reservations*:

"Florio captures the culture and poverty on reservations still suffering from greed and mismanagement in a ripped-from-the-headlines story with a shocking ending."—*Kirkus Reviews*

Praise for *Disgraced*:

"A gutsy series."—*The New York Times*

"A gut-wrenching mystery/thriller that explores prejudice and the incredible stress on soldiers in a seemingly unending war with no clear goals."—*Kirkus Reviews*

"A hallmark of the Lola Wicks series is Florio's seamless weaving of Native American communities into the narrative. The culture of the Blackfeet in Montana and North Dakota, the Shoshone in Wyoming, both on and off the reservation, come poignantly alive in characters."—*Montana Standard*

"It is the issues and ideas that [Florio] explores that got me invested in this novel … an entertaining read."—*Missoulian*

"A story that is gratifyingly real."—*Missoula Independent*

"Even as *Disgraced* pinpoints our political reality it never sacrifices its suspense."—*Bozeman Daily Chronicle*

"Lola Wicks is back and better than ever."—*Montana Quarterly*

"With the chops of a world-class journalist and an unsurpassed knowledge of the Rocky Mountain West, Gwen Florio weaves a compelling tapestry that combines family saga, social consciousness, and human frailty, making *Disgraced* difficult to put down."—Craig Johnson, author of the Walt Longmire Mysteries, the basis for the hit Netflix drama *Longmire*

"Gwen Florio achieves what few others can in the field of crime fiction. She creates characters with real depth and places them in a story that is so hard-hitting and believable, it's easy to imagine it being in tomorrow's headlines."—J.J. Hensley, award-winning author of *Resolve* and *Measure Twice*

Also by Gwen Florio
Montana
Dakota
Disgraced

RESERVATIONS

GWEN
FLORIO

MIDNIGHT INK
WOODBURY, MINNESOTA

MIDNIGHT
INK

FIRST EDITION
First Printing, 2017

Book format by Bob Gaul
Cover design by Ellen Lawson

Midnight Ink, an imprint of Llewellyn Worldwide Ltd.

Library of Congress Cataloging-in-Publication Data
Names: Florio, Gwen, author.
Title: Reservations / Gwen Florio.
Description: First edition. | Woodbury, Minnesota : Midnight Ink, [2017] |
    Series: A Lola Wicks mystery; #4
Identifiers: LCCN 2016049791 (print) | LCCN 2016059948 (ebook) | ISBN
    9780738750422 | ISBN 9780738750583
Subjects: LCSH: Women journalists—Fiction. | GSAFD: Mystery fiction.
Classification: LCC PS3606.L664 R47 2017 (print) | LCC PS3606.L664 (ebook) |
    DDC 813/.6—dc23
LC record available at https://lccn.loc.gov/2016049791

Midnight Ink
Llewellyn Worldwide Ltd.
2143 Wooddale Drive
Woodbury, MN 55125-2989
www.midnightinkbooks.com

Printed in the United States of America

For Sean, who insisted we see the dinosaur tracks.

ONE

THE DAY THAT WOULD see Ben Yazzie transformed into shreds of flesh in too many evidence bags began with a rare strong and satisfying piss. Ben leaned back against the stream, a veritable Niagara, not his usual dribble and hitch that put youth farther in the rearview mirror every day.

He shook off with a flourish, tucked himself in, and returned to the bedroom with a regretful glance toward the empty bed. Morning like this, he'd have woken his old woman with a proper tumble. Angelina, dead these five years now, liked a good frolicking right up to the end. He stood before the mirror, wound a wide red cloth band around his forehead to hold back his still-black hair, slid the chunk of turquoise and silver high on his throat to fasten his bolo tie, and draped three strands of hand-rolled turquoise beads interspersed with coral around his neck. Silver bracelets weighed down his wrists, and rings adorned his fingers to the knuckles. They sported lumpy, old-fashioned turquoise nuggets, not the glossy plastic-injected crap so often sold these days. He'd have worn them anyway, the jewelry his legacy from a silversmith grandfather, but there was the undeniable fact that tourists liked their Indians to look the part. Ben gazed into the mirror. But for the grin on his face, he was looking at a living, breathing, colorized version of an Edward S. Curtis photo. He forced his mouth into severe submission. Part of looking the part was a stoic solemnity.

In the kitchen, KTNN, the self-proclaimed Voice of the Navajo Nation, filled the room with Diné-language news, more and more of it these days about the unrest over the Conrad Coal mine. The deal allowing the whiteman-owned mine on reservation land had injected millions of dollars into Navajo and Hopi coffers for decades, but people increasingly contended that millions more were owed the tribes, and still others thought the mine shouldn't exist at all. It sucked water, already the most precious of commodities, from the land and returned it poisoned. Livestock died. People lived, but only by virtue of drinking bottled water. And now the mine wanted to expand. The newscaster reminded people that demonstrations against the development had edged close to violence the previous summer. A heavy police presence would likely accompany this new summer's protests—a fact omitted from the truncated English-language version of the news that followed. No use scaring the tourists who along with the mine were the financial lifeblood of the Navajo Nation.

Ben grabbed a day-old doughnut from a box on the counter and filled a thermos with coffee. He opened the front door, moving fast to prevent the bobtail dog lurking outside from slipping in. The dog, a dirt-colored creature indistinguishable from all the other strays roaming the rez, had showed up shortly after Angelina's death, somehow divining Ben's new fragility, a weakness that led him on an occasional evening to set the remains of a TV dinner outside the front door, or toss a crust of toast the dog's way as he headed to work in the morning. He usually left a little before noon, counting on the fact it would take the tourists a while to drive to a site far from the motels and campgrounds they favored. But on this Monday morning the forecast was for above-normal temperatures, and Ben expected that a few smart tourists would want to do their sightseeing before the blistering heat of midday.

The dog laid its ears back and slunk away as Ben loaded the thermos and a lawn chair into a car as unprepossessing as the dog. He stood a moment in the sun, calculating its eventual intensity, then went back indoors and retrieved an umbrella, its black cloth gone rusty with age. It likely had never deflected a single raindrop over the course of its long existence, but it would create a necessary patch of shade as the mercury climbed throughout the day. Finally, Ben placed three one-gallon milk jugs filled with water on the floor in front of the passenger's seat.

The car lurched over the road's rough surface, its suspension shot, the undercarriage just inches above the dirt. The water sloshed within the jugs. Billows of coppery dust marked Ben's progress, enveloping the car whenever he braked before an especially challenging pothole. Around him, towering rock formations beloved by professional and amateur photographers alike jabbed implacable red fingers into a perfect blue sky. The road ran lonely between them. Every few hundred yards, Ben pulled over and took a hand-lettered signboard from the car's back seat and placed it beside the road.

Dinosaur tracks.
Just ahead.
Navajo guide.
Free.

By the end of summer, the signs would be sun-faded and road-filthy. But this early in the tourist season, they gleamed white against the red dirt. Ben reached a pullout below a billboard that answered its own question: *Like Your Lights? Conrad Coal Keeps Them On.* The billboard depicted a cozy living room blazing with light, its big-screen TV showing a football game. A family gathered on its sofa, vaguely brown-skinned (but not too) and dark-haired (brunette, not jet black). Trying to have it both ways, Ben always thought when he saw it. He didn't much care for the billboard, except for the way its struts hid his car from passersby. Tourists liked the idea of an Indian guide, but found reminders of Indian poverty off-putting.

He settled himself in the lawn chair, the jugs of water beneath it, the umbrella in one hand, thermos in the other. The leafy-roofed shade houses where jewelry vendors displayed their wares for tourists were still empty. When the sightseers showed up, if they did, he'd lead them across the slickrock, then direct them to the vendors. "You look like good trackers," he'd tell them. "Indians can tell these things. See them yet?"

Their smiles at his praise would vanish as they searched the rock's surface, their winter-white faces reddening fast from a combination of sun and frustration. "Here." Ben would hoist his water jug. They always thought he brought it along so they wouldn't die of thirst in the desert, just yards from one of the reservation's main roads, in sight of a silvery stream of passing RVs. "The desert demands a lot," he'd tell them as they set out across the rocks. "You want to have water with you at all times. And let somebody know where you'll be. It's not a place to go wandering off on your own. Not even for us, and we've lived here since the beginning of time." Taking them seriously, looking out for them, wrapping it all up in a little bundle of mysticism. His fingers twitched in anticipation of tips. He would direct their energy to the water bottle, unscrewing the cap with deliberate slowness, holding the jug high, the falling water a line of prisms in the sunlight, the tourists' eyes following it down, down as it splashed onto the rocks, pooling in the imperceptible depression, running to its edges, stopping and backfilling until a perfect footprint glistened before them, like that of an ostrich only bigger, so much bigger. Gasps all around.

"They went this way." Ben in his element at that point, moving and pouring, moving and pouring, the dinosaurs' path across the desert leaping into sparkling relief, followed by camera phones held high. "Velociraptors," he'd say, painting a picture of a herd of ravenous carnivores loping across the desert, inexorably drawing closer to something small and scurrying, too light to have left the tracks imprinted by its pursuers. "They ran right past where that billboard is now. Imagine them chasing you." His audience would shiver, the day's heat forgotten. "No, no," Ben would protest as hands enfolded his, pressing the bills into his palm. "Sign says free. All right. If you insist. Thank you. Thank you kindly."

He patted his empty pockets in anticipation. Just around the bend, thankfully shielded from view by the leap of mesa, outsize machinery clanked and groaned at the mine whose gleanings, despite the maybe-Indian family in the billboard, mostly lit cities like Phoenix and Los Angeles. Ben shot a middle finger at the billboard, his daily greeting, set the umbrella aside, and unscrewed his thermos for some coffee before the day got too hot.

The earth shuddered beneath him. The umbrella gave a skip. Coffee leapt from the thermos. The ground buckled and blasted skyward, bits and pieces of Ben Yazzie soaring high and pouring back down in an unseasonable rain of red.

TWO

I WISH I COULD recapture the elation of that first moment, when the sound rolled over my perch among the rocks more than a hundred feet above the desert floor.

Even more than the sound, the feeling. I was a mile away, and out of sight around a bend, but still the rock beneath my feet quivered like a nervous horse, the air shoving hard against me so briefly I thought maybe I'd imagined it. Until I saw the smoke, a great dark cloud heavy with red earth. I lost my dignity then. Hollered, jumped up and down, punched the air with my fists. Forgot, for that moment, my doubts and protests. All those months of planning, and it actually worked exactly the way it was supposed to. Maybe it was the right thing to do after all. I went down the ladder twice as fast as I'd gone up and forced myself not to run the long circuit back to where I'd parked my car in a thicket of piñon and juniper on a side road. It wouldn't do for anyone to see someone running, not on this day, raising a line of dust that would mark my passage. I'd been told to stay away, but I couldn't pass up the chance to see the results of all those months of planning. Even as I sauntered, my excuse at the ready—an early morning trip to the cliff houses to be among the ancestors—I heard the sirens. A grin stretched my cheeks. No matter how they felt about the mine, everybody on the rez hated that damn sign with its damn fake Indians.

I figured I'd see matching smiles when I stopped by the café right at nine, just like I did whenever I was home from college. Set a pattern, I was told. Stick to it. To the minute. No Indian Time for this boy. But when I strolled through the door and asked for a cup of coffee with room for cream, Leona greeted me with reddened, puffy eyes. Her hair, usually bound in the traditional complicated knot at her nape, hung in ragged hanks about her face. She turned away with a hiccupping sound. I looked around the room. I'd expected a hum of excitement, the whole reservation buzzing with the biggest thing to have happened in a long time, the gossip pinging around even the farthest-flung chapter houses with an immediacy that mitigated the fact that the Internet was still a long way from reality in most parts of the rez.

The café wasn't much, just a prefab on a side street with a few mismatched tables. There was no menu, no need for one. Everybody knew it was eggs or pancakes in the morning, hamburgers or Navajo tacos for lunch and dinner, and spaghetti and meatballs on Fridays, when Leona packed the place. Its location meant that few tourists found their way to it, and the ones who did always looked around with apprehension, surprised at finding themselves surrounded by so many brown faces, sometimes backing out with embarrassed looks. Which was a shame, because it meant they were missing out on the best coffee on the rez. But you couldn't blame them for feeling overwhelmed. Most of the places they went, museums and cultural centers and trading posts and such, were designed just for them, meaning that while the waitresses or front desk people or sales clerks were Navajo or sometimes Hopi, the tourists were mostly among their own kind. Even if that kind included the German and French and Japanese tour groups whose members walked right up to the line of obsession with our culture, they all seemed to have more in common with one another than they did with us.

A sullen silence surrounded me, seeping into my bones. Leona thrust the coffee toward me. "Who died?" I asked, seeking a smile. She burst into tears.

I turned to the closest table, populated by the same elders who were there every time I came in. For all I knew, they never went home, just curled up on the floor at night, then rose and stretched stiff muscles each morning before ordering up Leona's pancakes. Courtesy demanded that I wait for them to speak first.

Harold Bitsinnie obliged, pursing his lips over toothless gums as if gathering strength for the words. He wore his Korea Veteran cap—*Forever Proud*—and he removed it now, twisting it in his permanently bent fingers as he spoke.

"Somebody blew up that big billboard this morning. You know, the coal one over by the dinosaur tracks." His voice shook.

Harold hated the coal company. So it could have been excitement playing games with his voice, but the look on his face, all the lines pulling downward, told me it was something else.

"This bombing. Did it mess up the dinosaur tracks? Those tracks, they're how *Shizhé'é* makes his living," I said, using the Diné term of respect, "My Father," applied to male elders. I felt sick. Through all the planning, that possibility had never once come up, and I voiced my fears before I could help myself. "At least he doesn't set up till late."

Again, that closed-in feeling in the room. Something clamped itself around my lungs. Squeezed. I struggled for air, and heard Harold's next words through my own rasping breaths.

"He set up early today."

THREE

THE OPEN DUFFEL GAPED a mockery at Lola Wicks.

In her days as a Kabul-based foreign correspondent, she'd kept a packing list in the back of her head like an open screen on her laptop, always mentally clicking it, seeing what needed to be replenished—Batteries? Outlet adapters? Pencils for when it got so cold that the ink froze in pens?—and what else she needed to add. She'd kept a go-bag with a few emergency essentials, along with a flak jacket that came down over her hips and whose reinforced collar stood up around her neck, protecting the vulnerable jugular and spine. Longer trips into Afghanistan's restive provinces had necessitated days' worth of planning, with items laid across the floor in an orderly row, the bulky generator at one end of the line, the suture kit—thankfully never used—at the other.

Now she sat in her bedroom in northwestern Montana, flummoxed by the prospect of a two-week vacation to Arizona that required nothing more than a few pairs of shorts and some T-shirts. Still.

"You don't want to go." The indictment harsh, the voice gentle. Her husband of two years, Charlie Laurendeau, father to their just-turned-seven-year-old daughter. It had taken him all of those years after Margaret's birth to persuade her to marry, and a few months beyond that to take this trip, their ostensible honeymoon. And then only after he'd couched it in terms of visiting his lone sibling, a brother who'd left their boyhood home on the nearby Blackfeet Nation years earlier to marry a Navajo woman.

Edgar hadn't been back since, not even for Lola and Charlie's wedding. Given what she'd learned during her time with Charlie about Indians' intense and all-inclusive version of family, Lola had drawn a few conclusions about Edgar because of that. But she kept them to herself, just as she had—at least, she thought she had—her feelings about this trip.

Charlie stood behind her, his blocky shadow dividing the shaft of sunlight through the open bedroom window. This far north, they didn't need screens, the only bugs a few mosquitoes peppering the air above the shallow sloughs that provided splashes of blue in the golden sea of surrounding prairie. Lola tore her eyes away from the accusing duffel and turned to the window, letting her gaze skim over the plains to the great jagged wall of the Rocky Mountain Front to the west. Dark ropes of cloud bound the peaks, sliding down the slopes to spit a mouthful of pebble-like hail or even stinging snowflakes at unwary hikers who foolishly trusted in summertime.

Every year people died in those mountains, shoved off narrow ledges by gleefully screaming winds, drenched into hypothermia by icy gray rains, or on the rarest of occasions, masticated into unrecognizability by irritable grizzlies. Lola, years removed from her job as a foreign correspondent, ended up writing about all of those things in her present job as a reporter for the local *Magpie Daily*

Express. Still, the sight of the mountains, with their unwavering demand for respect, always steadied her.

"I'll miss it here." Too late, Lola bit her lip. The words were already out. She had spent much of her life rejecting attachments to people or places; now she had a husband and child who brought with them an extended family of aunties and uncles and elders on the reservation.

"You'll like it even more after a break." Charlie dug the heels of his palms between her shoulder blades. "You're stiff as a two-by-four." He knuckled a stubborn knot of muscle. "A two-by-four layered with marbles. Sure you don't want to rethink counseling? Maybe when we get back."

Lola shrugged his hands away and took one in her own, twining her fingers in his, a basket weave of brown and white. "It's been a year. I'm fine."

"Sure you are."

It was as much as they ever talked about it. Lola had always been on the high-strung end of the spectrum, fresh from Afghanistan when they'd first met, still sizzling with adrenaline, a horse with a bit in its teeth and eyes rolling toward every possible escape. Charlie had been smart enough to know that only a very long rein sustained their relationship, although Lola periodically rebelled against it, even after Margaret had come along. Charlie accepted the danger inherent in his own job as county sheriff, but often fretted about Lola's penchant for putting herself in harm's path.

A year earlier, though, while reporting a story in Wyoming, that tendency had ended up getting not just herself but also Margaret nearly killed. At which point Lola had fled back to Magpie. There, she contented herself with covering her beat, the Blackfeet Reservation, but of necessity whatever else was happening around the region—

the usual small-town-newspaper fare of weather stories, farm reports, and the occasional tourist-related disaster on the Front. She acquired, as the saying went, a "mile-wide, inch-deep" knowledge of commodities prices, snowpack levels, wildfire movements, fracking, land-use disputes, local centenarians' birthdays, and, always and forever, weather. Some days, she even relaxed into a shimmering sort of stillness that another person might have identified as happiness.

Overall, though, her new passivity disturbed her husband as much, if not more, than the old recklessness. He hadn't even been able to drag her away from Magpie's endless howling winter for a long weekend in the warmth and brightness and people-on-the-streets cheer of Great Falls or Missoula. "No," she'd said, her eyes straying toward the window, the black wall of mountains barely visible beyond the billowing curtains of snow. "I don't think so." Followed, again, by "I'm fine."

The honeymoon to Arizona, then. "Dammit, you're not fine," Charlie had said when he proposed it. That was all it took. The old Lola raised her head. Curled her lip. Margaret stood by her father, both of them holding their breath. A look passed between them: *she's faking it.* Margaret owed the lankiness that was chasing baby fat from her bones to her mother, along with an unyielding jaw and gray eyes hard with skepticism. The obsidian hair, the brown skin, the unnerving calm, that was Charlie.

"A honeymoon," Lola had said. "Why not?" Fists clenched behind her back, nails clawing her palms, breaking the skin in stripes. "Arizona sounds nice."

Oxygen had flowed back into the room, and Lola gave thanks for a husband kind enough to pretend he believed her lie.

FOUR

Now, WEEKS AFTER CHARLIE had called her bluff, oxygen seemed in short supply.

Lola's breath juddered in her chest as Charlie went to her dresser and pulled underwear, shirts, and shorts from the tangled mess within. "I'll need my running clothes," she managed. "And shoes." Pretending to go along.

Running was the one good thing she'd brought back from Wyoming, urged into it against her will by a friend there, her first attempts almost as painful as they were resentful, calves screaming, lungs afire. Improbably, she'd persisted upon her return to Montana, describing wide circles around the house at first, dodging sagebrush, rocks, and the occasional rattler too startled to strike, but always keeping the frame bungalow, with Margaret inside, in view. It had taken a blowup on Charlie's part, full of invective about her presumptions of his incompetence as a father, to send her out on the gravel roads surrounding the ranch, and eventually farther up into the foothills, under the cool dimness of the lodgepole pines, their needles providing a springy cushion underfoot.

"Where will I run there?" she asked, even as Charlie double-bagged her beat-up running shoes and added them to the duffel filling with alarming rapidity. Lola gripped the edges of the bed.

"You probably won't," he said. "It'll be ninety degrees by seven in the morning, past a hundred by noon."

Lola imagined a vast fiery cauldron, an unwelcome change from a Montana summer that reliably offered see-your-breath mornings and sweatshirt-demanding evenings as a respite from the daytime heat. "Couldn't we wait until winter?" Her distaste for Montana's defining season lay in inverse proportion to her love of its summer.

"Margaret has school," Charlie reminded her. "Besides, Eddie—I mean, *Gar*—said summer was the best time for a visit, with the girls being out of school and all." Edgar had taken to calling himself Gar, a moniker Charlie had been slow to adopt. "How 'bout you call me Char?" Charlie had said to him in one telephone conversation. "Then we can rhyme. Gar and Char." Lola couldn't make out Edgar's words, but his laugh had rung loud through the phone. Charlie's face darkened and he'd changed the subject.

Gar probably figured that nobody in his right mind would come to Arizona in the summer, Lola thought now, but she kept silent about her suspicion. She consoled herself with the reminder that Charlie had promised to be back home by Indian Days, the Blackfeet Nation's annual Fourth of July powwow, so she'd still spend most of her summer in Montana.

Margaret appeared in the bedroom doorway, followed by Bub, a three-legged Border collie listing farther off balance than usual, his jaws locked around the handles of Margaret's small duffel, his tail tucked as far between his legs as it would go. "Mom, Dad, look. I

15

taught Bub to carry my suitcase. Aren't you ready yet? I thought we were supposed to leave right after breakfast. I want to meet Juliana." Edgar and Naomi's daughter was two years older than Margaret, who'd been talking for weeks about all the things she expected to learn from her big-girl cousin.

Charlie pointed to his own bag, zipped shut, beside the bedroom door. "I'm ready. Your mom's the one holding us up. And give that poor dog a break. He has better things to do than tote your bags. Drop it, Bub." Bub's jaws parted. His feathery tail resumed its usual lofty posture. His eyes, one blue, one brown, radiated gratitude. He padded to Charlie's side, standing proud with his savior.

"I'm almost ready." Lola ignored Margaret's pointed gaze at the open bag. "Five more minutes. Go say goodbye to the chickens and Spot." Margaret was responsible for the care and feeding of their Appaloosa, Spot, as well as a flock of recently acquired Buff Orpington chickens, extravagantly feathered against Montana's cold.

"You mean twenty-five minutes. Come on, Bub." Margaret swept from the room in wounded righteousness. The dog gave Charlie a final worshipful glance and trailed Margaret at a distance designed to discourage further assignments. Lola went into the bathroom and threw her toothbrush, deodorant, and a sample-size bottle of the hand lotion she used as face cream, her version of makeup, into her Dopp kit. They rattled against the small plastic bottles containing the fossilized antibiotics, industrial-strength painkillers, and sleeping pills from her foreign correspondent days, when medications were her only weapons against interminable flights and all-too-possible injury from accident or, more likely, attack. She tried to remember the woman she'd been then, jolting in a Soviet jeep over the red-painted rocks that bordered known minefields, or lying flat on a hotel balcony to transmit stories on a satellite phone while firefights rattled the streets below. That woman hadn't had a child, hadn't known what it was like to face losing that child.

Lola sorted through the bottles. The container for sleeping pills was empty, the prescription long outdated. She tossed it. She lifted the bottle of painkillers, twisted off the top, and held it over the toilet. Then she relented, capping it and replacing it in the kit. You never know, she told herself.

In the bedroom, Charlie's cellphone chimed. Lola's heart lifted. Maybe it was a last-minute emergency. Even though Charlie had recently acquired a deputy, a big case would require the attention of two people. They'd have to cancel their trip. She hovered in the doorway, waiting.

"Wait," Charlie said into the phone. "Slow down." He sat down hard on the bed. The tone in his voice bespoke bad news. Lola turned her back so he wouldn't see the hope lighting her face.

"God," he said. "No. An elder?"

So the reservation had lost another of its elders, Lola thought. She mentally subtracted four days, the time for the necessary funeral ceremonies, from their vacation. She eased onto the bed beside Charlie and pasted an expression of sympathy across her face. She wondered who'd died. All the elders she knew were in robust good health. She racked her brain for a name, and abandoned the effort with Charlie's next words.

"A bomb?"

Lola bounded to her feet. She scrabbled through the mess atop the dresser for her truck keys and phone and pens and notebook. If a bomb had killed an elder, it was a story, a big one. Too big for just Jan, her fellow reporter at the *Express*. Lola might have stopped chasing the big national stories, but the ones on her turf still sparked the old frisson, focus narrowing to a pinpoint, nerves zinging in anticipation, her senses on this day heightened further still by the welcome knowledge that she could kiss her vacation goodbye. She pursed her lips to whistle a happy tune, sucking her breath back in just in time.

Charlie clicked off his call. "Where are you going?"

"You just said there was a bomb. One that killed somebody. Not just any somebody, but an elder. I'm going to go cover it. I'll drop Margaret at Auntie Alice's on the way."

Charlie's smile contained not a hint of mirth. The hair on Lola's arms stood up.

"Better gas up the truck. You've got a long ride ahead."

Lola shifted from one foot to another, impatient to hit the road. If he talked much longer, Jan would make it to the bombing long before she got there. Jan had probably already heard it on the scanner and would be on her way, leaving Lola with mop-up, the secondary interviews with experts, none of the drama from the scene. On the other hand, Charlie knew the bomb's location. "Why? Where is it? Babb? Heart Butte?" She named communities in the reservation's far reaches. Even though Charlie worked off-reservation, he got called in, along with the FBI, when the Blackfeet reported possible felonies.

"Gaitero."

In all her years of covering the rez, Lola had never heard of Gaitero. "Where's that?"

Charlie's smile stretched wider, some actual humor infiltrating it. "That was my brother on the phone. This bombing you're so hot to cover? It's in Arizona."

FIVE

Lola watched in the pickup's side mirror as the house grew smaller behind them.

Charlie swung the truck onto the main road. Once a shade of scarlet that made it a magnet for speeding tickets, the truck was the legacy of Lola's friend Mary Alice, who'd splurged on it with her buyout money from the Baltimore newspaper where she and Lola had worked together as young reporters, before Mary Alice had headed off to Montana and Lola to Afghanistan. Lola had ended up in Montana as a result of Mary Alice's murder, acquiring both Charlie and the truck in the process. After years of clocking more miles on gravel roads than paved, the truck's candy-apple exterior was dull and pitted as scrap metal, and it no longer so readily caught the Highway Patrol's eyes, not even when Charlie, a legendary leadfoot, was behind the wheel.

The prairie whipped past, tawny grasses rippling wavelike, washing around the legs of glossy Angus cattle. Horses roamed among them, paints and buckskins and blue-tick roans, so different from the monotone Thoroughbreds that had populated the paddocks of Lola's wealthier childhood acquaintances. Unlike the stolid cattle, the horses tossed their heads and frisked, chasing one another head-high to presumably better pasture. Beyond, the mountains stood unmoving. The house disappeared from view. At Lola's request, they made a long looping detour so that she could say goodbye to Ninah-stako, named Chief Mountain by whitemen. The lone butte hard by the Canadian border was sacred to the Blackfeet. Early in their relationship, Charlie had told Lola he wanted to be buried within sight of it. "Me, too," Lola had said. Even without the cultural heritage, Ninahstako had a way of getting under one's skin.

She wrapped her arms around herself. Magpie was the first place that had felt like home after leaving her parents' house on Maryland's Eastern Shore at the age of eighteen. Until she'd arrived in Montana in her early thirties, she'd spent the intervening years in a series of dorm rooms, then a Baltimore apartment before and (briefly) after a years-long stint in Kabul, where she'd shared with other journalists a rented villa that came with its own exorbitantly paid contingent of Kalashnikov-toting security guards.

In Afghanistan, such weaponry was on constant and casual display, toted by boys barely into their teens and elders with chest-length beards. She'd gotten used to the possibility of violence there. Even after her return to the United States, her reporting had brought the occasional death threat. But not until she'd worked briefly in Wyoming had the threats involved Margaret. Lola's stomach lurched at the memory. "I think I might be getting carsick."

Charlie turned toward her. The wind rushed through the open window with a noise like tearing cloth. It caught his hair and flung it about his face. Early in his stint as sheriff, sensitive to his status as the first Indian cop—back then, the only cop—in a white county, he'd adopted a buzz cut. He'd since relaxed and now his hair was longer than Lola's, hanging past his shoulders on the days he decided to forego braids. "About the bombing," he said. He'd long ago learned that news was the best way to distract her.

Lola let herself be played. "Who would want to kill an elder?"

Charlie's mouth twisted. On anyone else, that mouth would have been too wide, lips too full, but it provided a necessary balance between the assertiveness of chin and nose that dominated his square face. "Actually, Eddie"—Lola guessed he wouldn't resort to "Gar" until they crossed the Arizona line—"thinks they were trying to kill the sign."

"A sign?"

"Billboard, actually. For a coal mine."

Lola tried to figure out how a billboard could prompt a bomb. "Does somebody want to build a coal mine?" After years of sporadic, low-level resistance to coal, the fast-moving reality of climate change had finally prompted real, widespread opposition around much of the country. Even in the regulation-hating, job-hungry West, a billboard promoting a new mine probably wouldn't go over well.

"Nah, the mine's been there for years. Decades. They want to expand it, I guess."

"Where does the elder come in?"

"That's the problem," said Charlie. "He came in."

The truck blew past a small metal oblong that informed them they'd passed into the next county. There were plenty of counties to go. They'd be in Montana for nearly a third of their thousand-mile trip, assuming the bombing had distracted Charlie from his plan to stop at every kitschy attraction within twenty miles of the highway.

"The elder is sort of a local attraction," he explained. "He guides people to dinosaur tracks."

21

"Dinosaurs?" Margaret sat up in the jump seat behind them. Bub, who'd draped himself across her lap, shook himself off with a grumble, not taking kindly to being disturbed.

"Just their tracks," Charlie said. "We'll see them when we're there. Anyhow," he said to Lola, "he does this all summer long. But nobody expected him to be out there that early in the morning. Just a wrong place, wrong time sort of thing. Whoever set that bomb was probably trying to demolish the billboard. Unfortunately, the elder was sitting right next to it. Not much left of either of them, from what Eddie said."

Lola worked her phone, trying to find a site for an Arizona newspaper that could give her more information. *No signal*, the phone taunted her. She looked at the map accordioned on the console between her and Charlie. From the looks of their route, largely free of the dots that signaled towns of any size, they'd be in no-signal territory for a good part of their trip.

Charlie enfolded her phone hand in his own, effortlessly steering one-handed around serpentine curves that traced their way down the side of a long ridge. The truck barely slowed at all. Beyond the driver's side, the road yawned away into emptiness.

"Withdrawal setting in already?" he asked. Lola always checked her phone incessantly, even on her days off, fearful of missing a story. "When does the twitching start? And what do I need to do about it?"

Take me home, Lola thought. The road unkinked. For what would be the last time in two weeks, she fixed her gaze upon the peaks of the Front, the defining feature of her home. How would she feel in a place without its reliable boundary, the visual touchstone by which she oriented herself daily?

———

Seven and a half hours, two warnings, and one actual ticket later—Charlie had never adjusted to Montana's belated imposition of a speed limit and believed the old no-limit rule should apply everywhere—saw them in Salt Lake City, where Charlie tried, to no avail, to lure Lola into a mall. "They've got a Macy's and a Nordstrom and everything. I don't think there's a Nordstrom in all of Montana."

Lola looked as though he'd suggested they wallow in a rattlesnake den. "What would I possibly want from Nordstrom?"

"I thought women liked shopping," Charlie said, even as he conceded the point. Lola's wardrobe—jeans and cargo pants, winter turtlenecks and summer T-shirts, with a few shorts and tank tops that would have gotten her killed or worse in Afghanistan—was long on service and short on fashion.

The pickup cruised wide, scary-clean boulevards. "There's the mall," Charlie nodded. "Right across from the temple." Lola ignored the temple's Oz-like spires, the golden angel Moroni trumpeting defiantly atop the tallest, and tapped at her phone, flush with four bars. "Looks like there's an Apple store near Nordstrom. I don't suppose you'd planned to duck in there while you dumped me at Nordstrom. You know that you can order their stuff online, right?"

She sneaked a glance at Charlie and bit her lip to keep from laughing. His own lip thrust forward. Margaret came by her epic pout honestly, Lola thought. Charlie had been making noises about an iPad for his birthday after the county refused to pony up for one for the sheriff's office, despite his lengthy memo on its myriad uses.

Lola's fingers stilled on the phone. "I found it."

Margaret, who'd fallen asleep, stirred. "Found what?"

"A story about the bombing."

"And?" Charlie lifted his wrist and studied his watch. Despite his newfound crush on technology, he'd yet to give up his sturdy Timex with its duct-taped band. "Mall's probably closed, anyhow. Let's find a motel." His sigh filled the pickup's cab.

"Pretty much what you said. Looks like the billboard was the target. Nobody expected the elder to be out there this time of year. Investigation continuing, no suspects yet, blah blah blah ... Hey. Your sister-in-law's quoted."

Charlie pulled up to a chain motel known for allowing dogs. "What'd she say?"

Lola tucked in her chin, straightened her shoulders, and spoke in pronouncements. "'No matter how people feel about the mine, this represents an inexcusable destruction of property, exponentially compounded by the unforgivable death—no, murder—of one of our most respected Diné elders,' said Naomi Nez Laurendeau, a prosecutor for the tribe. 'The full force of the law must be brought against the perpetrator or perpetrators,' added Laurendeau, whose husband, Edgar, is an attorney for the mine.'"

"Edgar, huh? Guess the tribe didn't get the memo about his new name." Charlie reached across the seat and took the phone from Lola's hand. "Let's turn this thing off for now. We're on vacation, remember?"

Lola slid her hands beneath her thighs to keep from grabbing the phone from him. She'd get it back when he went in to register.

Charlie tossed a grin her way and slid the phone into his pocket. "Back in a few. Don't worry that you're missing anything. Starting tomorrow night, we're probably going to hear more about this bombing than we ever wanted to. Sounds like Naomi's been assigned to the case."

SIX

For whatever reason—Lola decided not to question it—Charlie continued his abandonment of sightseeing excursions the next day, barreling toward Arizona through scenery reassuringly similar to that of Montana, juniper and piñon now mingling with the sagebrush, but mountains always visible somewhere on the horizon. Midway through the day, she relaxed into sleep. She awoke in a different universe.

She sat up and scrubbed the heels of her hands against her eyes. When she lowered her hands, things looked the same. "What happened?"

She glanced back. Margaret stared wide-eyed through the window, her expression mirroring her mother's, and stated the obvious. "Different."

The mountains had disappeared, along with nearly any hint of greenery. Red rock jutted from red earth, fairly glowing beneath a fierce sun whose heat burned every last cloud from the sky. The horizon, so emphatically defined in Montana, was somewhere in the wavering distance. It was as though someone had skinned the earth of its surface, peeling back grass and loam and trees to reveal the rounded muscular rocks beneath.

"What do you think?" said Charlie.

Lola looked around for a patch of hazy air over a slough, or a wandering line of trees that would signify a creek. People needed water, she thought. As did animals and birds and plants. She didn't see any of those things, and for sure, there was no water in sight. She touched her tongue to a crack in her lips. She couldn't remember whether it had been there before. Had the tender skin dried and pulled apart in just the short time she'd slept? Her tongue clogged her throat. She reached for the water bottle that sat in the console— Charlie never so much as drove to the convenience store without water in the truck—and drank deep, holding the cool liquid in her mouth. Parched cells plumped with relief.

She swallowed. "It's awfully dry."

"You've got to give the Navajo credit. The Hopi, too. Not to mention the Ancestral Puebloans. They all found a way to survive here."

"The who?"

"People used to call them the Anasazi. They lived here first. Farmed, too. Seems impossible, doesn't it? But they traded with people as far away as Mexico. Eddie and Naomi will probably want to take us to Chaco Canyon on this trip. Something like a thousand people lived there. Although, come to think of it, Eddie and Naomi might not have time for a trip like that now, what with this bombing case. But we can go on our own."

Lola thought she'd prefer that. They'd save money by staying with Edgar and Naomi, but Lola hated the idea of two weeks' worth of enforced togetherness with people she'd never met. It would be nice to have some time alone with Charlie and Margaret, or mostly alone, given that Juliana would probably tag along. Annual Christmas photos of the girl, a little older and more serious in each, marched across their refrigerator in Magpie. Early on, when Juliana was just a toddler and before Lola had arrived in Montana, Charlie had had custody of her during a rough patch in Edgar and Naomi's relationship. After a trial reconciliation in Arizona without his daughter, Edgar had finally made the decision to retrieve Juliana from the Blackfeet Reservation and permanently join Naomi there. Charlie hadn't seen Juliana—or his brother and sister-in-law—since. When Lola had first met Charlie, she'd been wary of gossip about a possible daughter, and then had been unaccountably relieved when she'd finally unraveled the real story.

"How much farther now?"

"Not much," Charlie said. "We're almost to Gaitero."

"Maybe you'd better fill me in on Edgar—Gar—and Naomi. How'd they meet, anyway?"

"College," Charlie said. His lips twisted again, in an expression that was becoming familiar to Lola whenever he talked about his brother. "Dartmouth."

Lola wondered how, in all her time with Charlie, she'd missed that detail. She thought she was beginning to understand the tension that crept into his voice whenever he talked about his brother. Charlie—and Edgar too, she supposed—had gotten a boost when their parents insisted they attend the adjoining county's white schools, not the best, but several notches above the chronically underfunded reservation schools. Charlie had spent two years at the reservation's junior college and finished up at the Montana University System school in the Hi-Line town of Havre, on the windscoured plains to the east. Lola knew Edgar had gone to law school at the University of Montana in Missoula, and she'd assumed he'd done his undergrad there, too. Bad enough that Edgar was a lawyer to Charlie's cop. But he'd snagged himself an Ivy League degree. Way to one-up the big brother, Lola thought.

"What about Naomi?"

"Navajo royalty, if there is such a thing. She comes from a long line of tribal presidents, council members, what have you."

"What's she like?"

"Dunno. Never met her."

So Charlie hadn't gone to his brother's wedding either. Tit for tat. "This vacation is sounding more fun by the moment."

"What's that?"

"Never mind." Lola guessed she was going to have to bite her tongue a lot during the next two weeks. She pointed to flimsy roadside shelters, their uprights made with twisted branches. Beneath them, darkness patched the scorching hearth of desert. "What are those?"

"Shade houses. People use them in the summer in the sheep camps. But these along the road, they're mostly for folks selling things to tourists."

Lola couldn't imagine the shelters offered much relief from the heat she could feel radiating up from the road, permeating the underside of the truck, toasting the soles of her feet through her customary hiking boots. She made a note to switch to her running shoes as soon as they arrived. "What's a sheep camp? And how do you know all these things?" Most of what Lola knew about the Navajo Nation was gleaned from a long-ago-read series of mystery novels and a quick spin through Google. Now she realized that she'd forgotten what little she'd learned.

"A sheep camp is where the people who still run sheep take them in the summer, up in the high country where it's cooler. Eddie filled

28

me in on some of this stuff when I came down here to bring Juliana back home, once he and Naomi had worked things out."

"Wait. You said you'd never met Naomi."

"She was away at a conference. She goes to a lot of them. You know how it is."

Lola hadn't, when she first met Charlie, but she'd learned. Between white groups eager to burnish their bona fides by featuring Indian speakers and Native groups flexing increasingly powerful legal muscle, the conference circuit could amount to a full-time job.

Charlie tapped the brakes just in time to slow for the speed-limit sign that announced the approach to Gaitero. The truck rolled through a town that looked too small for the adobe-style chain hotels on its outskirts. Lola said as much.

"It is," Charlie agreed. "But it's a good jumping-off point for places like Monument Valley and Canyon de Chelly, so it gets its share of tourists. Naomi and Edgar live outside town, far enough not to be bothered by them."

Town provided only the briefest of breaks from the barren surroundings. Lola looked at the map spread across her lap. "Doesn't Naomi work at tribal headquarters? That's got to be at least an hour away." She consulted the map again. "More. This reservation is huge."

"Biggest in the United States. You can ask her yourself in a few minutes. But she works in Gaitero—the rez is so big that there are court divisions in every major town. The mine has a satellite office in town, too. Best I can tell, they want an Indian face where people can see one, not hidden away up at the mine itself. It makes for a long commute on the days he has to be at the mine, though."

Lola was approaching a decade in the West, but she had yet to accustom herself to the distances people routinely drove. She considered herself lucky that she and Charlie lived just outside Magpie, where each of them worked. People on farther-flung ranches or reservation towns drove an hour each way just to get groceries. Her few remaining East Coast friends still marveled at the way she spoke of larger Montana towns as being "only" about five or six hours away.

The pickup slowed again, this time for a turn onto a gravel road. It hit the first two potholes hard. Red dust rose around them. Lola closed her window seconds too late. Margaret and Bub registered protests from the jump seats behind them, Bub in a series of sneezes, Margaret with a word—one of Lola's favorites.

"Quarter," Lola said automatically. A family rule imposed a fine of a quarter per curse word—applied in theory to anyone, but in practice mostly to Lola.

Charlie braked and waited for the curtain of dust to fall, revealing a house. Not a regular house.

Lola took it in. "A hogan."

"Sort of," said Charlie. But she heard the pleasure in his voice at the realization she'd done some homework, belatedly acquiring the thinnest veneer of knowledge during the insomnia of her final night in Magpie, surfing Navajo websites on her phone as Charlie slumbered oblivious beside her. The house was a larger, updated version of the traditional hexagonal dwelling, with adobe walls instead of chinked wood and wide, deep-set windows in place of the traditional rooftop smokehole that also let in light. A real door, one with a suburban trio of stairstep windows, had replaced the customary blanket, but still it faced east, the direction of thought. A telltale layer of metal roof shone beneath an earthen topping.

At first glance, it looked modest, low to the ground, its muted hues taking their tones from the surrounding earth. A muffled hum from a clump of junipers revealed a concealed central air-conditioning unit. "Sweet," said Lola, who'd spent the latter half of the drive wishing Mary Alice had invested in AC for the pickup. A late-model pickup, considerably larger than their own and clean, too, sat beside a Prius in the driveway.

"Not what you were expecting?" Charlie's tone hovered somewhere between pride and rebuke.

Lola accepted the censure as her due. She hadn't given much thought to what the house might be like, assuming the standard BIA shoebox, short on both charm and sturdiness. Some families gussied them up, tacking on porches, additions, sometimes even a second story that challenged the houses' already questionable stability. Most people didn't bother, accepting the fact that their homes would start falling down around them almost as soon as they went up. When she looked more closely at Edgar and Naomi's home, she could see it had an addition of its own, not immediately apparent to passersby. Lola calculated total square footage and whistled beneath her breath. She and Charlie and Margaret lived in about a third that space. A thatch-roofed patio, cool and welcoming, sat to one side of the main house. "A shade house?" she asked, even though it bore only the barest resemblance to the flimsy roadside shelters.

"Yes. Beautiful, isn't it?"

"Yes. No. There's beautiful." She pointed with her lips, in the Indian way she'd learned, toward the two people who had emerged to stand like sentinels in the doorway.

———

Assumptions always got Lola in trouble. Nonetheless, she'd taken for granted that Edgar would have his brother's height and bulk, along with the glowering square features that disguised the gentleness within. She'd imagined Naomi as equally imposing, one of those large severe women who commanded respect by their physical presence alone.

But the man and woman approaching the pickup were so similarly slight and slim-hipped that they looked more like brother and sister than husband and wife. Edgar was, if possible, the more beautiful, with the hooded eyes and arrogant aquiline features of a Goya portrait. He wore his hair short, swept up and away from his forehead in a high pompadour. Naomi's hung to her waist. She brushed it back from her face with slender fingers weighted with turquoise. She and Edgar each wore jeans and crisp white snap-front shirts, Western dress-up clothes, suitable for everything from rodeos to church to board meetings. A person could have cut himself on the precise creases down the front of the jeans and along the shirtsleeves buttoned at the wrist despite the heat. Lola felt self-conscious and worse for the wear in her travel-crumpled cargo pants and sweat-sticky T-shirt. Her feet sweltered in their hiking boots.

She got out of the truck and hung back as Charlie helped Margaret unlatch her seat belt. Bub wriggled across Margaret and jumped onto the red dirt, taking a second to balance himself on his three legs before lurching to the truck's back wheel and generously watering it.

A peal of laughter rang out beyond Edgar and Naomi. Margaret's head snapped up. Juliana emerged from behind her parents and made a beeline for Bub. With her first glimpse of Juliana's perfect parents, Lola had feared a miniature version of Edgar and Naomi, maybe decked out in one of those of *Sound of Music*-style sailor suits. But Juliana was small and sturdy in mismatched top and shorts, long hair tangled, hands reassuringly grubby. Charlie lifted Margaret from the truck and set her on the ground. Juliana veered from her pursuit of Bub and came to a halt in front of Margaret.

The girls eyed each other, Margaret two years younger and a head shorter. Her eyes simultaneously implored acceptance and flashed a warning should none be forthcoming. Juliana registered the latter and defused it. "Do you want to see my pony?" She held out her hand.

Margaret took it and they raced away, Bub unevenly hotfooting it behind them.

"That went well." Naomi's chuckle was a throaty burble. "*Ya'at'eeh.* Greetings. And welcome." She pressed her cheek to Lola's. Her skin was cool and smooth. The whisper of her shirt, with its elaborate top-stitched flower pattern across the shoulders, bespoke raw silk.

Lola closed her eyes and inhaled Naomi's light floral scent. She hugged her back, harder than she'd intended, overcome with memory. "My friend wore that same perfume."

"Your friend has good taste." Naomi's smile revealed a chipped front tooth, enough of an anomaly to be charming. Lola wondered if that was why she'd never had it capped.

"She's dead." Lola couldn't seem to stop herself. "Someone shot her."

Charlie stepped in to save Lola from herself. "It was a long time ago. That's how Lola and I met. I investigated the case."

"Looks like you investigated more than the case."

Three faces turned to Edgar. He had not, thought Lola, achieved his wife's level of urbanity, a bit of grimace in the smile, some vinegar in the tone.

"Charlie. Long time." Edgar held out his hand. Lola would have expected a man-hug, all exhalations and back-pounding with a few good-natured insults thrown in.

"Gar." Charlie's mouth twisted around the single syllable. The two men touched fingers the Indian way.

"You must be exhausted." Naomi took things in hand. "Let's relax in the shade house. We'll have some lemonade."

Lola hung back, scanning the broken land around her. Rocky ridges and buttes and arroyos. Hoodoos, their skinny sandstone bodies topped by flat pancakes of hardrock. But not a mountain in sight.

SEVEN

Lola was used to plastic pitchers full of faux-lemonade, a standard at events both on and off the reservation, the gritty flavored powder turned sludgy in the bottoms of paper cups. Naomi appeared on the patio bearing a tray with four glasses and a graceful rounded pitcher of heavy blue Mexican glass, ice cubes tinkling within, lemon slices sailing like vivid ships amid the transparent floes. Lola took an astringent sip and touched her tongue to her teeth, bursting capsules of pulp. The real thing.

Sunlight filtered through the willow branches roofing the shade house. The narrow dried leaves rustled pleasingly in the breeze. "We wanted it to be as traditional as possible, as well as being functional." Naomi ran a hand over the polished uprights. "You'll see shade houses like this all over the reservation."

Not exactly like this, Lola thought. One side of the shade house was taken up by a stone fireplace with a grill built into an extension. Water chuckled in a corner fountain, spilling over rounded river rocks into a shallow pool. Plants burst in cool green profusion from outsize ceramic pots with geometric designs; Lola, whose thumb was brown verging on black, had no idea what they were. The long picnic table where they sat could accommodate a dozen people. Lola thought the whole setup belonged in one of those fat, years-old magazines she perused in the dentist's office, turning pages worn to the consistency of soft cloth. First in Kabul and then in Montana, she'd lived so long apart from the good life portrayed in those photo spreads that they appeared to her as exotic as a National Geographic feature.

In Magpie, when people no longer felt like doing their outdoor entertaining among rattlesnake-concealing sagebrush, they spent a weekend tacking on a redwood deck, topping it with a one-piece picnic-table-and-bench combo Howard Gulbranson had banged together and sold outside his gas station, and called it good. People knew to tote their own bubba chairs to barbecues for the overflow.

Naomi's glance told Lola she'd registered her inventory, along with its attendant judgment. "We do a lot of entertaining. Lawyers, and, especially with Gar's job, corporate types. This helps. You understand."

Lola wished she didn't. Some of the lawyers and probably most of the corporate types would be white and affluent, raised and educated far from the reservation, barely able to mask their shock at its casual and pervasive poverty, the junked cars beside the rusting house trailers, the outhouses that signaled the lack of indoor plumbing, electrical lines nowhere in sight. They must have writhed within at the invitation to dinner at Edgar and Naomi's, fearing dirt floors, sheep shit in the driveway, unchained rez dogs. Then, this. Relief would gust like a summer squall, the ominous clouds of preconception shredding and wafting away. The conversation in the rental car on their drive back to the familiar confines of a chain motel: "Delightful people." "Yes. We can do business with them." "Ivy League–educated, you know."

Lola searched for a topic less fraught. "That's a beautiful shirt," she said. Idiot, she thought. She stiffened in preparation for Naomi's reaction. The woman was an attorney, for God's sake, and here she was, falling back on the inane woman-speak of clothes. Bad enough she'd already mentioned the perfume.

But Naomi preened. "I made it."

Lola's eyes widened, again taking in the top-stitching adorning the delicate fabric, the piping that outlined the yoke and placket, the pearly snaps. How did one attach snaps to a blouse, anyway? She imagined some sort of glue but figured that wasn't the case.

Naomi's shoulder lifted prettily, a modest shrug. "I never took to weaving. Sewing was always my thing."

Lola had wrestled with an apron—an apron! Who wore aprons anymore?—for weeks in a high school home ec class. A blouse like Naomi's looked like months of work. "How do you find the time?"

"I make the time. It helps me unwind. When I can't sleep at night, I'll go in and whip something up."

Lola revised her estimate of the time involved. Maybe a few days.

"You should see her sewing room," Edgar said. "Take the finest department store. Anything you see there, she can make herself, only better. At Dartmouth, nobody could figure out how this poor little Indian dressed better than all the white girls."

Lola noted the way he beamed upon his wife, as well as the barely suppressed grimace that crossed Naomi's face at his words. She took another stab at changing the subject, holding her glass against her cheek, absorbing the cool. "This is just what I needed. Our truck doesn't have air-conditioning."

Edgar cocked an eyebrow. "That's going to be a problem here. And that color isn't going to help." Even faded, the red paint would absorb the heat. He reached into his pocket. "Here."

A set of keys flew across the table. Charlie caught them one-handed. "What's this?"

Edgar pointed with his chin to the brawny white double-cab pickup in the driveway. "Use mine while you're here. Air-conditioning and more room besides. We've set up a tour for you at some nearby cliff houses tomorrow morning. A local guide will take you through them once you get there. I hope you don't mind bringing Juliana along with you. We had a whole raft of things planned to do with you, but it looks like you're going to be mostly on your own now. Both of us got sucked into this bombing case. Naomi even had to take some time off from her hours at the law school in Tempe."

"Do you teach there?" Lola asked. Good lord, she thought to herself. Was there nothing this woman couldn't do?

"Just once a week," Naomi said. "It's about a five-hour drive each way, so I have to spend the night. I usually keep the same hours in the summertime, to prep for the fall semester. It looks like I'll have to double up on them once this case is over."

Charlie shifted in his chair. "The bombing—have they caught the guy who did it?"

Edgar's head wagged back and forth. "Nobody yet."

A panting Bub appeared at Lola's side, Margaret and Juliana behind him. "Mom, can we ride Valentine? Margaret says she knows how."

"I do know how," Margaret chimed in. Both girls were breathless, their faces red, as though they'd run the whole way from wherever Valentine lived.

Naomi looked a question at Lola.

"She does," Lola said. Margaret had only been a few months old when Charlie had first boosted her in front of him on Spot. The upshot was that Margaret bossed Spot around even more decisively

38

than Spot bossed around Lola, who'd never attained complete confidence in her riding ability.

"All right," Naomi said. "But stay close to home."

Lola jerked in her seat. "You're letting them head out on their own with a suspect on the loose?"

Charlie shot Lola a look that she had no trouble deciphering: *Fine, my ass.* Another lecture about counseling no doubt awaited.

"The bombing was miles from here," Edgar said. "They'll be okay." The girls dashed away, dust puffing like smoke at their heels, before Lola could raise any more objections.

———

"What's your part in this?" Charlie returned to the subject at hand. "Seems to me it's the cops' show at this point. And the FBI's."

All four people at the table fell silent. Bombing was a federal crime no matter where it occurred, the FBI's involvement routine. But on Indian reservations the FBI was called in for any suspected felonies, creating a layer of resentment among local law enforcement who felt bigfooted on their own turf.

"Something like this, it's all hands on deck," Edgar said. "Besides, our—the mine's—billboard was destroyed. We don't know if the billboard was the target or the elder was. It's probably the billboard, though, so I'm doing some research into attacks on corporate sites, trying to identify likely suspects."

"If they catch the guy, the tribe will be ready to do its own prosecution," Naomi added. "That's where I come in."

"*When* they catch him," Edgar said.

"Of course." Naomi spoke into her glass.

"Seems like the FBI would have all that information on hand," Charlie said. "They've been investigating these kinds of cases for years."

"Well, we're looking into it anyway," Edgar said. "Think the FBI's going to share everything with the tribe? Let alone with the mine."

Charlie raised his glass in wry acknowledgment. "Any likely suspects?" He leaned forward in his chair. Hah, thought Lola. Charlie was always giving her a hard time about being unable to turn off her reporter instincts. But put a crime in front of him, even one far from his jurisdiction, and he shifted into cop overdrive.

"Too many," Edgar said. He ticked them off on his fingers. "The protesters. It's early yet, but last summer we had a whole army of elders out there every week, holding signs protesting the mine's expansion, trying to get the tourists' attention. Drove the Chamber of Commerce types crazy."

"Would elders know how to make a bomb?"

"It's hard to imagine, isn't it?" Naomi interjected. "A lot of them don't even have electricity. But we've also got the greenies, the white activists attaching themselves to the issue. Not that there aren't environmental concerns. There are, and they're huge. People living near the mine have lost their drinking water. But this has been a problem for years. These folks just started showing up recently."

Lola took another sip of lemonade and watched Charlie's face as he processed the information. He didn't change expression, didn't shift in his chair. But something, a tightening of the muscles around his eyes and the corners of his mouth, a deeper stillness, evidenced quickened interest.

"The usual hippie-dippies? Or … ?"

Edgar nodded understanding. "ELF," he said, meaning the radical Earth Liberation Front. "That was my thought, too. They did a number on Vail way back when, burning down that lodge. Along with a ranger station someplace, Oregon or Washington, I think. And didn't they set fire to a bunch of SUVs somewhere?"

"Right. But that's the thing. They're burners, not bombers."

Lola suppressed a smile. Charlie's knowledge of crime went well beyond the borders of his own isolated rural county. "You never know when they're going to show up here," he'd said once, when she twitted him about studying up on some obscure troublemaking group or other. When she'd first moved to the speck on the map that was Magpie, she found the notion laughable. Then she'd learned about the weeks-long standoff in the 1990s in remote eastern Montana between the FBI and an anti-government group calling themselves the Freemen. Another group, in the mountains of western Montana, created a hit list of local government officials so extensive as to include the dogcatcher. It had sounded like a joke to Lola until Charlie told her how agents had unearthed house trailers packed with dozens of guns and thousands of rounds of ammo, along with pipe bombs and booby traps. And, of course, the Unabomber had operated for years from a hard-luck Montana logging town, where his reclusive, off-the-grid lifestyle and unkempt appearance had attracted not a moment's notice.

"Could be a freelancer," Edgar said. "Some wannabe monkey-wrencher."

"Could be," Charlie agreed.

But it's probably not, Lola saw him thinking. Charlie's mantra, buttressed by years of experience, was that nearly always the perp was the most obvious suspect: the husband of the woman who "accidentally" drowned in the bathtub, the mother of the missing child, the disgruntled employee, the wronged spouse.

"The places with public computers, the library and such, already offered their hard drives to the FBI so they can check to see if anybody's been searching bomb-making instructions. And, of course, the mine is cooperating fully," Edgar said.

Lola had forgotten about Naomi until she felt slender fingers lace through her own. She fought an urge to pull her own unlovely hand away, to hide its freckled white skin, its blunt fingers with their bitten nails.

"What if it's a provocateur?" Naomi spoke almost in a whisper. "Someone from the mine, maybe, looking to paint the opponents as crazies." She stared at her husband as she spoke, her face still and straight, a line of tension twanging between them.

Edgar's hand twitched. Lemonade sloshed from his glass. "That's ridiculous," he said.

Naomi's hand tightened on Lola's. Lola bit the inside of her lip to keep from wincing. "It was just a thought," Naomi said.

Charlie nodded. "One that should be considered."

Naomi loosened her grip on Lola and threw Charlie a grateful smile.

A bee buzzed beneath the willow branches and landed in the puddle of spilled lemonade. A second joined it. Edgar set his glass down with a thump. The bees rose almost to the willow leaves and then drifted back to the table, lifting legs individually and placing them back down in the sticky moisture.

"We'd better show you two to your room so you can settle in," Edgar said. He reached out with thumb and forefinger, crushing first one bee and then the other with a small tight smile of satisfaction.

"Mommy, look." Twinned voices snagged the adults' attention. A piebald pony, all stubby legs and round stomach, jogged toward them, the two girls riding bareback, Margaret's arms wrapped Juliana's

42

waist. Her heels tattooed Valentine's distended flanks, urging the pony into a rocking canter. Behind them, Bub quickened his lopsided gait.

Four pairs of hands broke into applause. Four parental voices called their approval. Four heads jerked as one at the deafening bang.

The pony disappeared in a whirl of dust. When it cleared, two girls lay motionless on the ground.

EIGHT

CHARLIE HAD STRENGTH, BUT Lola a mother's desperation. She reached the girls first, flinging herself to the ground beside them, her face to Margaret's, her hand on her daughter's chest. Charlie fell to his knees beside her.

Margaret opened her eyes. "Ow."

Juliana sat up. "Double ow."

"Stay down," said Lola. "I don't know what that was. It was too loud for a gun. And that bomber's out there somewhere."

A new sound rang out. Laughter. Naomi and Edgar bent double, whooping, slapping their thighs. Edgar straightened first. "Bomber? You mean this miscreant?" He wiped tears of mirth from his eyes.

A young man walked around the corner of the house. He touched fingertips with Edgar, accepted a kiss on the cheek from Naomi. "What's so funny?" He continued on toward Lola and Charlie without waiting for an answer, stopping a few feet away. A hesitant smile vanished at the sight of the girls on the ground. "Juliana, are you all right? Who's this? What happened?"

Juliana hopped to her feet and dusted off her rear end. She reached a hand to Margaret and pulled her up. "This is my cousin, Margaret, the one I told you about. We were riding Valentine until your stupid car scared him. He bucked us off."

Charlie shook his head at Lola, trying not to smile. Lola's glance in return promised retribution.

The pony stood some feet away, reins dragging in the dirt. He stamped a hoof. "Come back here, Valentine," Juliana called. The pony gazed at a distant butte.

"Get him, Bub," Margaret said. Bub, who knew about horses' hind legs from long experience with Spot, nipped at Valentine's fetlock and then danced away before a sharp hoof could land. Valentine pinned his ears back. A second nip drew another ineffectual kick. When Bub darted in for a third, the pony turned and trudged toward them, ears still signaling extreme discontent.

"I'd keep that dog if I were you," the young man said. A thread of scar tissue along his cheekbone lifted with his slow smile. "I'm Thomas Benally. Owner of the stupid car." He shifted a bookbag from one shoulder to the other.

"Which Lola here thought was a stupid bomb." Edgar couldn't have looked more pleased with himself.

"You can't blame me," Lola said. "Given what happened here just a few days ago."

Naomi stepped between them. "Let's all go back into the house. It's cooler there. Girls, put Valentine away and feed him." She didn't invite Thomas to dinner. It was, in the Indian way, assumed.

Lola reached for Valentine's reins, smacking the pony's nose when he tried to take a bite out of her arm, and led him step by reluctant step to Juliana. The vacation had already begun to feel too long.

Thomas was a sort of ward, Naomi explained to Lola, putting it in white terms first, then narrating the clan kinships that Lola had never been able to sort out among the Blackfeet, let alone an unfamiliar tribe like the Navajo. Bottom line, he was a relative, even if not in the strict blood relationship understood in the white world.

What it came down to, in the end, was that Thomas had needed a place to live for some years and Naomi and Edgar provided. It was a practice—without the complicating and clueless machinations of government supervision—that Lola knew to be so commonplace among Indian families as to go unremarked. Now, Naomi said, he spent most of his time at the tribal college in Tsaile, about an hour and a half away, but still stayed with them during holidays and summer breaks. "He's pre-law. Not officially, of course. But that's the goal." Striving for casual, failing to keep the pride from creeping in. Diné College, like all thirty-four tribal colleges around the country, was a two-year program. "He'll go to the University of Arizona from here, and then their law school, or better yet, one of the Ivies. After that he'll come back and work for the tribe."

He *will* go, Lola noted. He *will* come back and work for the tribe. She hoped Thomas was on board with the program.

As Naomi spoke, she pulled things from the refrigerator, assembling the meal with an efficiency Lola envied. She peeled plastic wrap from a bowl of pasta salad heavy on vegetables and light on dressing. Lola ran her hands, useless, unoccupied, over the counter's polished moss-green surface. Granite? She realized that she wouldn't know.

"Refill on that?" Naomi lifted her chin towards Lola's lemonade glass.

"Sure."

Naomi refilled her own glass as well. She glanced over her shoulder and took from the cupboard a large bottle of clear liquid, hand-labeled as almond flavoring.

"I didn't know that came so big," said Lola. She was pretty sure that somewhere in her own cupboards, among all the other unused things, she had some almond flavoring, albeit about a quarter of the size of the bottle in Naomi's hand. She wondered if she should be putting almond in more things—especially given that she'd never put it in anything at all.

"It doesn't." Naomi flashed a conspiratorial grin and waved the open bottle under Lola's nose—whatever was in it wasn't almond—and then gestured toward the window, where the sky glowed orange and gold, a final burst of glory before the sun slid behind the rampart of butte. "Sun's over the yardarm, I'd say." A slug of "almond" went into her lemonade. "Lola?"

Lola thought of the tension between the brothers, of the girls on the ground, of the bomber possibly lurking somewhere on the vast reservation. She could have kissed Naomi for her offer. She held out her glass.

"Between us," said Naomi.

"Definitely." Lola filed that away for future reference, too.

Naomi called to Edgar and handed him a pan of lamb kabobs marinating in olive oil and fragrant herbs. Lola held her breath as he brushed past her in the kitchen, even though she probably didn't need to. She was pretty sure the "almond" was vodka, less incriminating than gin.

"You can grill these now," Naomi said to him. "From our garden," she told Lola. "The herbs, the vegetables, all of it. Edgar built raised beds and rigged up a drip irrigation system. And the lamb is from our own sheep. My family ran them on the mesa until—" Her face darkened.

"Until?" Lola prompted.

"Let's wait until dinner. Or after, when the girls have gone to bed."

Lola picked up the bowl of pasta salad and carried it across the kitchen. She bumped the door open with her hip and turned toward the shade house. The sun already was gone. Dusk shrouded the yard. Movement caught her eye, a blur of gray against the dun of desert. She froze and waited. Sure enough, a coyote trotted from behind a rock. It stopped and turned toward her. Then it stood on its hind legs, barely visible in the fast-deepening gloom. Lola gasped and stepped back. The salad bowl tilted in her hands. She checked to make sure none had spilled. When she looked up again, the coyote was gone.

———

Silence, broken only by the hiss of flames in the fireplace, fell over the table after the girls departed. With full nightfall, the shade house grew cool and then cold, surprisingly fast. Chairs scraped across the flagstones as people dragged them from the table to the fire, which provided the only light. The wavering flames threw faces into high relief and deep shadow, exaggerating dominant features. Charlie looked fiercer, Edgar haughtier, Naomi lovelier. Lola didn't want to think what she looked like. Haggard, she imagined. Thomas sat apart from the rest, alone in the shadows. The fountain's murmur, subsumed during the evening's conversation, asserted itself. Lola remarked upon it.

"Like the creek at home," Edgar said to Charlie. *Crick.* "Remember how Mom always yelled at us? 'You boys keep away from that crick.'"

Affection softened Charlie's voice. "Told us the Under Water People would get us, and as if that wasn't bad enough, told us the herons were Boy Eaters. That they'd spear us with those long beaks and roast us over a hot fire."

"No!" Lola and Naomi chorused.

"Yes," Edgar said. "And not just at the creek. There was water everywhere at home." Lola saw the motion that was Charlie's nod. Finally, the brothers, whatever strain had kept them apart for so long, were in sync, united by memory. "Sloughs, the Two Medicine River, all the lakes in Glacier," Edgar went on. The Blackfeet Reservation, bumped up against Glacier National Park, had even encompassed it at one point until whitemen decided they knew best how to manage the land—and make a pretty penny from tourism, too—where tribes had roamed from time immemorial.

"You miss it." The way Charlie said it, it wasn't a question.

"Be crazy not to. All that water, so clear and cold and good. And not just the water itself. The grass, tender and green in the spring before summer fries it. And the air. It's softer back home. Doesn't attack you the way it does here, sucking you dry. And the way the sage smells after rain."

"The best," said Charlie. He and Lola each liked to break off bits of sagebrush, crushing the leaves in their palms, holding their hands to their faces, breathing in. If water were nearby, Charlie would dip sage sprigs into it, intensifying the scent still more.

"Speaking of home," Lola said. "I saw something tonight that reminded me of Montana."

Charlie and Edgar looked into the darkness beyond the shade house, as though they could still see the distinctly un-Montana-like rock formations. "What's that?"

"A coyote."

Charlie shot her a warning look that Lola couldn't interpret. Naomi and Edgar locked eyes for a moment. Thomas made a choking noise.

Lola soldiered on. "It was so strange. It stood up on its hind legs. I've never seen one do that before."

Naomi bent in a spasm of coughing. Edgar pounded her back. "You were mistaken," he said. Not allowing for any possibility that maybe she wasn't.

Naomi rose and ran to the kitchen. Lola and Charlie followed in time to see her scoop something from a container on the counter. Naomi opened the door and looked at Lola. "Where was he?"

Lola pointed with her chin. Naomi stepped into the yard and sprinkled something on the ground. "Corn pollen," she said as she brushed past Lola on her way back to the shade house.

Charlie put his hand to Lola's arm to hold her a moment in the kitchen. "Coyote's a trickster here, just like at home, but he can be bad luck, too. He likes to set the world on fire."

Lola dropped her head in her hands. Yet another reminder of her whiteness. Gratitude washed through her when, with everyone back in the shade house, Naomi returned to the subject of Charlie and Edgar's homeland.

"At least it's still there, your creek." The words sliced knifelike through the conversation, all the good feeling leaking away like blood from a wound not yet recognized as mortal. "Your creeks, your lakes." She threw Edgar's own words back at him. "All *clear* and *cold* and *good*. You can still drink it. And you can go back there. Spare me your nostalgia."

Thomas rose from his chair and joined their circle, crouching beside her. The firelight flickered across his face. "It's okay," he said. "He loves his home just as much as we loved—still love—ours."

"You see," Edgar said, "Naomi and Thomas, they're from the mesa."

Lola didn't see, and said as much.

So Naomi told her.

NINE

BOTH THE NAVAJO AND Hopi lived on the mesa, the Hopi clustered in their traditional high-rise adobe dwellings to the south, the Navajo scattered about, a few still in hogans but most in the trailers and BIA bungalows that replaced them, tending sheep. Both groups depended on the profusion of springs that seeped from the desert rock, the Hopi for their ingeniously irrigated agricultural plots, the Navajo to water their sheep. And, of course, all the people for drinking water.

"It was so for centuries. Millennia," Naomi said, words easing into a singsong. Lola thought of the elders at home reciting Blackfeet history, passing it down among the generations, rhythm and beauty given equal weight with facts in their choice of words. The fire flared and receded, underscoring the cadence of the words.

"The whitemen at first found no value in the land. Too high, too dry. If the Indian people wanted to scratch a living from its surface, then let them. The whitemen laughed and went away." She paused and drew a long breath. A piñon log collapsed into radiant coals, throwing out a shower of sparks along with its beguiling fragrance.

"But they came back," she whispered. Thomas took her hands. She bent her head to his, the circle of their bodies forming a sort of sculpture, graven, unmoving, until the fire's glow highlighted the tears sliding down Naomi's cheeks.

"But they came back," Thomas echoed. "And this time they looked below the surface. They peeled it back with their giant machines, machines larger than even the dinosaurs that roamed the land without destroying it. Their machines bit into the earth, into the black rock beneath."

"Coal," Lola breathed.

"The more they took, the hungrier they became. And to take even more, they needed water."

Naomi freed her hands from Thomas's grip and pushed herself up from her chair. Indian people normally spoke in low, quiet tones, almost a whisper, which made Lola, however she tried to match it, feel loud and unmannerly in comparison. Now Naomi's voice rose to a white level, a shout by Indian standards, a raw, ragged thing. "The springs dried up. The water that was left became brackish. Crops withered. Sheep sickened and died. Babies, too. Our precious children. No longer did they need bullets to kill us."

Thomas unbent himself to stand beside her and again took up the narrative. He was taller than Naomi and his presence beside her had a visible calming effect, her rigid shoulders relaxing by millimeters, fists unclenching. "But the people persisted. They drove hundreds of miles every week to the towns, bringing back clean water. Tried to hold on. Until—"

The silence lengthened liked a stretched rubber band, the tension unbearable with the knowledge that the pain to follow would be worse. Lola held out as long as she could. "Until?"

"Until the whitemen went after the people, too." Naomi again, her voice back to normal, if anything so layered with anguish could be considered normal. "Ordered them to leave the lands that were the pathetic remnant they were allotted as reservations."

Lola struggled to put it into some sort of historical context. Tribes all around the country were only a few generations removed from the genocide that had accompanied the arrival of Europeans. Even so, Naomi and Thomas's torment seemed unusually intense. "They tried to move your grandparents? Your great-grandparents?"

"Not my grandparents. My parents! Me! I was born on the mesa. I lived there until I was a teenager. Thomas was a toddler, but still he remembers."

"My grandparents wouldn't leave," Thomas said. "We went to visit them there. All alone in a hogan, no electricity, no plumbing, hanging on in the old way. We'd bring them water, food, driving in at night with no lights so the whitemen wouldn't get us for aiding and abetting the trespassers."

"The land where they'd lived forever. *Trespassers.*" Naomi again.

Lola couldn't make sense of this new information. The history of the reservations was one of relentless betrayal. In recent decades, though, tribes had turned whitemen's weapons back on them, wielding the law as a far more effective defense than guns had ever been. And when white lawyers let them down, they sent their own young people to faraway law schools, trusting that they'd come back and advocate on behalf of the tribe. Edgar and Naomi would have been among that first wave, Lola knew, Naomi with her work for the tribal courts and Edgar on the corporate front, making sure the tribe, even though its people were not his own, got the money coming to it from the companies investing in its resources.

"How could this happen?" she asked. "Surely there were lawsuits. Congressional hearings."

"Of course there were. And in most cases, they'd have been effective." Edgar spoke quickly, quietly, a foil to the raw emotion emanating from Naomi and Thomas. "But this is Conrad Coal."

Lola had heard of it before, vaguely. One of those big corporations whose names showed up regularly in headlines on the financial pages she never really read. "I take it they have money?"

"More than God. ExxonMobil type money. Walmart money. Aramco money. They're not just national but international."

"Oh, no." No matter how many smart Indian lawyers the tribes threw at the case, no matter how many high-priced white lobbyists they hired in Washington, they'd be outmatched. That kind of money trumped everything else, every time. Lola had covered too many lawsuits and even criminal cases that dragged on forever, endless waves of appeals financed by limitless bank accounts, thousand-dollar-an-hour corporate lawyers with their buttery leather briefcases and retinues of paralegals and assistants arrayed against local prosecutors, in cheap scuffed shoes, trying to do justice to the biggest cases of their lives without shorting the rest of their crushing caseloads.

"Like the Russians," Lola murmured.

"Pardon?"

"Something my father always said. The reason nobody could ever conquer Russia. Not Napoleon, not the Germans. Because the Russians had an endless supply of bodies to throw at invaders. Each time a row of them was mowed down, another row popped up to take its place. They could lose millions and millions and still have millions more left. Of course, nowadays I suppose that theory applies to the Chinese. And to dollars, of course. These companies have millions."

"Billions," Edgar corrected her. "Many, many billions."

"You're so screwed," Lola blurted. She couldn't figure out a tactful way to voice her question, so she made it a simple statement. "But you work for the mine." She thought she was beginning to understand the strain between Edgar and his wife.

Naomi moved closer to the fire. She wrapped her arms around her torso, clad in its thin layer of silk, and disabused Lola of her theory. "It was my idea," she said, as Edgar nodded agreement. "I thought it would be a good idea to have somebody on the inside."

Lola was reminded of how Naomi seemed to have Thomas's career planned out. It appeared she'd likewise dictated her husband's path. She wondered if the considerable salary Edgar almost certainly pulled down from the mine had played into Naomi's recommendation.

"It seemed like a good idea at the time," Naomi added, "given how Conrad Coal doesn't fight fair. But now it looks as though somebody's decided we shouldn't either."

Maybe it was the contrast between the dancing shadows thrown by the flames and the moonlit desert beyond, the landscape edged in hard bright lines of black and white, everything a little weird, out of kilter. Lola's blood hummed in her veins. The air felt supercharged, jittery with overactive ions, as though readying itself for a crashing storm still hours from its appearance on the horizon.

"You mean the bombing," Lola said slowly. "Terrorism. Ecoterrorism, I guess they call it."

"Not terrorism." Lola didn't know if it was a trick of the firelight, but Naomi seemed to be smiling. "War."

TEN

ONE MINUTE I'M DRIVING up to Gar and Naomi's, giving it some gas because I'm late. The next, people are hitting the dirt like I'm one of those World Trade Center bombers. Guess I'd better not make jokes about bombing, though. Not with what happened at the billboard.

There were two of them, Gar's brother and his white wife. Oh, and their little girl. That's three. Four if you count their three-legged dog. The brother, Charlie, doesn't look anything like Gar. Taller and twice as wide. Not fat, though. Solid, the way a lot of our people are. Got that cop look to him. Alert. Makes you nervous, like you've done something wrong. Which I haven't. Not intentionally. The wife, just about as tall as he is. On the scrawny side, kind of like Naomi, only Naomi wears it better, always dressed in something stylish. This woman looks like she throws her clothes on in the morning without taking a good look at what she's pulled out of the drawer. Lots of curly hair, fair skin. She's not doing well in the heat, you can tell. Neck all red and blotchy. I'll give her credit for one thing: she's not all Indianed up like a lot of white women who marry our men. No turquoise, no feather earrings. No T-shirt with an image of armed Apaches and a message reading *Homeland Security: Fighting Terrorism Since 1492*. Not a dream catcher in sight.

Their little girl, though. She's all Indian except for her eyes. Those are light like her mother's, and they drill right through you. Falling off Valentine knocked the wind out of her. But when I went to help her up, she gave me a look and told me she'd get herself up, thank you very much. They're going to have their hands full with that one. Maybe they already do.

Naomi and Gar acted like it was all a big joke, the way that woman thought my car backfiring was a bomb, or shots, or something. I didn't think it was so funny even though I laughed and went along. Their being here complicates an already complicated situation. Charlie's a cop, like I said. Not a Navajo cop, but cops can't help themselves. Something goes wrong, especially something like this, and their noses start twitching like dogs on the hunt. And it turns out the woman is a reporter. You ask me, that's worse. Cops, at least they follow rules, most of them anyhow. You get crosswise with them once or twice, as I might have done—stupid kid stuff, no permanent record—and you know how they work. The way they see things. If something doesn't fit, it's not like they throw it away completely, but it goes off to one side, ready to be retrieved if something else comes up.

I haven't dealt with reporters as much; not at all, really. But I've seen them at tribal council meetings, the way they sidle up to people afterward, hit them with questions nobody saw coming. Far as I can tell, they don't have any rules. And, like cops, they're always on the clock. This woman, Lola. The way she was asking questions after dinner last night, you'd think she was a hotshot for the *Navajo Times*. And that business about Coyote. If I didn't know better, I'd say she'd made it up just to mess with me. But how can she possibly know about Coyote?

I fed her the story about the mesa. That always gets them. Fits into the whole Indians-screwed-by-whitemen narrative. It helps that it's true. Here's the thing. Most people, white people and, hell, even Indians, they hear that and it's enough. But this woman just kept those gray eyes of hers on me after I'd finished talking, not saying anything. Thinking. Turning it over in her brain, looking for the piece that didn't fit. Like she was on to me, even if her cop husband wasn't. Yet.

We're going to have to decide what to do about her. About both of them.

ELEVEN

Lola had set her phone alarm for six, hoping to ease into the day alone before confronting the relentless perfection of Edgar and Naomi's life.

Charlie, normally an early riser, lay like the dead beside her. All that driving, she thought. She lingered a moment, savoring the cool of the room. The breeze slipping through the blinds at the open window had a scrubbed, sparkling feel, the aftermath of the storm that had rumbled through at about four in the morning, lots of wind and crashing drama but, as far as Lola could tell before she'd fallen back asleep, only a brief patter of rain. Still, it was enough to release the heady scent of damp earth and aromatic sage.

A run was in order, she thought. Something to clear her head of the previous day's bombardment of information and emotion, the way the storm had cleared the air of heat and dust. She rooted in her duffel for the caffeine-laced jellybeans that she ate before her runs— the better to avoid the pee stop mandated by carelessly calculated

60

coffee intake—and slipped from the room, hoping to get in a few miles before the sun blasted opportunity into impossibility.

Not a chance. The aroma of fresh-ground and brewed coffee greeted her as she entered the kitchen; that, and the scent of waffles arising from an old-fashioned iron atop the stove. Bowls of sliced fruit sat around the island, next to a pair of iPads in identical leather cases. Lola wondered how Naomi and Edgar told them apart. The same pretty pitcher from the previous night now held orange juice. Wrung-out orange hulls sat in a heap on a cutting board. Lola entertained the sour suspicion that Naomi had waited to throw them away so Lola would know that, just as with the lemonade, there was nothing store-bought about her orange juice. The front door stood open, Naomi silhouetted within it, facing outward. She turned, training a brilliant smile upon Lola. It vanished fast.

"I always greet the dawn ... oh dear." She poured a hasty cup of coffee and thrust it into Lola's hands. "You're one of those."

The coffee burned its way down Lola's throat, so much better than the caffeinated candies. Something sparked in her brain, a flaring match, a flipped switch. She risked words. They came out in a croak. "One of those?"

"One of those people who isn't really awake until after that first cup of coffee. Gar's the same way. Charlie, too? I'm a tea person myself." She gestured to a cup on the counter, wisps of steam curling from the pale liquid within.

Of course you are, Lola thought, thankful that the coffee had already done enough of its work that the words didn't slip from her mouth. "You're up early," she said instead. Even though she knew that six wasn't particularly early, that lots of seemingly normal people, Charlie among them despite his uncharacteristic decision to sleep in, were awake and even functioning at that hour.

61

"Always," Naomi said.

You're one of those, Lola thought, tempted to throw Naomi's own words back at her. On a typical day, Naomi was probably in the office by seven, and filing briefs or whatever lawyers did by eight.

"Morning's my alone-time," Naomi offered, and Lola felt some of her prejudices melt away as their eyes met in quick understanding. "You know how it is," she said. "Husband, kid, texts, emails. Somebody always wants something from me, all day, every day. At least that's how it feels. Early morning is the only time I'm free of it."

Lola raised her coffee cup. "Amen to that."

The corner of Naomi's mouth twitched. "Are you toasting me or do you want a refill?"

"Both." They laughed together. Which is how Charlie and Edgar found them when they belatedly arrived on the scene. Charlie cast an envious glance at the iPads, then turned his attention to his wife and sister-in-law. "This could be trouble," he joked to Edgar.

The smile faded from Lola's face as she noticed Edgar's shoulders stiffen in a sign that he agreed—and that he didn't see it as a joking matter.

––––––––

"Watch your step," warned their guide, looking up at her from the base of the soaring ladder that led to the cliff houses.

The site, Edgar had said over breakfast, would be a good introduction. "It's small, not as overwhelming as places like Canyon de Chelly or Chaco Canyon, and it won't be overrun with tourists. When I first came here, Naomi took me to all of the sites. They got mixed up in my head. I'd never seen so many cliff dwellings and kivas in my life. You know us Piikani … " He threw a glance at Charlie, watching him catch the Blackfeet language reference to their people. "The most we ever left behind was some tepee rings."

"And a lot of scared-ass Crow," Charlie said, of the traditional enemies of the Blackfeet.

Lola had taken the joshing to mean that the dissonance between the brothers was starting to ease. Good, she thought. That would make for a more relaxed stay.

Naomi broke in. "With the cliff dwellings and kivas you'll see today, the people were more like the Hopi. Even though we Diné live here now, we're more closely related to the Piikani than the Hopi. We're all Athabascan, the people who migrated over the land bridge from Siberia."

She had looked at Lola as she spoke. Grateful as Lola was for the history lesson, she'd thought it also emphasized her status as a white-skinned outsider. She wondered if Naomi's innocent-seeming lectures were a way of keeping her firmly on her own side of the fence, no matter what they had in common as stressed-out working mothers.

Now, as Lola clung to the wooden ladder halfway up a cliff, a more immediate concern asserted itself. Before they'd left the house, she'd divined that climbing would be involved. "How high?" she'd asked.

"Oh, it's not bad," Naomi had told her. "Unless you don't like heights." Luckily, Charlie hadn't been in the room to take exception to Lola's swift denial.

To say she didn't like heights was an understatement. Lola thought of all the things she hated: Vacation. Wearing suits or, worse yet, dresses. Acting like a lady. But she'd have gone on vacation for a month, in a cocktail frock and pearls, trailing air-kisses in her wake, if it meant she could have avoided going more than three feet off the ground. When she'd first come to Montana, the man who'd killed Mary Alice had tried to kill her, too, by forcing her off a precipice, which hadn't exactly helped her acrophobia. Yet now she was easily fifty feet up the side of the cliff, with fifty more to go, and aware that surviving until she reached the ledge at the top only meant that she'd face the even more agonizing trip back down.

Charlie's booted feet receded above her. The girls had gone first, scampering like mountain goats up the ladder, their dexterity worrying even the guide. "Don't go running around up there until I get there," he'd called, climbing faster. "You two okay behind me?" he yelled back to Lola and Charlie. "I'll wait for you at the top."

Even though it was bolted to the cliff, the ladder swayed whenever Charlie took a step. Each time it moved, Lola stopped and clung white-knuckled, pressing against its rungs. Whenever Charlie stopped, she lifted a trembling leg, placed it on the next round rung, and hauled herself up, willing herself to look only at the rock wall beyond the rungs, its rough surface the color of sunset. An elegantly striped lizard with a blue-gray whiptail skittered across the rock. It stopped and turned its head toward Lola. The soft white pouch of its throat pulsed. Lola swallowed in response. Her own throat was dry. She dared not free a hand to retrieve the water bottle dangling from a carabiner hooked through a belt loop. She refused to look up, for fear of seeing how far she had to go. And to look down would only remind her of how very far her fall would be, the plunge that would end with her head split open like a gourd, bones shattered, her final words a whispered, "I told you this was a bad idea."

"Mom, hurry up." Margaret's voice, closer than she'd thought, banged against the wall of panic that surrounded her. A strong hand clasped her wrist. "I've got you," said Charlie. He pitched his voice low and reassuring. Lola loved Charlie for all sorts of reasons, but at this moment, the one that outshone all others was that he never made fun of her fears. She scrambled onto the ledge on all fours and clung to Charlie as he helped her to her feet, not releasing her grip on him until her knees stopped shaking. She took a breath and looked around. "Whoa."

The guide nodded, accepting the amazement as his due. "Worth the climb?"

"Almost." Lola remained unwilling to grant that anything was worth that sort of torture. She stood within the welcome cool of a rock overhang that soared several stories above them, adobe houses stacked one atop the other within it. Lola reached out a still-shaking hand and touched a wall.

"Those bricks are a thousand years old," the guide said.

She snatched her hand away.

"You won't hurt it. But we ask that people not touch the things that are here—the pot shards, the beams, the rock art. We're lucky, though. We're small enough, and enough out of the way, that we don't have the problems here that they see at Chaco Canyon."

Lola put her face close to the brick, close enough to see the twigs and grasses that held the mud together. Heat radiated from it, bringing the scent of earth and—she had to be imagining this—thousand-year-old dung. She tilted her head back, no longer afraid to look up now that her feet were planted on rock instead of rung. The houses seemed all of a piece with the land surrounding them, the same dusty reddish color, pleasingly proportional, large homes at the base with small single-room structures perched at the top. She gazed out over the desert, far—very far—below, and tried to imagine it quilted with vegetable plots. This time of day, the people probably would have retreated to the cool of the houses, the woman chatting companionably as they ground the corn so efficiently grown across the region with so very little water. "What happens at Chaco Canyon?"

The guide's face darkened. "New Agers kept sneaking in, holding their ceremonies—such as they were—in the large kivas," he said of the circular underground rooms used for ceremonies. "We had to close them off to the public. Those people tried to tell us they were honoring us. But those are our sacred spaces. Imagine if Catholics decided to hold a Mass in a synagogue or mosque and told Jews or Muslims they should feel flattered."

Lola rolled her eyes. She'd been with Charlie long enough, and had spent enough time on the reservation, to be well acquainted with the phenomenon of white people either claiming a long-ago Indian ancestor or, worse yet, proclaiming themselves "Native American" in spirit. "Try fifty—or sixty or even seventy—percent unemployment," she always wanted to say. "Try an Indian Health Service that's underfunded by half its budget. Try a life that's more than cool feathers and beads." Or, she thought, in the case of the Southwest, silver and turquoise. On their stops on the way to the reservation, she'd already seen elderly white women with squash blossom necklaces worth thousands of dollars bouncing around on their leathery, too-bare chests. Each time, she forced herself to re-member that the sale of that necklace probably had supported a family for months.

"What's that?" Lola pointed west, toward an industrial-looking tower beside an elongated heap of black rock that dwarfed the hub-bub of truck traffic around it. Even from several miles away, the op-eration was impressively large.

"The mine." The guide cut off the words with a finality that dis-couraged further questions. He spat into the dust. The damp blotch disappeared almost immediately.

Lola turned away from the modern intrusion into the ancient landscape and peered through a small square window in one of the cliff houses. The room within was cool and dim. Behind her, the guide explained that the houses' thick-walled construction provided refuge from summer's fierce heat. In winter, a small fire easily warmed them. "Speaking of fire," Lola called to him, "has the charcoal survived all this time because it's so dry?"

"What do you mean?"

Lola pointed through the window to a few sticks of charred piñon in the middle of the floor. Charlie leaned in close behind her. The guide went around through the door and stooped over the wood. He poked at it with his finger, lifted one of the sticks, and sniffed it. Charlie joined him. A long look passed between them.

"Oh, for heaven's sake," Lola said. The strong silent cop thing only went so far. "It's fresh, isn't it?" She went around to the door and bent low to enter the room. Either the Ancestral Puebloans had been tiny or they'd bumped their heads a lot, she thought.

Charlie held up his hand. "Stay right there." His eyes scanned the room, fastening on something in a dark corner. Wide, horizontal marks striped the dirt floor. "He swept behind him," Charlie said. "We're not going to find any footprints." Having established that, he walked to the corner, Lola and the guide close behind.

Margaret's voice floated through the window. "Mom, where are you?"

"In here, honey."

Margaret and Juliana piled through the door. "Juliana showed me some rock art. Come see." They stopped at the sight of the adults' grim expressions.

"What's going on?" said Juliana.

"Looks like somebody's been using this house," said the guide. "That's illegal. Whoever it was made a fire. And, look over there." He pursed his lips in the direction of the corner, where Charlie reached for a small bookbag.

"Don't touch that!" The guide's voice was urgent. "This is Navajo Nation land. I'll have to call the tribal police. And the National Park police too, probably."

"I'm a sheriff," Charlie said.

"Not here, you're not."

Margaret and Juliana edged around the two men. The bookbag was a few feet beyond them, a little larger than the one Margaret carried to school but forest-green and battered, not the bright primary-color variety carried by younger kids. It lay nearly flat, collapsed upon itself. Empty, or nearly so, thought Lola. She wondered what it had held. A key chain adorned with a miniature Navajo rug dangled from one of its loops.

"No keys, dammit," Charlie said. "That would have helped."

"Come on." Juliana tugged hard at his hand. "Let's get out of here. This place scares me."

"Wait a minute," said Charlie. He fumbled for his cellphone. "I want to take a picture."

"No!" said Juliana. The single word trembled. "This is a sacred place. It's disrespectful."

Lola could almost feel the battle within Charlie, cop versus tribal member. But not a member of this tribe. And not a cop in this state. He lowered the phone.

"Let's go back down," the guide said. "Do you mind? I want to let the higher-ups know about this before another group comes through."

The only person who minded was Lola, and only because it meant she had to face the damnable ladder again, sooner than she had planned. She lagged behind as the others moved to the edge of the cliff, grateful when Juliana asked for a delay. "I have to go to the bathroom. Don't worry, I'll go over there." She pointed to a nondescript space far to the end of the ledge. "You go ahead."

Lola was pretty sure that peeing was on the list of forbidden things at the site, and said as much. "Can't you wait until we get down?"

Juliana danced from one foot to another. "I don't think so."

Charlie began to shake his head. "I'll wait for her," Lola said. Anything that gave her another few minutes before the climb back down. You can do this, she chanted to herself. Juliana reappeared sooner than she would have liked. "You'd better go ahead of me," Lola said. "I'm going to take forever."

"Okay." Juliana brushed past her, swung herself onto the ladder, and clambered down with impressive alacrity. Lola, as promised, moved far more slowly. First, because she was at least as afraid climbing down as she'd been ascending the ladder. But also because she was trying to process the sight of the key chain's little rug dangling from Juliana's pocket.

TWELVE

Juliana reached the bottom of the ladder before Lola was half-way down. At least, that's what Lola surmised by the chorus of voices floating upward, dominated by Margaret's high-pitched "Mom, come on. Hurry."

Hurry, she said to herself. That's a good one. Her sweaty hands slipped on the wood. She wanted, desperately, to wipe one and then the other on her pants but dared not release her hold. The same lizard that had greeted her on the way up appeared not to have moved. It flicked its tongue at her as she leaned against the rungs and tried to steady her breathing. She blew out a long stream of air and thought that the ancient ones were almost diabolically resourceful in terms of defense. If anyone attacked, all they needed to do was raise the ladders. She'd noted with intense gratitude the heavy iron bolts that held the present-day ladder in place. Even as she'd praised it, the guide had pointed to the cliff wall. "Look there." Her gaze traced the faintest of ledges and footholds along the side of the cliff. If enemies had been so foolish as to dare the perilous ascent, they'd have had to do so single-file, in easily picked-off fashion. And if they'd tried to lay siege, the guide told them, the pueblos would have been stocked with plentiful stores, pots the size of children filled with ground corn, even tall water jars, their bottoms indented to fit a bearer's head. Given their imperviousness to conquest, the mystery still bedeviling historians was why their civilization had decamped from the region. Some sort of natural disaster was the prevailing opinion. Years or even decades of drought, probably. Nothing like the man-made disaster that was the mine.

Lola's vantage point on the ladder allowed her to gaze across the miles at the mine without looking down. The mountain of coal, awaiting transport to belching power plants, was a miniature version of the sacred mesa atop which it sat. She reminded herself, as she always did when confronted with man's despoiling of natural beauty, that she liked her electricity just fine. And that the mine, according to what Edgar and Naomi had told them the night before, provided hundreds of jobs in an otherwise-remote area. As she watched, one of the trucks detached itself from the swarm around the coal and lumbered along the access road.

Lola lifted a reluctant foot from the security of the rung and lowered herself inch by inch until she felt the next rung beneath her foot. She eased her other foot down and let her hands slide along the ladder. She took a shuddering breath and paused before the next step. The truck turned out of the mine entrance onto the main road that led past the turnoff to the ruins, growing larger as it approached.

Margaret's voice wafted her way, chased by Charlie's. "Almost done, Mom."

"No hurry, Lola. We've got nothing to do for the next hour or so."

Lola blew another breath. *When the truck passes*, she told herself, *I'll take another step down*. The truck moved closer, and then, with a blast that shook the ladder in its fastenings, petaled into an orange bloom of flame.

———————

Lola was on the ladder and then she was on the ground, the last several steps accomplished with a speed she'd not have believed possible. The guide had already taken off, dust churning in his wake as his tribal-issue pickup barreled down the road. Charlie and the girls were in Edgar's truck, which barely slowed to pick up Lola.

"Holy shit." Lola struggled to fasten her seat belt as Charlie swung the truck in a quick turn that flung her against the door. "What was that?"

"You know what it was." He spat the words as if cursing.

"Where are we going?" As if she didn't know.

Charlie's grip on the wheel was fierce, his eyes narrowed, lips pressed together. "To see if we can help that poor trucker."

That poor trucker was beyond help, Lola knew. She'd seen the aftermath of too many bombings in Afghanistan to hold out hope. "The girls," she said. They didn't need to be exposed to that sort of thing.

"You're going to stay with them," said Charlie. The pickup leapt forward. Charlie muttered something about the benefits of a V8 engine.

"Like hell I am." The strands of breaking-news DNA, tamped into a deep place more than a year earlier, began to move about, stretching and uncoiling, crowding the walls of their confinement, in a sensation that was nearly physical. Lola pushed her hands against her gut and spoke as much to herself as Charlie. "You can't go there. It's like the guide said. We're outsiders. You are."

"Uncle Charlie." Juliana's voice trembled. "I don't want to go. I'm scared. We should go home."

Charlie didn't reply. The truck rocketed along another half-mile before he lifted his foot from the accelerator and touched it to the brake pedal. His U-turn was unnecessarily exaggerated, accompanied by great plumes of red dust. Lola looked in the rearview mirror, caught Margaret's eye, and shook her head. Not the time for conversation, she tried to convey. Margaret turned to Juliana and laid her finger across her lips. Charlie's temper, rarely exhibited, was of the silent variety and usually quick to pass. Lola knew he would be more angry at himself for wanting to do something so clearly ill-advised, given the girls' presence. Usually that sort of impulse was Lola's territory. Lola promised herself she wouldn't bring it up the next time they fought, even though she knew very well it was a promise she'd likely break, just as she knew Charlie would probably forgive her for bringing it up.

They rode in silence for a half-hour, until Charlie turned off the main road onto the long track that led back to his brother's house. Lola took a moment to appreciate the fact that their relationship was at the point where they'd made their peace with one another's imperfections, and wondered if Edgar and Naomi, sprinting down the driveway toward the pickup, had reached that same stage.

———

"We knew you'd gone to the cliff houses." Naomi's voice was muffled, her face buried in her daughter's hair. "We tried to call. But there's no cell service there."

"We were afraid you might have been on the road when—" Edgar added, wrapping his arms around wife and daughter.

Just like that, Lola was back in Wyoming, fearing for Margaret's life. *Fear* being wholly inadequate to encompass the certainty that if anything had happened to Margaret, her own life would cease to matter. The feeling rushed back now, the cessation of breath before she'd realized that day that Margaret was safe, the need to touch her child everywhere, to inhale her scent, to press her lips again and again to Margaret's soft skin. Now, before she could turn to her daughter, Margaret's hand was in hers, the child sensing the mother's need. Deep within Lola, the breaking-news DNA that had responded to the bombing spiraled tight and quieted.

"Coffee, I think, is in order," she said, trying for normalcy. She thought back to the previous night, to the way Naomi had dosed her lemonade. "Or maybe lemonade." From the grateful look Naomi threw her, she knew she'd divined the woman's need. She wondered how deep it went.

"Girls," Edgar said, "why don't you go inside where it's cooler? Stay close. No riding Valentine."

"We don't want to, anyway," Juliana said. Lola surmised they were more rattled than they wanted to let on. They twined their arms and bent their heads toward one another, dark hair flowing together, and slipped from the room silent as water.

The adults settled themselves in the shade house and sipped at the beverages of their choice. It was midday, an hour that defeated even the shade house. But the chill of violent death lay over them all. Despite acknowledging Naomi's need for her doctored lemonade, Lola opted for coffee, her own drug of choice, wrapping her hands around her mug, absorbing its warmth.

Edgar waited until the door had closed behind the girls. "No solid information yet," he said in answer to Charlie's unspoken query. "The truck driver is dead, of course," he added before anyone could ask the next likely question. "Which is the scary thing. The elder, that was probably an accident. Nobody expected him to be there when the sign blew. But there was no way anyone could have expected the truck driver to survive today. Only two incidents, but the guy who did this—if it *is* a guy, and if it's the same guy—is already upping the ante."

"Here's what I don't get," said Charlie. "With the billboard, there was still some room for doubt that this was a protest against the mine. After today, I think we can safely presume that the mine is the target."

The line between assume and presume was so thin as to be nearly invisible, but Lola knew Charlie was right. Once again, she reminded herself that when it came to crime, the most likely theories usually proved correct.

"Possibly," said Edgar.

Maybe lawyers were more skeptical, Lola thought.

"When people do something like this as a protest, they usually want the world to know," Charlie continued, pushing past Edgar's hesitance. Lola wondered if anyone else caught the annoyance in his tone.

"Go on."

"Nobody's claimed responsibility. No communiqués, no manifestos, no blathering on the Internet, right?"

"Oh, there's plenty of Internet chatter," Edgar said.

"I'll bet," said Charlie, and Edgar looked pleased. "But chatter about the bombings, right? Nobody saying, 'Look what we did. And guess what else we're going to do if—what?' The mine isn't shut down? Or, at least, the expansion halted?"

"Nothing like that," said Naomi when Edgar remained silent. "I've been watching." Her tall glass was half empty. With a manicured nail, she etched patterns in the rime of frost on its side.

"It's too soon for anything about the truck," Edgar protested.

"Not necessarily," said Lola. "The Taliban gabbed online within minutes of some of their attacks. I always thought it was funny how fast they took to the Internet, given the whole anti-technology thing they started with."

"How long since you've been in Afghanistan?"

Edgar had mastered the lawyer's art of tone-as-dismissal, Lola thought. "Almost ten years."

"Well, then." Advantage, Edgar.

"Is it possible that these were done by different people?" Naomi ventured. "Not just by different people, but different groups?

"Wrong question." Charlie spoke to Naomi, but Lola guessed his response was directed at Edgar. "Of course it's possible. But is it probable? It just isn't. How's that research coming?"

Edgar slumped and ran his hand over his face. "Along with our own digging, we're getting regular updates from both the tribal police and the FBI. It's like you said, the MO doesn't fit the usual suspects. On the other hand, they're the ones with the skill to pull this sort of thing off. Not giving them credit. Just being realistic."

"Whoever did it had some serious chops," Lola said. "Two different kinds of bombs—that doesn't seem easy."

Edgar snapped to attention. "What do you mean, two different kinds?"

"I'm guessing the one that took out the billboard—and the elder—was your basic timer device. Your guy probably set it up at night when nobody was around to see him, and timed it to go off in the morning before things got too busy. The billboard was far enough off the road that even if a car had been driving past, it might have been damaged but not destroyed."

"Unlike the elder, who had the misfortune to be sitting right next to it," Edgar said. "What about the other one?"

"You wouldn't want to use a timer on that one," Lola said. "Not if you were trying to take out a truck or some other vehicle from the mine. You'd have no way of knowing when it would pass. So you'd want some sort of trigger device, like a cellphone."

"I don't get how that rules out the same person for both," Edgar said.

Charlie came to Lola's defense. "It doesn't. But again, people who do these sorts of things tend to learn one method and stick with it. Maybe we've got a copycat here—somebody who saw the billboard blow up and decided he could make an even bigger splash."

Lola switched sides, playing devil's advocate. "Or we could have a lone wolf on our hands." That wriggle within was back, uncoiling faster, more insistently. She twisted in her seat and ignored the arch of Charlie's eyebrow at the word *our*. "Someone like a McVeigh. Or that guy who attacked abortion clinics down South and then hid out for years in the woods? Wasn't he a bomber, too?"

"He was," said Charlie. "And now he's in SuperMax in Colorado, cooling his jets there with McVeigh's partner and the men who planned the first World Trade Center bombing. Anyway, his thing was abortionists and gays, not environmental stuff. And McVeigh hated the government."

"But their methods," said Lola. "The bombings, the business of working alone. It throws people off the scent. Remember how everybody thought Islamic terrorists were behind Oklahoma City? And how they blamed the Olympics bombing in Atlanta on some poor security guard? Neither of the guys who actually did it went around bragging about what they'd done. In fact, each did their damnedest to get away with it. What if the same thing is at work here?"

At which point, given the looks on everyone else's faces, Lola wished she'd just kept her mouth shut. They'd all been thinking the same thing. It was, as Charlie so devoutly espoused, the most likely scenario.

But it was also the scenario that would prove the toughest case to crack. Meaning, Lola knew, that more people were probably going to die.

THIRTEEN

I DIDN'T DO ANYTHING this time. At least, that's what I keep telling myself. "I'm out," I said a couple of days ago. "This killing—"

The reply came cool and quiet as spring water. *That was an accident.* The same words I'd told *Shizhé'é* when he came to me, after.

But at least I got a promise: *Never again. Not for you.*

Which didn't mean I was done. There was another job for me, a strange one this time, so strange I should have known. I was to go to the road outside the mine between ten in the morning and ten fifteen and leave a large gym bag in the westbound lane, just to one side of the center line. The idea was, it would look like the bag had fallen off a car. The tourists are always tying all of their shit on top of their cars. The bag was already scuffed up pretty bad, just like it had bounced along the road a ways. It even had some clothes inside, men's jeans and T-shirts and underwear and socks. An old disposable razor, a ratty toothbrush, a half-squeezed tube of off-brand toothpaste. The clothes were worn, like someone had had them for a long time. I figure maybe they came from a secondhand store.

There's a few on the reservation, people giving us their castoffs—even their underwear, for Chrissakes—rather than letting us develop businesses where we could work jobs that would let us buy our own damn clothes. Businesses other than the mine, I mean.

"What's this for?" I asked, hefting the bag. I just got a look, one that said *Don't ask.* My chest seized up. A Dopp kit was added to the bag. I didn't look in it. I guess you could say I knew after all.

Between ten a.m. and ten fifteen. Westbound lane. A little off the center line. Then get out of there.

So I did it. Spent the night in my hiding spot, high up the cliff, in one of the houses of the ancients. I crept down at first light, sat in brush a few yards back from the road for four hours, shifting a pebble from one side of my mouth to the other to fight thirst, fretting over a mistake I'd made. I'd left my bookbag behind. By the time I realized I'd forgotten it, it was too late. The cliff dwelling tours would have started. All I could hope was that nobody would find it. I went over all the things that could go wrong and ended up feeling as good as I could under the circumstances. Nothing in the bookbag would identify me. I'd taken out my books the night before so as not to have any extra weight. Just a water bottle and a sandwich. Even when my brain went all CSI and I started worrying about fingerprints and DNA, I calmed myself down by remembering that mine weren't on record anywhere. Besides, I'd worn gloves against the night's chill, and their fabric had probably wiped the bottle clean of my fingerprints. The plastic wrap around the sandwich, thank God, I'd crumpled up and stuffed into my pocket so as not to leave trash.

The key chain bothered me a little. I don't use it for keys, just carry it because I like it. Half the people on the reservation, and even more tourists, have those key chains. Betty Begay makes them. Once she realized how much money she could make stocking trading posts around the reservation with those little trinkets she could turn out in no time at all, compared to the months it took to weave a good-sized rug, she turned mostly to them—which had the effect, of course, of making her true rugs all the more rare and therefore worth even more than they'd been before. Betty Begay could have taught the supply and demand segment of my Econ 101 course in about five minutes flat.

I sat under that brush, alternately worrying and reassuring myself, until ten. Each time I started out from under my shelter, I'd hear a car approach. By ten after, I was sweating. At twelve after, the road was bare. I dashed out and positioned the bag just so, laying it on its side so it would look even more like it had just fallen, and sprinted back to the brush. I waited a few minutes, then began a retreat, dodging from one clump of brush to the next. I could hear tires screeching as cars approached the bag and swerved around it. They had to be careful. The shoulder there was soft. I was almost to the side road where I'd parked my car when I heard a deeper rumble. One of the trucks from the mine, I figured. I didn't look back.

Until I did.

The blast was bigger this time, or maybe I was just closer. The air did that thing again, pushing against me, sucking back. Long time ago, my parents took me to California, to the ocean. I stood in water up to my thighs, feeling it tug at me. That's what the air was like. Again the cloud of smoke and dirt, bits and pieces of truck kicked into the sky by the blast, the red dirt swirling counterclockwise across the desert floor. I fell to my knees and wrapped my arms around my head.

"I didn't do it," I whispered. "I didn't." Even though I knew that, in some crucial way, I had.

FOURTEEN

The sense of something wrong jolted Lola from sleep.

She lay in the woolly dead-of-night stillness, letting herself come fully awake. The room was quiet. Too quiet. That was it. Charlie was the soundest of sleepers, falling off within seconds of his head touching the pillow, his deep breaths just short of a snore. Now he lay tense and alert beside her. She rolled onto her side and ran her fingers over his chest, feeling the muscles tighten with the motion. "You're awake. What's up?"

"Thought I heard a car."

Lola listened. Nothing. "Probably out on the main road."

"That road's a long way away. Besides, it wasn't the engine. A door."

"Maybe somebody stopped on the road. Sound travels at night." She faked a yawn, hoping he'd take the hint. If he stopped talking, there was a chance she'd sink back into sleep. Then she heard it too, a faint whirring.

"There it is. I thought you said it wasn't an engine sound."

Charlie chuckled. "It's not. Haven't you ever heard a sewing machine?"

"Do I look like I have? I barely made it through home ec in high school. I think Naomi's is the first I've seen up close since then." Lola had faked appreciation when Naomi pointed out the sewing machine sitting atop a table with a flounced and flowered skirt, showing off an instrument panel that would have done credit to a jetliner,. She'd narrated all the things it could do, things about which Lola cared not a whit.

"Guess Naomi can't sleep either. Besides, that's not what I heard. It was definitely a car door."

"Maybe Naomi or your brother left something in the car and went out and got it. Besides, what do you mean, you can't sleep either?" Lola, an insomniac who nightly marveled at the profound restfulness of Charlie's sleep, had jerked fully awake. He might as well have told her the sky was green and the grass was blue. He never couldn't sleep. "What's on your mind?"

"What do you think?"

They lay quietly together, thinking of the two innocent men shredded by someone's murderous impulse. Lola reached for the light blanket at the foot of the bed and pulled it over them. Naomi and Edgar turned off the air-conditioning at sunset and threw open the windows to admit the cool night air. Lola's and Charlie's room overlooked the shade house. The breeze whispered through its rooftop branches. Something skritched across the patio's flagstones. Lola remembered the lizard she'd seen earlier in the day. When she'd told Naomi about it, Naomi had assured her they were harmless. "But watch out at night. That's when the tarantulas come out. Sometimes when you're driving, the headlights will catch them crossing the road. They look scary, but they're not poisonous."

Lola resolved never to go anywhere barefoot at night in this place. Which, she hoped, wasn't a place she'd be much longer.

She broached the subject to Charlie. "Your brother and Naomi are going to be even busier than before. Maybe we should just go home." Even though he couldn't see her hands in the dark, she slid them beneath the blanket and crossed her fingers.

"I thought that, too," Charlie said. Lola uncrossed her fingers. Too soon.

"But the girls are getting along so well." His voice a murmur, barely audible. "Besides, there's something else."

"What?" Lola tried to soften her snappishness. "Yes, it's nice about the girls." Why oh why couldn't Juliana have been the Miss Priss she'd expected, the kind of ruffle-bedecked child who'd present Margaret with Barbie dolls and dress-up clothes? Along with her gray eyes, frequently narrowed in suspicion, Margaret also had inherited her mother's horror of all things girly.

"Eddie ordered me to go."

"What do you mean, ordered?" Lola thought Charlie was probably exaggerating. Edgar had likely made the same sort of suggestion Lola had just proffered. "They're probably worried about not being able to be the perfect hosts because they're so busy with the bombings."

Charlie shook his head so emphatically that Lola's own pillow shifted. "We'd just put the girls to bed. We closed the door behind them and he looked at me and said, 'Go home.' Just like that. I started to ask him about it and he walked away. Went to his and Naomi's room and damn near slammed the door."

"What the hell?"

"Yeah. That's what I thought." Telling his story seemed to have drained the tension from Charlie. His breathing lengthened and deepened. "Anyhow. He's my only brother. I haven't seen him for years. Things haven't been right between us for all this time. Somehow we've gotten too far apart, and I'm not sure why. I don't want to go anywhere until we fix it." His words now almost a whisper, fading into the night and ending on a faint snore.

Lola tamped down her disappointment. But as long as they were staying, she had a few things of her own she wanted to resolve before they left. She nudged Charlie to make sure he was well and truly asleep. A snore stopped short before resuming its leisurely rhythm. Lola started to swing her feet over the side of the bed and then remembered what Naomi had said about tarantulas being nocturnal. They couldn't get in the house, could they? Back home in Magpie, she'd made the rounds at night before going to sleep, making sure that doors were locked and windows were fastened no more than four inches open—too little room for anyone to squeeze through—a habit dating to her Baltimore days, and one shared by almost no one else she'd met in the West. Especially on the reservations, where knocking was considered rude and people just strolled into one another's homes and helped themselves to coffee. What if Naomi and Edgar were like everyone else, leaving windows propped high and doors never ever locked, an open invitation to whomever—or whatever—wanted to creep in?

Lola wished she'd brought slippers. Then considered the fact that a tarantula might find the toe of a slipper very much to its liking, reminiscent of its own desert burrow. She felt around on the nightstand for her phone, clicked on the flashlight app, and shined it across the floor. Nothing scurried.

She eased from the bed, held the phone close to the floor, and followed its glowing path into the hallway. The girls' door stood ajar, easy admission both for tarantulas and a snooping adult. Lola didn't see any of the former and didn't plan on either of the girls seeing the latter. She lingered in the doorway, assuring herself of the girls' deep breathing. She flashed the light across the floor—nothing—then held it close to her body as she crossed the room to Juliana's low dresser, its surface covered with a detritus of interestingly shaped stones, feathers, and fast-drying plants—the same sorts of things Margaret picked up on her own rambles. Out of habit, Lola held a bit of sage to her face and inhaled, smiling at the scent that lingered within its brittle leaves. She put it down and flashed the light across the dresser to make sure she hadn't missed the key chain. It wasn't there. She turned around, checked on the girls, and slid open one drawer after another, running her fingers through the clothes within. Nothing but socks and underwear, shorts and T-shirts, and a single pair of jeans, all folded and stacked in neat rows. Lola turned to the nightstand beside Juliana's bed. She held her breath and stepped to the table. But its top, in contrast to the dresser, was distressingly clear.

Something brushed her bare feet. She gasped and jumped back, fumbling for the phone's flashlight. A weak laugh escaped her lips. She'd stepped on Juliana's clothes, abandoned on the floor beside her bed. Margaret wasn't the only one who couldn't seem to remember to use a hamper. Lola bent and lifted the clothing. The key chain's metal ring clanked against the floor, and Lola froze for a long moment. Silence. She felt around on the floor until her fingers closed on the tiny woven rug.

Words rent the darkness. "What the hell do you think you're doing?

———————

The words were grown-up. The voice wasn't. Lola responded to the former. "I might ask you the same thing," she hissed to Juliana. "What the hell is this?"

She held the key chain before Juliana's face, shining the light on it. Juliana snatched at it. "Give me that!"

Lola held it high and switched off the light. "Not a chance, missy."

"It's mine. You're a thief. I'm going to tell my dad."

Lola crouched beside the bed and lowered her voice so that it could barely be heard, forcing Juliana to lean toward her. She didn't want to risk waking Margaret, especially given what she was about to say. "And you're a liar. This isn't yours. You took it from that bookbag today. Do you realize that's a crime? Maybe I'm the one who's going to talk to your father." Lola reminded herself that she was playing hardball with a nine-year-old. She vowed to soften her next remarks.

She might have been ready to back off, but Juliana wasn't. "He won't believe you. You're white."

Lola sat on the floor with an audible thud. She and Juliana each held their breath for a minute, reassuring themselves that Margaret's slumber continued unbroken.

You little shit, Lola thought, barely choking back the words. She said aloud, "We'll see whether he believes me or not. You can take that chance—or you can tell me why you lifted the key chain."

Just like that, Juliana's defiance broke. "You can't tell him. You can't tell anybody. Please." Her voice, so assured moments earlier, quivered and broke.

Lola suspected an act, then reminded herself yet again of the girl's age. She touched a tentative hand to Juliana's back. It quivered through her thin pajamas. Lola rubbed in a circular motion. "It's okay. Just tell me what's going on. Why'd you take it?"

Juliana trembled so hard her teeth chattered. Tears glinted in the moonlight slicing through the blinds. "Because someone will get hurt."

"Having the key chain will hurt someone? That doesn't make sense." Lola wished for a cup of coffee. Her synapses were firing entirely too slowly. She belatedly answered her own question. "Not because of just having it. Because the key chain will lead them to whoever owns the bookbag."

Juliana sobbed aloud. In the other bed, Margaret stirred.

"Juliana." Lola's whisper was urgent. "Do you know whose bag that was?"

Maybe there was a "no" in Juliana's wail. Lola couldn't tell. Margaret rolled over. Lola needed to calm Juliana, and quickly. "Listen. All kinds of things could lead them to the owner. Whatever's inside the bookbag, for starters. We might as well just give them the key chain. I'll help you think of a reason why you took it. Maybe you could say you just liked it and took it before you realized the bookbag might be evidence. For heaven's sake, Juliana, you're just a kid. The worst thing you're going to face is a lecture. I've already been meaner to you than anybody else will be."

Juliana hiccupped. "You're pretty mean."

"So I've been told."

Juliana's hand, damp with tears, found its way to hers. "Can I have it back for now?"

Lola hesitated, wrestling with her conscience over the fact that she didn't trust a nine-year-old and what kind of person did that make her? Juliana interrupted her internal monologue by sliding the key chain from her fingers. Lola reached to retrieve it, then froze at the sound of footsteps outside.

The door swung open.

"Everything okay in here?" Edgar asked.

———

"I thought I heard Margaret," Lola said. "So I went to check."

They were in the kitchen, Edgar busying himself at the stove. "I'm guessing, given the hour, that decaf is in order." It wasn't a question. "Milk? Sugar?"

"Neither." Lola would have preferred high-test but didn't want to distract Edgar, whose movements were purposeful to the point of being abrupt. Something was on his mind. Lola figured the longer she kept quiet, the quicker he'd get to the point.

He set the mugs on the island and took a seat across from her. "When do you think you and Charlie will be taking off? This can't be much fun for you, with us being so busy."

Lola raised the mug to her lips as a way to avoid answering. She'd thought that maybe Charlie was exaggerating Edgar's desire to have them gone. Now she wondered. She swallowed her coffee and parroted Charlie. "You know, the girls are getting along so well. It's a shame to cut the visit short." Even though she didn't think it was a shame at all. But she wanted to see how Edgar reacted.

"That's another thing." Objects dissolved into shadow in the dim glow of the light above the stove. Lola couldn't discern Edgar's expression.

"What's another thing?"

"This friendship between the girls. I'm not sure it's good."

"How so?"

Edgar drained his mug in a long swallow. "I don't know how to say this nicely."

Lola's fingers tightened around the mug. "Just say it."

"I think your being here confuses Juliana."

"Why?"

Edgar got up and poured himself more coffee, ignoring Lola's cup. "Naomi and I, we could have gone anywhere," he said, his back to her.

"Could have taken our Ivy League degrees and cashed in. You know how many corporations would love to check a diversity box with an Indian? Unique among minorities! But we made a conscious decision to work for the tribe, to raise our daughter here among her people."

Given what she figured he was about to say, Lola allowed herself a jab. "Among her mother's people, you mean."

Edgar turned and faced her. "Among *Indian* people."

There it was. He started to say something else. Lola raised her hand. "I get it."

"I don't think you do. If you did, you'd have never married my brother. But you did, and you've got this white child, and my brother works and lives off the reservation instead of with his own people—"

"Margaret's an enrolled member of the Blackfeet tribe," Lola interrupted. No need to mention the fact that her daughter met the blood quantum requirement by only about a single drop of blood. "She spends every day, when we're working, on the rez with one of her aunties. She's with her own people all the time. And Charlie was already working off the rez when I met him."

She tried to think of a single reason not to bounce the heavy coffee mug off Edgar's head. Back off, she told herself. Before you say or do something you'll regret. "I'm so sorry you feel this way," she said finally, falling back on the standard not-apology of practiced politicians. "It's late and I'm tired. I'm going back to bed."

She stalked from the kitchen with as much dignity as possible, given her limping gait due to toes curled against the possibility of lurking tarantulas. She slipped into bed beside Charlie and dug an elbow into his ribs. He woke—almost—with a snort.

"Your brother's an asshole."

"Whaaaa ... " His voice trailed away.

"I'll explain in the morning." She paused. She could have sworn she'd heard a car. She listened hard but detected only the wind. She reminded herself of her own words to Charlie earlier—sound travels at night. "But don't worry about cutting our vacation short. We're not going anywhere."

That wriggle within again, not so deep this time, something stretching and expanding, insistent almost to the point of anger, as Lola Wicks silently echoed the vow Charlie had made earlier: to figure out what the hell was going on.

FIFTEEN

No MATTER HOW EARLY she got up, Lola thought as she registered voices in the kitchen, someone in this household was always ahead of her.

Naomi stood at the stove, flipping pancakes with the insouciance of an orchestra conductor. Thomas perched on a stool, his long legs in faded denim wound around its metal ones. The face he turned to Lola was all haggard lines and under-eye circles so dark it looked as though someone had punched him. His wan "Morning" ended in a choking cough. A yellow legal pad sat at his elbow. Some sort of list ran halfway down the page. He turned it over when he saw Lola looking.

She shrugged her way past him, pretending she hadn't been caught, and poured coffee into the largest mug she could find. "I knew I heard a car." Her eyes wandered to the pad again, its blank cardboard backing a mockery. "What time did you get in?"

"Late," he said. "Or early, depending on how you look at it. I was … out with friends."

"You must have gotten the car fixed," Lola said. "It's a lot quieter. No backfires. And I could have sworn I heard that car twice. Were you coming and going in the middle of the night? You and your friends must have had quite a time."

Naomi shushed her with a hiss. She reached for the radio that sat on the counter and turned it up louder. It spat a stream of agitated Diné, high and low tones punctuated by glottal stops. A pancake bubbled and turned brown around the edges, then black, as Naomi stared at the radio. An occasional English phrase leaked through. *Conrad Coal. FBI.* Thomas put down his coffee. The *Navajo Times* lay open before him. A photo spread showed the truck's charred metal skeleton and grim-faced headshots of faces both white—Conrad Coal executives—and Indian. Lola recognized the elder's portrait, bordered in black, among them, and surmised that the second black-bordered photo was that of the truck driver.

Smoke rose from the skillet. Naomi slid the spatula beneath the charred round and sent it soaring into the sink. Country music replaced the newscast, a guy trying to figure out whether he preferred his girl to his truck, the homespun sentimentality jarring in contrast to the lurid photographs in the newspaper.

Naomi dripped another circle of batter on the skillet. "There's going to be a meeting," she said. "At the high school outside Window Rock."

The music faded with a final twang. The announcer broke in, with the same sense of urgency. Naomi froze. Lola stepped to her side, took the spatula from her hand, and turned the pancake. Another song, this time traditional. Naomi's breath caught. "It's an honor song." The wailing tune rose above the drum's parade beat as the singers gave tribute to those who had passed on.

Lola slid the pancake onto a plate and offered it to Thomas. He waved it away. "Not hungry," he said.

Lola was always hungry. *The way you eat, you should be the size of a house*, Charlie had often marveled. She slathered the pancake with butter, drowned it with syrup, and dug in. Thomas turned the pad back over and jotted more notes. Lola nodded toward it. "What's that?"

"I thought I could get a jump start on next semester, maybe collect stuff for a paper about these bombings for my political science class. The meeting should give me some good information."

Lola would have thought the information would better apply to a criminology class, and said as much.

Thomas's mouth twisted downward. "People will be scoring political points all over the place at this meeting. People who like the mine, people who hate it. I'll be up even later tonight than I was last night. *Studying*."

Naomi nodded approval. "It'll be good practice for you to see how something like that works. The more you learn about tribal government now, the better."

She'd said Thomas would go to law school. Apparently politics was next on the agenda, Lola thought. Once again, she found herself hoping Thomas was on board with the plan. "Where's Window Rock?" she asked. She'd studied a map of the reservation during their drive down, but beyond being impressed at its immense size, sprawling into three states and surrounding the Hopi Reservation, she had little concept of what was where.

"It's on the New Mexico border, a couple of hours away. They're going to hold the meeting this afternoon to give people from all over the reservation time to get there, and then get home again safe. Window Rock's near Gallup," Naomi said, as though that explained something.

Lola lifted a shoulder. "So?"

"Gallup's off-rez."

Lola's shoulder fell. "Oh."

Naomi didn't have to say anything else. The Navajo Reservation, like so many, was dry. The outskirts of Gallup, then, would be lined with liquor stores run by people who self-righteously proclaimed that no one forced their customers to overindulge. Lola thought of people going into town to tie one on, and then making the two-hour drive home—or more, depending on where they lived—weaving their way through the blackness on unlit two-lane roads, maybe with kids and elders in the car. The shoulders of rural roads all over the West were dotted with white crosses. Indian reservations, with their disproportionate struggles with alcoholism, too often featured whole forests of the grim markers.

"We'll want to get on the road early, then." Lola's words were a reminder to herself, but she spoke aloud.

Naomi resumed her station at the stove, turning pancakes with renewed assurance. "Gar! Charlie! Girls!" she called. "Lola's eating your breakfast. Sorry," she said to Lola as the others entered the kitchen, the girls shouldering their way past their fathers. Juliana went directly to Thomas and wrapped her arms around one of his legs. He reached down and hugged her.

"We've all got a long day ahead of us," Naomi said. "But you won't have anything to worry about. You'll be long gone by the time the meeting starts. And besides, your route home doesn't take you anywhere near Window Rock, so there won't be any traffic." She pulled four plates from the cupboard and placed a pancake on each.

Margaret looked from Naomi to Lola. "We're going home?"

"You're going home?" echoed Thomas. The closest thing Lola had seen to a smile crossed his face.

"Yes," Edgar answered for Lola. "They're going home."

Lola permitted herself a small smile in return. "No," she said. "We're not going anywhere."

———————

Lola tapped into the domestic goddess buried very deeply within, once again taking the spatula from Naomi. She urged her to sit with the others. "After all," she said, the sweetness dripping from her voice rivaling that of the syrup that Charlie sloshed across his plate, "you're putting us up. We should be waiting on you."

"That's right." Charlie threw Lola a look that told her he didn't know what she was up to, but that he was willing to go along. He poured orange juice. "Margaret? Juliana? Big glass or little?"

"Little, please," said Juliana. Margaret's eyes narrowed to slits. Like her father, she knew something was up. Unlike him, she'd yet to acquire a poker face.

Lola saw the storm clouds gathering above Margaret, ready to rain questions, and moved quickly to clear them. "We can see that you two are going to be buried with work, at least until somebody catches this guy," she said to Naomi and Edgar. "It only makes sense that we stay and help you out on the home front." Margaret's eyebrows shot skyward. All Lola had done was raise more questions in her daughter's mind. Lola turned to Naomi and inserted the knife. "And the girls are getting along so well. Juliana is Margaret's only cousin—only first cousin," she quickly amended. As far as she could tell, Indian people regarded every other member of their tribe as some sort of cousin. She jiggled the knife. "It seems a shame to rob them of this time together."

"I don't know—" Edgar began. He'd yet to tame his hair into its styled pompadour and it stood up in clumps. A few unshaven hairs bristled from his chin. He rubbed the back of his hand against them.

"Our talk last night," Lola said to him. "That made it easy to stay."

"What talk?" Naomi and Charlie said together.

"I couldn't sleep," Lola said. "So I went to the kitchen for a glass of water. Eddie—Gar—was up, too. Somehow we got into the importance of family. It made me realize how crazy it would be to squander this time, even if we adults don't get to see much of one another." Lola turned back to the stove so Edgar wouldn't see the way her saccharine smile kept twitching toward a wolfish grin. Nothing like a giant unspoken fuck you to start the day, she thought.

Quickly, while the room was still awash in good feeling, however feigned, Lola gave the knife a last twist. "And we'd like to go to the meeting today, too."

"What was that about?"

Charlie stood next to Lola at the sink, his arms deep in soapy water. Beside him, Lola wielded a towel on the clean dishes. Naomi had urged them to use the dishwasher, but Charlie insisted upon washing them by hand. "Cleaner that way," he said, casually insulting Naomi's Miele.

"You won't believe what your brother said to me last night," Lola whispered. Quickly, with an eye on the door, she recounted her conversation with Edgar. "There's something weird going on here. Everything all nicey-nice by day, and then we get the bum's rush."

There was that business with Juliana and the key chain, too. Lola started to say something, then thought better of it. Somehow, it felt like a betrayal to the girl. She'd wait until the subject of the bookbag came up on its own.

Charlie dunked another dish in the rinse water and handed it to Lola. "Eddie can be full of himself. I remember him before he was a jerk. He and I need to get back to that place. So I'm glad you want to stay. Maybe we can work things out."

Lola polished the dish until it shone. "I thought maybe you were jealous."

A plate slipped from Charlie's hands and fell back into the water with a splash. "Of what?"

"His law degree. This." Lola flapped the towel at the kitchen—the polished stone countertops, Mexican-tile backsplash, and stainless appliances insistently bringing to mind their own kitchen, stuck in the linoleum and avocado-appliance era of Charlie's parents. "*Her.*"

Charlie withdrew his arms from the water, shook off the soap-suds, and wrapped them around Lola. Damp seeped through her shirt. "What good would fancy degrees do me in Magpie? They'd just price me out of the one place where I want to live. And what would you do with a kitchen like this? Cook? I don't think so." Lola, her face buried in his chest, let a laugh escape. "As to her—if you ever start running around in makeup and designer jeans, I'll know you've taken up with some other guy. Because this one likes you the way you are. Well, except for the fact that you *are* a little pale."

Lola pulled free, gave the dishtowel a twirl, and popped it against his butt. She danced away laughing as he came after her with a pan of soapy water, threatening to dump it over that curly head of hers if he could only catch her.

"Whoa," Charlie said, behind her. "We've got company."

Margaret and Juliana stood in the doorway, Margaret shaking her head at her parents' antics with the resigned patience of one entirely too familiar with the scenario. Juliana looked baffled.

"It's okay," Lola reassured her. "Your Uncle Charlie is a bit of a goofball, that's all."

"Auntie Lola is the one who's the goofball," Charlie said.

Something swelled up within Lola. Auntie. A term much in use on the reservation, applied to the women who occupied the indeterminate range between young marrieds and elders, Auntie was a term of respect, one that Lola had never thought of as applying to herself.

Apparently she wasn't the only one.

Juliana's faced smoothed as she returned to more surefooted ground. "Daddy says I don't have to call you Aunt. I can just call you Lola." A remark that somehow stung more than all the other insults Lola had endured since her arrival in Arizona.

Apparently unaware of the effect of her words, Juliana prattled on. "Mom and Dad are leaving early for the meeting. Can I go later with you? We can stop and see the dinosaur tracks on the way. I know where they are."

"I don't know—" Lola began. What if the crime scene tape was still up? Or the rocks still bloodstained?

"Canyon de Chelly's on the way, too." Juliana rushed on, undeterred. "We can stop and look for a few minutes. But if you want to go down into it, you need a guide, just like yesterday. Only it's bigger, way bigger. We should go back there another day."

Maybe, Lola thought as her niece basked in her own expertise, Juliana was just trying to curry favor after their middle-of-the-night standoff. She decided to follow the girl's lead. "Probably not today. We'll be leaving Bub home long enough as is. But I'd love for you to show us another time." At least Juliana seemed to have no qualms about spending the rest of the day with her. She wished Juliana's parents felt the same way.

SIXTEEN

THE TRUCK SAILED ALONG in the stream of vehicles flowing toward Window Rock, their roofs glinting like sun-swept wavelets. Lola drove, steering around the battered pickups and elderly sedans listing on busted shocks. An occasional Subaru or SUV bespoke a family of tourists, probably wondering how they ended up in the middle of what appeared to be the entire Navajo Nation on the move.

The landscape changed from red to dun and back again, the rocky surface improbably dotted with junipers, the colors reminiscent of Lola's little-used spice shelf—the dull gold of turmeric, the russet of cinnamon, the faded green of oregano.

Lola wondered how the trees' roots found enough soil for purchase. Small houses and trailers sat back from the road at miles-apart intervals, most accompanied by hogans. Lola marveled at the variety of the latter—everything from modern stucco or prefab, complete with windows, to makeshift tarpaper-covered frames to old-school log or even, rarely, earth.

An occasional band of sheep foraged among the slim pickings. Most were of the fluffy modern variety that children depicted as cotton balls on legs, but every so often Lola saw a few churro sheep, elegant with their silky long hair, the rams sporting four extravagantly curved horns.

Charlie pointed his chin at the sheep. "It's a miracle any are left." He recounted a story Naomi had told him, about how, back in the day, the federal government had deemed the Navajo Nation overgrazed. Their solution—to eliminate the majority of the sheep that were very nearly as important to the Diné as the bison had been to the Plains tribes.

"Sometimes they killed the sheep right in front of the people's homes. She said the elders told her it was like watching their family being slaughtered. But anybody who objected was arrested."

Just once, Lola thought, she'd like to hear a story about the tribes that didn't involve betrayal and death. She knew better than to hold her breath. Such stories always provoked an urge to pull Margaret close, to shield her from the inevitabilities of doubt and prejudice that awaited her. At least, Lola thought, they were a century past the killing years of the Navajo Long March and Cherokee Trail of Tears and Potawatomi Trail of Death, and all the massacres, Sand Creek and Wounded Knee and the Marias and the others. Yet the poverty and substance abuse that arose from the reservations' isolation and chronic lack of resources took nearly as deadly a toll, albeit one slower-moving and less in the public eye.

"Hey. Lola. Careful. Here's the turn for Window Rock."

Lola jerked her attention from the bloody past to the bloody present. The bombings' death toll was minuscule by comparison to those events chiseled into collective Indian memory, but their outsize effect was evident in the near-traffic jam approaching the Navajo Nation's capital.

A long coppery bluff sheltered one end of the town. The iconic rock, an upended shelf with a circular opening, overlooked the complex that housed the nation's headquarters. Lola braked as they passed the Council Chambers and gaped, oblivious to the vehicles backing up behind her. Naomi and Edgar's house might have been modeled on a traditional hogan, but the chambers upped the ante by several degrees. Inside, Charlie told her, reading from information on his phone, seats for the council's eighty-eight members were arranged in semicircular rows. Above them, massive logs spoked from a center circle that mimicked a smoke hole.

The meeting was in the local high school, a few miles outside town in the smaller community of Fort Defiance. Lola fell back on her years of reporting and parked as far from the entrance as possible, backing into a space. "Quicker getaway," she explained when the girls grumbled. "We'll have to walk farther, but at least we won't be stuck in traffic." The high school's gym, one of the largest in the country, could hold as many as seven thousand people—Charlie, still reading from his phone, supplied the facts as they hurried toward the doors—and appeared to be fast filling to capacity.

"Over there." Charlie looked across the vast space toward Edgar and Naomi and Thomas, who'd driven together in the Prius. He and Lola each took a girl's hand and eased through the crowd.

"We saved you seats," Edgar said. "Good thing you got here when you did. I don't think we could have held on to these much longer."

Juliana squeezed in next to Thomas. His whispered "*Ya'at'eeh*" came at the end of a long, wheezing breath. Lola wondered if he had asthma.

She turned her attention to the people around her. The younger people were in the universal uniform of T-shirts and jeans, the boys' baggy and drooping, the girls' tight across high young butts that made Lola sigh in envious remembrance. Elders clustered in the front seats, the grandmothers wearing the long flounced shirts and velveteen tunics that Lola had thought were the stuff of coffee-table books and postcards featuring scenes of long ago. Nearly everyone in the room was brown save for a skinny disheveled guy a couple of rows ahead, whom Lola pegged for an activist, and the reporters corralled in a far corner. Naomi pointed out a group of Hopi sitting together on one side of the room. "The mine affects them, too," she explained. "The tribes share in the profits."

Earlier in the day, Lola had shoved her long sleeves up above the elbow because of the heat. Now she unrolled them and tugged them over her wrists, hiding her pale arms. She ducked her head. Not much she could do about the chestnut tangles that fell to her shoulders, an anomaly in a sea of gleaming black hair. She was used to being the lone white person in the room on the Blackfeet Reservation, but there she knew most people. The sting of difference had long since eased. Now it flared anew. Something else, too. Around her, older people chatted easily in Diné.

"The whole meeting will be in our language," Naomi said. "It's a rule. But they'll translate. They'll have to. Because of him." She lifted her chin toward a whiteman who sat with several tribal members at the dais. Like them, he wore an open-collared shirt and jeans, but he'd added a blazer. Lola wondered if he took it off when he went outdoors. Studying him more closely, she doubted it. He had the smooth, well-fed look of executives the world over, men who'd reached a stature where the everyday aggravations of mere mortals—heat and hunger, for example—dared not trouble them. She remembered the herds of young studs from white-shoe firms who roamed Baltimore's streets at lunchtime and after work, in full suits with ties tightly knotted even in the wet-washcloth humidity of a Charm City summer. Or Kabul, where humidity was removed from the equation but the mercury climbed even higher and the sun shone more viciously. Even there, the higherups at the UN offices flaunted their suits like uniforms, somehow retaining their starched stiffness, shoes gleaming despite the film of dust that clung to everything else.

The guy on the dais would have fit right in, his incipient paunch kept in check by regular workouts, hair cropped almost close enough to have qualified for shaved, a far better solution to male-pattern baldness than a comb-over. Another white guy sat next to him. No trendy cut for him, just a classic crew. No paunch, either. Even from a distance, Lola could tell that his blue shirt buttoned over a toned abdomen. He likewise wore a blazer, its seams straining across a commanding breadth of shoulder, its hem hiding the gun that almost certainly rode at his hip. Lola pegged him as a cop, probably FBI.

"Who's he?" Lola indicated the first man.

"Jeff Kerns. Mine manager." Naomi's voice retained its same low musicality. And nothing changed in her face, not so much as a twitch in her cheek or a tightening of the skin at the corners of her eyes.

Those eyes, though. Lola hoped she'd never see a tarantula, but she imagined it might have the same sort of gaze, flat and focused and deadly. She was glad she'd pulled her sleeves down so her sudden goose bumps wouldn't show. She looked away, toward the reporters aiming long lenses at the elders, theirs cameras sounding a dry-leaf rustle of constant clicks.

The story, with its irresistible elements of downtrodden tribe versus big bad corporation, had attracted a scrum of journalists from national organizations and even, if Lola guessed correctly, contingents from France and Germany, countries with a long fascination with all things Native American. The elders in their turquoise jewelry and traditional dress made for irresistible images. Lola studied the reporters, hoping to see a familiar face. There was none. She'd been gone too long from the big-story world, the one that attracted the same predictable group to every unfolding tragedy of sufficient magnitude. The Vultures, they'd called themselves, defiantly adopting the sobriquet sometimes hurled at them by unappreciative subjects. Her own tribe, she thought. Among them, she'd known the rules. Crack relentlessly wise. Be quick with a question and sharp with an elbow when the flock swerved as one toward a particularly interesting subject. Even now, after so many years away from that world, she missed that feeling of surefootedness, of belonging.

Had she stuck with the Baltimore newspaper's assignment of a stateside post once the Kabul bureau was shuttered, she still might have ended up in Window Rock this very day. Might have talked her way out of that stupid suburban job the paper offered her and into one that at least let her roam the country, if no longer the world. She felt a tug of longing so sharp she bent her head toward her knees.

Maybe, she thought as she studied the weave of faded denim across her thighs, she should try to snag herself a freelance assignment on the bombings, possibly to one of the foreign news services like Agence France-Presse. She didn't dare approach an American outfit. A year earlier, she'd written a story from Wyoming for a national website, but it ended badly when Lola herself became part of the story in the showdown that had threatened Margaret's safety. The memory tripped the old fearfulness, set her heart to hammering, and forced the air from her lungs. Around her, people turned. Lola faked a cough, braced her hands on her thighs, and talked sense to herself.

She'd been alone on that story, alone but for her daughter and a vulnerable, traumatized friend. Not surrounded, as the journalists were here, by dozens of her own kind. Safety in numbers, the mantra that had governed her years in Kabul. She took an experimental breath. It came easier. Her heart steadied, lub-dubbing away like an old reliable horse clopping along a familiar route, no surprises to send it shying and skittering across the track. A familiar seduction whispered. The bombings on the Navajo Nation were a story, a big one, the kind of story she used to own. The notion like a sweet hot breath against her ear: *Like riding a bicycle. You could do this one with your eyes shut.*

The story could not possibly involve Margaret in any way. Just a few phone calls on Lola's part, maybe a couple of in-person interviews. Something to fill the time, given that they were going to hang around for a while. Not to mention some extra money besides. Lola's salary at the *Express* was a fraction of what it had been at the Baltimore newspaper, and Charlie, like all local government employees, was woefully underpaid.

Charlie. His hand tightened on hers. She saw him following her gaze, his own quizzical and concerned. Too late, she looked away.

"You miss it."

The compassion in his voice startled her. For a very long time after Wyoming, there'd been only anger. She'd spoken brave defiant words then, had insisted to him that her work as a journalist defined her as much as her role as Margaret's mother. She wouldn't give it up, she told him. But then the nightmares started, the face of the man who'd threatened her taunting her in her sleep. And, too, Margaret's own face, distorted in terror. So she'd given up the big stories after all, easy enough to do in Magpie, and gradually the dreams had faded. She'd never talked to Charlie about them.

Now he awaited a reply. The room's lowering volume saved her. The meeting was about to begin.

SEVENTEEN

THE MAN ON THE other side of Kerns stood. "Tribal president," Naomi whispered.

"*Shik'éí dóó shidine'é*," he said.

"My family. My people," Naomi translated, leaning close. Once again, Lola inhaled Mary Alice's perfume. Her heart clenched, reminding her that no matter how many years passed, she'd never stop missing her friend. She forced herself to pay attention to Naomi's whispered, disjointed translation.

"Our treasured elder murdered … and now another man, a tribal member, supporting his extended family by driving truck for the mine … Our people, our nation, are under attack."

He spoke on. The silence in the room was absolute. Even the children sat motionless. Lola wondered if they understood Navajo. Margaret had the glazed look she hid behind on the rare occasions that demanded the family's presence in church. Lola couldn't tell if Juliana was paying attention. The girl pressed her face against Thomas's shoulder and clung with both hands to his left arm. Good thing Thomas was right-handed, Lola thought as he continued to fill pages of his pad with notes.

The silence deepened. Lola looked back toward the dais. The tribal president sat. Kerns rose and addressed him. "My friend."

A translator leaned toward a microphone, maintaining the meeting's Diné-language integrity. "*Shi'kis.*"

Thomas's pen scratched across the pad. Lola's fingers itched for pen and paper of her own. She slid her phone from her pocket, sat it on her knee, and hit the *record* app in hopes that it would preserve at least some of the speechifying.

"We at Conrad Coal grieve with you for your losses." Pause for translation.

"Because of course they are our losses, too."

Lola watched the room as he spoke. With each sentence, faces hardened into pitiless lines, the younger people reacting to the English, the elders' expressions shading darker with each new translation.

"Ben Yazzie." The room stirred. "Everyone who worked at the mine drove past his signs every day. Most of us stopped to see those dinosaur tracks at one time or another.

"And Daniel Tsosie." Small sounds of dismay again flowed along the benches. "He was one of ours, as well as yours."

The truck driver, Lola thought. She wondered why Kerns kept drawing the distinction between *yours* and *ours*. Unnecessarily divisive, she thought. "Man needs a better PR pro," she murmured to Charlie, only to attract a flash of Naomi's spider-eye. She pressed her lips together lest more words escape.

"One of our Conrad Coal family, just like hundreds of other members of your tribes," Kerns went on. "I don't have to remind you that the mine is the largest employer on the reservation. Both reservations."

Lola winced at the clumsiness of it all. Whatever Kerns was trying to say, his words only underscored the sense that the tribes owed their financial well-being, such as it was, to this whiteman-owned enterprise.

"I think we"—Lola sighed in relief as Kerns belatedly turned to inclusiveness—"need to avoid a rush to judgment." Too soon, she thought as her spine stiffened. In her experience, the words *rush to judgment* usually preceded some world-class ass-covering. "Two terrible things have happened," Kerns stated unnecessarily. "One, the tragedy that befell Mr. Yazzie. We don't know the cause. And the second, ah, incident could have been anything. A truck malfunction, perhaps."

"Bullshit!" Lola's exclamation was, thankfully, covered by the collective rustle and murmuring of a very large and crowded room. She'd never seen the actual moment of a roadside bombing in Afghanistan, but she'd viewed the immediate aftermath enough times to know that the stricken vehicles looked exactly like the front-page photo of the mangled remains of the Conrad Coal truck. Also, in a room full of Indian people, who proportionally had the highest representation of any ethnic group in the armed forces, she'd bet there was more than one person who'd witnessed such bombings firsthand, maybe even suffered terrible wounds as a result. Kerns, she thought, had picked the wrong place to float his crap theory.

Amid the hubbub, the cop rose and introduced himself as Special Agent Fred Jardine. Lola had been right that he was from the FBI. By the way he beckoned the Navajo officer beside him to stand also, Lola deduced he'd worked on the rez for a while. Kerns could take lessons from this guy, she thought as the two lawmen gave the necessarily bland legal description of their efforts to track down the perpetrator or perpetrators—"in the event, of course," Jardine said with a grim nod toward Kerns, "that the second incident turns out to be more than a malfunction." He pointed with his chin—another small but welcome sign of cultural sensitivity—to someone in the audience. "You have a question?"

The woman who rose to speak was so tiny that her head barely topped those of people who remained sitting. She wore traditional dress. Lola wondered at the weight of all that fabric and wondered how the style had evolved. It looked hot. Then she remembered her time in Afghanistan, where she had encountered a sun so cruel that the only defense against it was to put on more clothes, layer upon layer between its rays and easily burned flesh, rather than strip down to the barest essentials. As the woman collected herself, the resentment that had permeated the room after Kerns's speech leached away, replaced by a sizzling air of expectation.

Lola jumped when the woman finally spoke, so firm and self-assured was the voice that issued from such a small person. She spoke first in Diné and then translated her own words, sentence by sentence. "My question is for the man from the mine."

She didn't use his name, Lola noted, even though she had to know it. The mine, as he had so thoughtlessly just pointed out, probably employed some of her relatives.

Fred Jardine sat down with palpable relief, proportionate to Kerns's obvious discomfort as he stood again.

"That mine there." The woman's tone was severe, accusatory. Her eyes, sparkling black within the collapsed foundations of a face that had endured decades of harsh sun and scouring wind, shone with intelligence and that most dangerous of weapons, humor. Lola guessed it would be a foolish man who underestimated her. She also guessed the woman had run across a lot of foolish men in her life, one of whom visibly sweated as he now confronted her.

"Conrad Coal, you mean." Kerns, so cool and composed moments earlier, blotted his high forehead with a snowy handkerchief.

Lola squinted and gave an audible snort, drawing another venomous glance from Naomi. Was that a monogram? All the men she knew used bandanas and called it good.

"I know what I mean."

Chuckles ran around the room. Even Naomi's glare softened.

"No mine, no troubles," the woman added. "Nobody killing people no more. No reason if the mine is not here." She paused.

"Now, Betty. Mrs. Begay."

Lola's eyebrows shot up. The fact that Kerns knew the woman's name, and that he'd used it—switching quickly from the familiar to the formal—when she'd so deliberately snubbed him, indicated the woman's stature went beyond even the usual respect accorded an elder.

"The mine is here to stay." Kerns's tone, all hearty indulgence, was dropped from the translation. "And as we've just noted, the second incident may very well have been a tragic accident."

"Ac-ci-dent." Mrs. Begay drew the word out, let it linger awhile before speaking again. "Same thing applies. No mine, no more accidents. You go away. Nobody else dies."

The response crackled through the crowd, not a chuckle, not given the subject matter, but appreciative nonetheless. Lola studied people's faces and reassessed. Some discomfort there, most apparent among the men but in some women, too. Mine employees and their families, Lola figured, torn between their loyalties to their people and their land—the two inseparable, after all—and the knowledge that, should the mine vanish tomorrow, they'd be shit out of luck on the job front. One of them, a stocky fellow in his thirties, shuffled to his feet, even as the woman sitting with him tried to tug him back into his chair. She held an infant to her breast. Two other children squirmed in the seats to either side of the couple.

The man ducked his head toward Betty Begay in shamed acknowledgment of the fact that he was about to contradict an elder. "The, ah, the thing is."

"Yes, Rich?" Again, Lola noted that Kerns knew the man. Probably a mine worker, although he lacked the subtle air of authority that would have marked him as a supervisor. Unusual, then, she thought, that someone so highly placed as Kerns would be on a first-name basis with him.

"The thing is, if these things keep happening, what happens to people's jobs? What if, ah … " The man paused, then forced the word in a rush. "What if something hits the mine itself? What if the mine has to … shut down?"

Kerns flung his arms out in approval. Lola thought that if Rich had been any closer, instead of deep within the crowd, Kerns would have enfolded him in a hug. She wondered if Rich's next paycheck would contain a little extra something, or if that deal had already been made under the table. The latter, she guessed.

"Exactly, Rich," Kerns said. "What if the mine has to shut down?" Although Rich had practically whispered the words, Kerns nearly shouted them, adding a layer of fearful certainty. "How many people will be out of work? How many children will have nothing to eat? How many car loans will go unpaid?"

"And if mine stays open?" Betty Begay again, the spark in her eyes flashing anger now instead of humor. "How many people die?"

Rich sank into his seat as Betty's accusations continued. "How much more water poisoned? How much more ash from the sky?"

Kerns ran his finger around the inside of his collar, twisting his neck like a man trying to wiggle out of a noose. "Any other questions?" No one spoke.

Mrs. Begay, summarily dismissed, remained standing anyway, through the meeting's formal ending by the tribal chairman, even as people began to file from the room. She swept the rows with her gaze as people retreated. Her eyes stopped at Lola, took in Charlie and Margaret, and noted their proximity to Naomi and Edgar. She nodded a greeting, then turned and followed the others toward the door. The skinny white guy Lola had noticed earlier hurried after her, apologizing his way through the crowd.

Lola curled her fingers around the edge of her seat, anchoring herself against a fierce impulse to follow Mrs. Begay outside, to take her by her twiglike arm, to gently steer her away from the others to a place where she could ask all the questions bursting from her brain.

The woman's words echoed. *You go away. Nobody else dies.*

With their implied promise: *Stay and more will die.*

Lola wanted, badly, to find out why Mrs. Begay was so very sure about that.

———

"What's Betty Begay's story?"

Lola twirled pasta around her fork, waiting for Charlie to stiffen at the word *story*, at any hint that she might find a way, no matter how unlikely, to work on a newspaper article during their honeymoon. But he leaned over his own plate of pasta and echoed Lola's question. "I was wondering the same thing. Who is she?"

After the meeting, Charlie and Lola had met Edgar and Naomi, along with Thomas and the girls, at an Italian restaurant in nearby Gallup, just over the state line in New Mexico. "After all," Edgar said, referring to the main fare in the tourism-focused restaurants in the rez towns, "you can only eat so many Navajo tacos." Lola didn't necessarily agree. Navajo tacos heaped spicy meat atop fry bread, a lard-and-carb bit of heaven forbidden in their household but guiltily permissible on vacation, when Lola ordered it at every opportunity.

A *trompe l'oleil* harborscape covered one wall of Trattoria Amalfi, its depiction of fishing boats and waves lapping at a beach incongruous given the window view of rocky bluffs scoured bare by the wind. A mishmash of a fountain, with a miniature Michelangelo's David poised in seashell, burbled in the center of the room. In all her years in Montana, Lola didn't think she'd seen a single fountain. In the past few days, she'd seen two. A bulwark against the desert, she supposed, the audible trickle a soothing denial of reality.

"Betty Begay," Naomi said now. She and Thomas traded long looks. "I guess you could say she's our hero."

Lola sensed another wrenching tale. She got one. Betty Begay grew up tending sheep on the mesa, as had her parents and their parents and grandparents before. But for the addition of motorized vehicles, it was a way of life virtually unchanged for centuries. No electricity or plumbing. Nearby springs provided adequate fresh water, given their sparing use by the people. As Naomi sketched the outlines of Betty's life, Lola thought back to the rural villages she'd visited in Afghanistan, so steeped in ancient times that the appearance, say, of someone on a bicycle jolted her with its reminder of modernity.

"Not a lavish life," Naomi said. "Nothing like ours. But it was enough. Sometimes I wonder if we'd all have been better off if we'd just stayed that way." Edgar paid sudden close attention to his eggplant Parmesan.

"But we couldn't stay that way." Thomas chased a meatball around his plate, stabbing at it with furious concentration. "The mine made us move."

115

"As we told you the other night," Naomi said, "they relocated people. Promised them all sorts of things—houses, wells, new corrals for their sheep—then never followed through."

Thomas sliced his meatball into quarters and swallowed them fast, one after the other. "Betty, though. She was smart enough not to go anywhere."

Naomi took up the tale again. Betty lived just far enough away from the mine site that her hogan—she still lived traditionally—was beyond its borders. Still, the mine wanted her gone, holding out ever-increasing incentives over the years.

"Like what?" Lola asked. "What is there beyond the house and the rest of it?"

Naomi rubbed her fingers together. "Money. The only thing the whiteman understands."

Lola squirmed, again feeling that impulse to hide her hands, her face, with their damning light skin.

Thomas's laugh was short and sharp. "They don't understand that money is meaningless to her. She already has her sheep, her home, her water, everything she needs. What else would she buy?"

Naomi tag-teamed again. "So they started taking things away. Even though they might not have realized what they were doing."

Lola poked at her salad, a few leaves of wilted iceberg lettuce topped by pale tomato wedges and mushroom slices going black and curled around the edges. She picked up a supermarket crouton in her fingers, popped it into her mouth, and crunched. "What things?"

"The water. The air."

"I don't understand."

Naomi's plate of linguine *alle vongole* sat nearly untouched before her. "The mine needed water for its slurry pipeline. It sucked it from the aquifer. The springs began to dry up. Betty had to drive her sheep farther and farther to find water for them and for her, too. Can you imagine, a woman her age, walking miles and miles every day, carrying water on her back all the way home at night?"

Lola couldn't imagine. Even the Afghan villages had wells, the biblical variety, yes, with the hand winches that took all a woman's strength to turn as she brought up individual buckets of water. But centrally located nonetheless, only steps from the villagers' mud huts—which were not unlike the homes of the Ancestral Puebloans she'd seen two days earlier, Lola thought. "And the air?"

Naomi pushed her plate away. "The air is full of coal dust. When I was a girl, you could see the mountains from miles away. Now, on some days, you can barely see to the edge of the mesa. All the people who stayed on the mesa, and even some of the ones who left, too, have lung problems. Not to mention the ones who work at the mine."

"At least they have jobs."

Lola's head snapped up. Edgar had sat silent through the conversation, polishing his plate clean as his wife and Thomas talked.

"This way, they die of lung disease," Edgar said as his wife prodded the wizened clams on her plate. "Without jobs, they fall into unemployment and alcoholism and now drugs, too. The Mexican cartels recruit the kids, show them the kind of money they can't earn anywhere but the mine. Which is worse? People have to eat, Naomi. Support their families."

It was an argument Lola had heard in various forms since her arrival in the rural West. The reservations, by dint of their far-flung locations on barren lands, had it worse, with unemployment rates approaching or even exceeding seventy percent, but life wasn't much easier for the region's white residents, many of whom lived too far from cities to commute to jobs there. The oil boom in western North Dakota had brought a tsunami of job seekers—along with crime, drug abuse, and forced prostitution, not to mention the effects on the environment. And yet the state's residents largely supported the oil companies because, for the first time in decades, people earned something that resembled a living wage.

Lola's thoughts were able to run on entirely too long, a product of the sullen hush that blanketed the table. The girls shifted in their seats. They'd long since devoured their food. "Can we go throw pennies in the fountain?" Juliana asked.

"May we?" Naomi said. "Sure." She dug through her purse.

Lola slid her hands around in her pockets. The pennies she retrieved were dull and furred with lint. She handed them under the table to Margaret, sorry to see her leave. The girls' departure left the adults alone in their stew of unspoken conflicts. She fished for a diversionary topic.

Charlie came to her rescue. "Edgar's asked me to come along with him to work tomorrow, get an idea of what he does here, how it compares to things on our rez."

Nice, thought Lola. Maybe Edgar's invitation was an olive branch, a way for the brothers to spend their first significant amount of time alone together in years.

Her appreciation was short-lived.

"Your rez? The one where you don't actually live." Naomi with her verbal knife again. Lola imagined a tiny silver rapier, flicking unseen, sheathed again before its victim realized he was bleeding.

"That's right," said Charlie. Lola knew it as one of his techniques. Agree with an accuser until he or she inevitably took things too far. *Let them get themselves into trouble,* he often counseled Lola, whose own response to insults, perceived or otherwise, was to fire back. "You and the girls can find a way to amuse yourselves tomorrow, right?" he asked her now.

"Of course," she said, with a reassuring smile that banished the plea for forgiveness in his eyes. "I've been wanting to explore, anyway. I'll take plenty of pictures so you can see what you've missed."

"I could go with you," Naomi said, her reluctance obvious. "Or send Thomas along."

"No, no. You're far too busy." Lola brushed the offers away. "It'll be nice, just me and the girls. Honestly." She saw no reason to add that she intended to explore her way right to the door of Betty Begay's hogan.

EIGHTEEN

EVER SINCE MARGARET'S BIRTH, Lola and Charlie had perfected the art of silent lovemaking. Strange beds, though, were always a challenge, prone to telltale creaks and groans. The guest bed in Naomi and Edgar's house offered no such betrayal, standing firm against a prolonged assault.

"Ahhh," Lola breathed afterward. She rolled off Charlie and fell back onto the mattress and patted it. "Good bed."

"Good woman." Charlie laughed beneath his breath. "Think Naomi and Edgar have it this good?"

Competitive even in bed, Lola thought. *Men*. She lay her head on his chest, slicked with sweat, and tried to pretend the incandescent feeling was simply the glow of toe-curling sex and had nothing to do with actual happiness. Her mind automatically rejected the word, an old superstition. Admit to its reality and something, or someone, would snatch it away.

Lola had left the blinds open. Moonlight splashed silver across the sheets. In the next room, the sewing machine whirred. Lola thought she and Charlie had been quiet. Now she wondered if they'd been quiet enough.

"Did you see those two at dinner tonight?" She didn't really expect an answer, so accustomed she was to Charlie's one-two-three-*out* fall into sleep.

But his response was strong and alert. "What do you mean?"

Lola shook her head. "Can't put my finger on it. Just—something was bothering them. I can't believe he defended the mine to her given how she feels about it."

"She's the one who wanted him to work there," Charlie reminded her.

"Working there is one thing. Buying into it, though. She probably didn't plan on that. No wonder she's pissed at him."

"Can you blame her?"

Lola wondered how she'd feel if Charlie went to work for one of the oil companies so eager to drill wells on or around the Blackfeet Reservation, on land considered sacred for millennia. She'd never have the same spiritual connection to the area that the tribe had, but in her relatively short time in Montana, she'd developed a sensibility about the land that defied logic, so much so that she struggled to maintain objectivity whenever she had to write stories about the drilling leases. No amount of money, she thought, would be enough to tempt her to work for one of the oil companies, and if it tempted Charlie, she'd be tempted to show him the door. She said as much and was relieved, if not surprised, by his laughing dismissal.

"Not a chance. But something was bothering you tonight, too. Those reporters."

"What about them?"

"I said it earlier. You miss it. Your tribe. The same way Eddie misses ours."

"No, I don't."

"Yes, you do. And I miss you."

Lola slid her hand across his chest and spread her fingers, savoring the feel of him, the safety of it. Since her return from Wyoming they'd not spent a single night apart. Now that sense of safety creaked like skim ice beneath her, more fragile than she'd realized. "I'm right here. How can you miss me?"

"I miss the way you were."

One of the things Lola loved about Charlie was that they never dissected their relationship, a neurotic exercise that, in Lola's opinion, seemed to affect too many columns and books aimed at women. Whatever she and Charlie had, it worked. Usually they left it at that. She held her breath, hoping that if she ignored him, he'd let it go. She stiffened as he pulled her closer.

"When I first met you, you were fearless. You had that crazy short hair"—Lola, fresh off the plane from Afghanistan, had shown up in Montana with hair cropped to within an inch of her head—"and an attitude that screamed 'Don't fuck with me' from forty paces."

"I took too many risks. You said so."

"Yes, you did. But listen, Lola." He released her and pushed himself up. Lola's head slid from his chest. She propped herself on one elbow and studied his silhouette, waiting. In the next room, the sound of the sewing machine halted. Even the wind stopped, as though in anticipation of his next words.

"I've been thinking about this ever since we got here and saw what Eddie's turned into. Maybe you took it too far. Just like he did with this bougie Indian lawyer thing he and Naomi have got going on. He's not himself anymore, and you aren't either."

"I thought you liked me this way." Lola groaned inwardly at the sound of her own words. Oh, lord. When had she become the kind of woman who changed to please a man? Although she knew it went past that—what she'd done was even worse. She hadn't changed to please Charlie. In her fear, she'd backed away from herself.

Charlie interrupted her psyche's wrestling match with itself. "I thought I liked you better this way, too. But you're different now. You don't get fired up about things anymore. Don't get me wrong." He held up his hand as Lola began to protest. "When you caught the scent of something big, you were a royal pain in the ass. But watching you go after it—that was a helluva spectacle."

"Huh. You make me sound like Bub." Lola was equal parts pleased and a little hurt. Where had that woman gone? The one who had once declared that working a breaking story was even better than sex—and meant it?

"All I'm saying," Charlie said, "is if you want a piece of this one, you have my blessing. Remember when you were learning to ride?"

Lola had told him about her solo struggle to learn to ride Spot after she'd inherited him from Mary Alice. She'd fallen off, and fallen off, and fallen off again, ordering herself back astride the Appaloosa each time until she finally learned to stay on.

"It's time to get back on the horse," Charlie said. Then, quickly, keeping things light, he changed the subject, combing his fingers through her curls. "Why'd you grow your hair out, anyway?"

Lola had to think back. "It was easier to keep it clean when it was short. Water was almost nonexistent in Afghanistan. I used baby wipes for my 'shower'. But keeping my hair short meant always having to cut it. Here, it's easier to take care of long. Now I can just pull it back in a ponytail."

As she spoke, the thing that had been knotted up inside her ever since Wyoming relaxed and expanded, stretching, testing its limits. It sought pain. Felt none. Maybe Charlie was right, that it was time to get past it. A pleasurable warmth spread through her. She pulled Charlie back down beside her. "Anyhow, what makes you think I need your blessing for anything? Here's what I want a piece of."

And, despite Charlie's protestations that it had been many, many years since he was a teenager and what was she thinking, pestering a man who needed his sleep, she got it.

———————

A few hours later, Lola and Charlie sashayed into a kitchen that held all the warmth and conviviality of the Arctic in mid-January.

"Whoa." They moved apart. "What's going on?"

Edgar and Naomi faced off over the island, eyes narrowed, lips compressed. Even in anger, Lola thought, they looked alike.

"Here." Naomi slid an envelope along the countertop without looking their way. "Read this."

Edgar slammed his hand against the marbled green surface. "Don't touch it!"

Lola drew back. She and Charlie stared at the envelope. It was made of cheap white paper, the kind with the visible blue cross-hatchings within and the stickum on the flap that never quite sealed. Someone had typed Naomi's name and address into a computer, printed it out, and then cut out the rectangle and Scotch-taped it onto the envelope.

"It's like those ransom notes with cut-out magazine letters," said Lola. "Only lazier."

"Look inside." Naomi's voice was hoarse.

"Don't touch it!" This time, Charlie's voice joined Edgar's.

"Oh for God's sake. My fingerprints are already all over it." Naomi extracted a folded sheet of paper from the envelope, holding it by a corner. She shook it out so that Lola and Charlie could read it. The paper quivered in her hand.

Again, a computer printout.

Back off, bitch, or your next. And keep your mouth shut. If you think you can catch me, your a dumb ass.

"I don't know what's worse," blurted Lola. "The improper 'your' is bad enough. And everyone knows dumbass is one word." She looked at the faces around the island. "And, uh, it's really scary."

"Damn straight it is. But someone doesn't think we should call the cops." A vein pulsed in Edgar's throat.

Naomi's scowl matched his own. "That's just giving him what he wants. More attention."

"As if killing people hasn't given him enough attention already. Assuming it's the bomber. Which I think is a safe assumption."

Bub, drawn by the palpable anxiety within the house, emerged from the girls' room and circled the island, whining softly.

"Guys, guys." Charlie's tone came from long practice with domestic disputes, barroom drunks, and the occasional out-of-control high school football crowd. Lola stepped back and let him do his work. "Naomi, when did you find this?"

Distracting her with details, Lola thought. The best thing about that tactic—it usually worked.

"This morning." Naomi looked toward the door.

"There?"

"Yes. When I stepped outside to face the sun."

"Show me."

Even at the early hour, heat and a handful of red dust shoved their way inside when Naomi opened the door. "There. On the top step. See that rock?" She pointed to a stone the size of a fist. "It was on top of the envelope, I guess to keep it from blowing away. I picked it up."

"And opened it? With an envelope looking like that?" Incredulity messed with Charlie's calm.

Letter bombs, Lola thought. The Unabomber and his ilk. Or the anthrax-filled envelopes sent to federal offices and media outlets after the September 11, 2001, attacks. That shit killed people.

"My question exactly." Edgar's grim satisfaction was evident. "I came in about then. You should have seen her face. Like she'd seen a ghost."

"And with good reason," said Charlie. "There's no stamp on this. So the guy who left it either walked or drove up to the house. Either of you hear anything last night?"

Naomi's hair swung back and forth in emphatic denial.

"Me, neither," said Edgar. "What about you two?"

Otherwise occupied, thought Lola, but contented herself with shaking her head, trying to ignore the slight reddening of Charlie's ears.

"Bub, stay." Charlie held up his hand to keep the dog away from the steps. He scanned the ground around them. "No footprints, but the wind could have taken care of that." He crossed to the driveway and spent some moments scrutinizing the tires on the vehicles there. His gaze swept the dirt again. "I don't see anything here, but it doesn't mean much. He could have parked on the main road and walked in from any of a hundred directions."

Or he could have come from inside the house, Lola thought. "Where's Thomas?" she said.

When they'd entered the kitchen, she'd thought Naomi was as angry as she'd ever seen her. Now she realized she'd been wrong.

"Why. Do. You. Ask." Each word like a separate sharp stone hurled Lola's way.

"Sleeping in. Look. His car's still here." Edgar moved between them, pointing out the obvious.

Again, Charlie went for distraction. "Naomi, do you have a baggie?" He wrapped it around his hand, then went back outside and retrieved the rock, sealing it in the bag. It sat on the counter, a garden-variety chunk of desert sandstone turned menacing. "Maybe this will be useful. We need to talk about calling the police."

They stood around the island, its granite expanse a demilitarized zone between them. Bub sat to one side, head cocked, eyes fixed upon them. Guarding them, Lola thought, keeping them safe. Naomi spoke first, simply ignoring the fact that Thomas had been raised as a possibility. "If we ignore it, maybe whomever left this will think I never saw it. The wind could have blown it away. There's no reason to call anybody."

"We can't take that risk," Charlie said. "For all we know, he was out there watching to see you open it."

They all turned toward the door. Naomi rose and drew the curtains on the window above the sink. The darkness made the usually bright kitchen feel claustrophobic, foreboding.

Charlie took charge. "Here's what we do. First, we make coffee." That got the reluctant smiles he'd intended. Lola took her cue and busied herself with the coffeemaker. "Next, we call the cops. And the FBI. No, Naomi, hear me out," he said as she began to object. "None of this has to get out. The cops can keep a lid on it so that he—assuming it's a he and not a she—won't get any extra attention from this. But this is a clear threat to you. We can't screw around. And they'll want to examine the rock and this note."

Naomi accepted the coffee Lola handed her, took a sip, and then quaffed more deeply, signaling her appreciation with an exaggerated sigh; Lola had taken advantage of Charlie's little speech to splash some "almond flavoring" into the mug.

"You're going to need some sort of protection," Charlie said.

Again, Naomi tried to protest.

Charlie shook his head. "We have to take this seriously—"

"Christ, Naomi." Edgar interrupted him, motioning away the coffee, undoctored, that Lola offered. "We've already got two dead. If nothing else, think about Juliana." Lola recognized the fear that flashed across Naomi's face.

"Won't having cops hanging around make me even more of a target?" Naomi's voice faltered as she posed the question.

"She has a point," Edgar said. "If there's a cop with her, whoever sent this will know she told."

Charlie rubbed a hand over his face and looked toward the hallway. The girls would be up soon. They'd need to have this resolved before then. All of them were entirely too aware of the unerring antennae of the young for anything out of the ordinary.

"Wait a minute," said Lola. "She's already got protection. A cop hanging around." She jutted her chin toward Charlie. "You. For all the rest of the world knows, you're just the visiting brother-in-law. It's perfect."

Too late, she bit her tongue. Reached out a hand as if to capture the words, crush them in her fist. Because, even as Charlie and Naomi and Edgar all nodded eager assent, she realized she'd just put her husband squarely in the sights of the bomber.

NINETEEN

CHARLIE'S SERVICE WEAPON ALWAYS traveled with him. But once they'd arrived in Arizona, he'd stashed it on a high shelf in the bedroom closet. Now he retrieved it, tucked it into a waistband holster, and changed into a loose, dark shirt that hung over it.

"So much for spending more time with Eddie. But this is a good idea. I'll go with Naomi to her office. At least I'll get to drive the Prius. I've always wondered what those things are like. Anybody asks—and I can't imagine anyone will—I'm shadowing her to see how Navajo prosecutors coordinate with the off-rez authorities. Wish I could go with you and the girls today."

"I wish you could, too." Lola moved behind him and put her arms around him. The gun pressed against her. He'd shown her how to shoot one, even offered to buy her one of her own, but she'd always demurred. "I'd do something stupid. My luck, I'd shoot my foot off before I ever got a bad guy. Or you."

She'd done too many stories over the years on fatal gun accidents, and not a single one about a gun successfully used in self-defense, to feel comfortable carrying one herself. Instead she contented herself with the bear spray that everyone back in their part of Montana carried as routine protection against the grizzlies that favored the same hiking trails, campgrounds, and huckleberry patches as their human counterparts.

She was glad Charlie had a gun, though, and especially glad he'd have one under these circumstances. She didn't say what she was thinking: that the kind of guy who could brazenly walk up to Edgar and Naomi's house to deposit a threatening note wasn't the type to give Charlie an opportunity to shoot first. *Be careful out there*, she wanted to say. *Stay safe. Watch your back.* All the clichés.

She didn't say anything, though—especially not the words her brain screamed at him: that he should be most alert around those closest to him.

Lola may have been worried about Charlie, but everyone else seemed worried about her. By the time she and the girls set out for their excursion, she felt as though she'd reassured the universe that she would be fine on her own.

"Really, it'll be fun," she told Charlie. "No, not as much fun," she added with a wicked grin, trying to lighten the mood with a reference to the previous night. Were those circles under his eyes?

When Edgar asked, she said, "I just want to drive around, get a sense of the place. All I've seen is the road to your house, and then to Window Rock and Gallup. I want to see where people live."

"I swear I won't get lost," she told Naomi.

She started to say something pre-emptive to Thomas, but he ducked his head and turned toward the door. Something had come over him since they'd first met. He seemed angry—or maybe exhausted from a night of typing threats and depositing them on the front step. "Bye," he said, and left without saying where he was going. No one asked. Minutes later, he departed in a series of blasts from his car's dragging tailpipe.

"I thought he got his car fixed," Lola said. "When he drove in the other night, I didn't hear all that noise."

"Maybe whatever got fixed broke again." Naomi handed her an insulated bag. "I packed sandwiches for you. You can have a picnic."

Lola had promised the girls lunch, although she'd imagined something in an air-conditioned restaurant after she finished visiting with Mrs. Begay. From what she'd seen so far, their surroundings did not lend themselves to outdoor dining, unless one enjoyed being baked crispy by a sun only too happy to oblige. But things might be different off the beaten path. Maybe Mrs. Begay could point them to some shady, secluded spot, one that once sheltered a spring of clear, cold water reduced to a bitter trickle.

"Take this, too." Naomi handed her a jug of water. "Don't drink it. Keep it in the car in case you break down."

"Thanks. You saved me a stop at Bashas," Lola said. Even though she'd still stop at the reservation's main grocery store to ask directions to Betty Begay's place.

At the store, the checkout clerk's response jolted her. "Are you some kind of reporter?"

"Excuse me?" Lola wondered if she gave off some sort of invisible vibe. She'd emailed a couple of contacts at Agence France-Presse and Der Spiegel before she'd left the house that morning; both had already written stories on the bombings, but Lola offered to keep tabs on the situation to save them the expense of keeping their own correspondents—who were supremely skilled, in the way of foreign correspondents the world over, of running expense accounts sky-high—in Window Rock.

"Reporters are always looking for her," the clerk said. "Like him." She pointed with her chin.

A rawboned white guy examining a rack of snack food turned at the clerk's words. Lola recognized him from the meeting. "And I found her," he said. He shifted a bag of trail mix to his left hand and held his right out to Lola. "Jim Andersen."

"You're a reporter?" Lola tried to keep the incredulousness from her voice. Even by the admittedly loose standards of a newsroom, up close Jim Andersen proved a scruffy specimen, clothes in need of a wash and hair in need of a comb. If she hadn't seen him at the meeting, she'd have taken him for a backpacker. "You weren't sitting with the other reporters at the meeting."

"I'm not mainstream media." He gave the words a derisive twist. "I write for the Green Coalition newsletter." He dug in a pocket. "Here's my card."

Everything fell into place. The Green Coalition was a loose affiliation of environmental groups that fell beyond the establishment boundaries of organizations like the Wilderness Society and the Sierra Club, but still on the right side of the line crossed by ELF. Or at least it purported to be. Lola knew them as one of the groups on Charlie's radar. If Jim Andersen looked like a backpacker, it's probably because he was, traveling on a shoestring, staying as close to the land as possible out of a combined concern over his carbon footprint and lack of finances. Lola wouldn't have put it past him to have hitchhiked to the reservation from wherever he was based. Which was where, she asked him now.

"Wherever I need to be. I came down here from the tar sands in Alberta. I was up there for most of the winter. Now I'm in Arizona in the summer, writing about the mine. I froze there, I'm cooking here. I need a better system."

You need a bath, Lola thought. He wafted scents of woodsmoke and sweat, common to campers everywhere. But there was something about him, a tense wariness, a shoulders-back, light-on-the-feet stance, ready for quick action. The hair falling to his shoulders was just for show, she decided. "You're military."

"Ex," he agreed.

"How long out?"

"Few years." He bounced once on the balls of his feet.

"Where?"

"Iraq. We done here?"

Lola wasn't, but knew she needed to be. She hazarded a single question more. "You've already talked to Mrs. Begay?"

"Yeah." He smacked the trail mix down on the counter and lay a bill beside them. He might not have been a traditional reporter, but he had the same sort of proprietary gleam in his eye that told Lola she wasn't going to get anything else out of him. "What's your interest in her?"

Lola pointed through the window toward the girls in the truck that, local-style, she'd left running so as to keep the air-conditioning going and gave him the shorthand version of another of the complex clan relationships Naomi had described. "She's my niece's grandmother." She saw the question in his eyes and offered what she hoped was a plausible explanation as to why, given her family's close connections to Mrs. Begay, she needed help finding the place. "She told me how to get there, but I wasn't quite clear. I thought I'd better double-check here." Hell would freeze over before she asked Jim Andersen for directions. She blew a sigh of relief when he nodded apparent acceptance, scooped up his trail mix, and left.

The clerk rang up her sixteen-ounce bottle of water. "Mrs. Begay is the only person standing up to the mine. Well, not the only one. But the main one. The leader, I suppose." She paused with her hands over the keys. "You want me to ring up a couple gallons of water? People usually bring her some when they go to see her. What she's got up there isn't fit to drink."

"Make it five," said Lola.

It took two trips to tote the heavy plastic jugs to the truck, but when she left the store, she had directions to Betty Begay's hogan in hand.

TWENTY

LOLA HAD TOLD THE truth when she said she wanted to see what the reservation looked like off the beaten path, especially considering that the beaten path itself consisted of nothing more than a handful of two-lane roads.

But first, she saw the mine. The clerk hadn't mentioned it in her directions, but towering wire fences, topped with razor wire, presaged its presence. Small signs sported the company logo of stacked *C*'s. Lola wondered if she could drive directly onto the mine's property, maybe even ask for a tour. Industrial sites usually were locked up tighter than CIA safe houses, but things in the West tended to be more relaxed and open.

A large warning near the mine's entrance exploded Lola's hopes of a friendly western howdy. *EMPLOYEES ONLY. VIOLATORS WILL BE PROSECUTED*, it shouted.

"Prosecuted, huh?" Lola glanced back at the girls. If she'd been alone, she might have risked it. Sometimes, stupid—"What sign? I didn't see a sign"—actually worked. A handful of protesters lounged in bubba chairs about a hundred yards from the gate. As the pickup approached, they rose and brandished signs.

Coal Kills.

Say No to Mine Expansion.

And, in a play on the company's *Conrad Coal Keeps Them On* motto, *Turn Off the Lights.*

Lola noted a couple of elders in traditional clothing. The others were young, white, and in shorts and T-shirts, the hippie-dippies that Charlie and Edgar had discussed. Lola gave them a nod of acknowledgment. As soon as she'd passed, they sank back into their chairs.

A truck, just like the one destroyed by the bomb, rumbled through gates manned by security guards. It turned toward Lola, who fought an urge to swing the pickup entirely off the road in an effort to give the truck as wide a berth as possible. What if someone detonated another bomb? She hit the accelerator, ignoring the girls' cries of protest and Bub's muttering, and turned onto a dirt track, only the smallest of signs indicating the road the store clerk had told her to take. The pickup's hotshot suspension failed the challenge of the higher speed she demanded in her effort to put as much distance between them and the mining truck as possible.

———

The track kinked. The main road with its other vehicles and occasional buildings vanished behind them. Just like that, Lola was beyond civilization.

She thought she'd seen desolation in North Dakota, where the plains rolled on forever, or Wyoming, with its treeless stretches of sagebrush. But at least the tight-packed sagebrush had represented signs of an abundant, if toughened, life. Here, even the sagebrush appeared cowed, only a few lonely clumps dotting expanses of bare rock. An occasional butte reared from the desert floor. Hawks soared on the downdrafts, specks against the painful glare of sky. Lola wondered what they possibly could be hunting. It seemed as though nothing could survive the frying pan of desert floor. She caught Juliana's eyes in the rearview mirror. "Do sheep really graze here?"

"Of course."

"Whatever in the world do they eat?"

Juliana looked as though she didn't understand the question. Her mother had described the land as bountiful and generous to the Navajo and Hopi people. Once again, Lola realized—as she had when she'd been assigned to Afghanistan, and then again when she'd ended up in Montana—that she was going to have to learn a new way of looking at things. Arizona must have hidden charms, or at least benefits, which her untrained eye had yet to detect. Maybe Betty Begay could explain them to her. In fact, Lola thought, that would be a good way to start their conversation. Assuming Betty was home. From what Naomi and Edgar had said, Lola knew it was entirely possible that Betty might be miles from her home, trailing a band of skinny sheep across the redrock.

"Auntie Lola! Auntie Lola!"

At Juliana's unexpected and welcome use of *auntie*, Lola eased her foot from the accelerator.

"There's *Shimá's* house."

Lola had nearly missed the turnoff. She steered the truck toward the bump on the horizon that eventually resolved itself into a hogan and worked on persuading Juliana about coincidence.

"Do you visit Mrs. Begay a lot?"

Juliana nodded. "With my mom," she added.

"Then we should stop and see her, too," Lola said. Let Juliana think everything had happened by chance while they were out exploring.

A familiar small figure emerged from the hogan as Lola parked the truck. Juliana wriggled out first. "I brought my new friends," she announced.

"*Ya'at'eeh*," Betty said.

Lola mumbled the greeting back, uncertain of her ability to get the breaks in the right places, to pronounce the final syllable as *eh* instead of *ay*.

Betty Begay directed a shrewd smile at her. "You're from the meeting. Now you're here to see me."

Lola rubbed her foot in the dirt and offered a vague semblance of truth. "We were just driving. Sightseeing. And then when we took this road, Juliana told me you lived here."

"Hmph." Betty Begay's skepticism could not have been more obvious.

"We brought you some water. Girls, help me out, please." She handed each of the girls a gallon jug and balanced the other three in her arms.

"You bring water even though you don't plan to see me? You must be a mind reader, know that somewhere on the mesa, an old lady needs more water."

For just a moment, Lola felt sorry for the mine managers or anyone else who tried to bullshit Betty Begay.

"I had it in the truck in case we got stuck somewhere—" Lola began, but Betty cut her off with another "Hmph."

"You come on," she added, and led the way into the hogan. "You girls want some lemonade?"

Lola motioned Bub to stay outside. She thought the hogan might be stifling, given the small space and the day's heat. But the thick mud walls pushed back against the sun, and the interior was cool and dim and soothing. An oil-drum stove stood beneath the smoke-hole. A pallet of sheepskins lay against one wall. A photo dangled from a nail. The oval frame surrounded the image of a middle-aged woman with softly permed hair and a severe expression lightened by a crinkle at the corners of her eyes.

Betty saw her looking. "She was my daughter."

"Oh, no. When did she ... ?"

"No. Not that. She was taken from me. By those people. To convert her, civilize her."

"A boarding school?" That story, at least, Lola knew. Religious warriors of various denominations had long waged battle on the tribes' so-called heathen ways. The Blackfeet had endured the Jesuits; the Salish and Kootenai, the Sisters of Mercy. In California, Father Junipero Serra—a Franciscan elevated to sainthood—persuaded people to Catholicism with the help of a lash. And everywhere, the forced removal of Indian children from their homes to the boarding schools, where nuns and priests cut their hair and forbade them from speaking their own language or following their own spiritual practices.

"Worse than boarding school. Worse than the Jesus people."

Lola couldn't imagine what might be worse, and said as much.

"The Mormons. They took our children, adopted them outright. Legally, my Loretta is their daughter."

Lola's head jerked involuntarily to look for Margaret. She could hear the girls chattering in the shade house. She tried to imagine what it would be like if people took Margaret from her and claimed her as their own, a vision that included a strong probability of herself ending up in prison for murder. She dusted her hands together, as if to rid herself of the unthinkable. Compared to the removal of a people's lifeblood, the problems posed by the mine suddenly seemed manageable.

Lola looked again at the photo. Betty's daughter was not a young woman. "It seems as though you've been in touch over the years."

"Oh, yes. She says she has two families. Me. And those people."

Betty appeared to have forgiven her daughter, Lola thought, but not the family who'd taken her. She couldn't blame her. "Does she live here now?

"Salt Lake." A quick, sly smile added another crease to Betty's features. "She's an adoption lawyer."

Lola returned the smile. No matter that other people had raised her; Betty's daughter appeared to have inherited her mother's subversive tendencies.

Betty took three metal cups from a shelf, poured water from one of the jugs into them, and mixed in the off-brand powdered lemonade so familiar to Lola. The cups were small. Lola glanced around the hogan. Empty water jugs sat in stacks against one wall. It appeared that the five gallons she'd brought represented the whole of Betty's water supply, making the offer of a drink even more precious. Betty herself, Lola noted, drank nothing. As Lola watched, she furtively touched her tongue to her lips. Lola set her own cup down.

"You know what? I'm not as thirsty as I thought. Would you like it?" She expected another "Hmph," but Betty sipped in silence.

"*Shimá*"—Juliana glanced toward Lola, and this time translated—"my mother, can I show Margaret around?"

Lola couldn't imagine there was much to see, but Betty nodded permission. Lola waited until the girls' chatter receded. "How many other people live up here?"

Betty's sigh plumbed depths. "Now? Hardly any. Most left. Some few way over there"—she waved vaguely—"but up here, just me."

"Isn't it lonely?"

Betty's laugh, like her voice, was full and rich, and startling from such a small frame. "Lonely? I have sheep. And every day, birds, hawks, lizards." The laugh trailed away.

"But?"

"Not so many anymore. They all need water, too."

Lola held up one of the jugs. "Speaking of water. How do you get it?"

Not a full laugh this time, but a delightful chortle nonetheless. "You bring me!" And others, too, Betty said. "Anybody who drives by, knows to bring me water. If I run out, I fetch from the spring, carry it on my back." She made sketching motions with her hands, indicating a sort of sling. Lola winced as she recalled the weight of the water as she'd carried the short distance from the truck to the hogan.

"I thought all the springs dried up."

"Not all. One about five miles that way." Again, the vague wave.

"Five miles!"

"Nice and close, not like the others."

Lola couldn't tell if Betty was serious or having some fun at her expense.

"Juliana knows where. You get her to show you. Nice and cool there. Good spot for a picnic."

Again, Lola searched Betty's expression for signs of mischief. Was it possible that the woman had somehow communicated with Naomi, that she knew Lola and the girls were planning a picnic? She banished the thought as absurd. The hogan lacked plumbing and electricity, along with phone lines, and for sure cellphones didn't work on the mesa; Lola had checked hers repeatedly on the drive. When Betty finished her lemonade, she gathered up the cups and sat them in a plastic basin. Lola wondered if she'd scour them with sand rather than water. She wondered what sorts of things she herself would do if every drop counted. Betty turned toward the door. The visit appeared to be ending.

"We passed the mine on the way here," Lola said quickly. Clumsy, she chided herself. The only way to the hogan—at least from the road—was past the mine.

But Betty seemed to have anticipated the subject. "You want to know about it."

"Everyone seems to think the bombings are directed at it."

Betty's smile lit up the hogan's dark interior. "Everybody's right."

"But who would do such a thing?"

The question hovered between them like a hummingbird, cheeky and demanding attention, the air around it vibrating with intensity.

"Anybody. Everybody. Maybe even me. Little Betty is big bomber. Boom!" She raised her arms, pantomiming an explosion.

Lola's laugh was a beat too late. She followed Betty into the sun with relief. "Girls!"

They charged around the side of the hogan. Bub jolted behind them on his three legs, tongue dangling nearly to the ground. "We were under the shade house," Margaret said. "Mom, come see what Betty does there."

"No," said Juliana. "We don't have time." She grabbed Lola's hand and dragged at it, pulling her toward the truck. "Come on, Auntie Lola," she said, with all the considerable winsomeness a nine-year-old has at her disposal.

"Plenty of time, girl."

Betty's rebuke was mild, but Juliana dropped Lola's hand. "Please," the girl said. "I want to go." A trembling lip replaced her smile.

"Just two minutes," Betty said. "You come see. You'll like this."

The shade house backed up to the hogan, a tiny makeshift version of Edgar and Naomi's lavish patio. Still, it featured the same deep shadows and pleasantly rustling branches. A card table and folding chair sat beneath it, strewn with miniature versions of patterned rugs attached to key rings.

"I make these," Betty announced. "Sell them at markets and the trading posts." She selected one. "Here. You take."

Lola tried to thank her, glad when Betty brushed her words away before she could utter them, leaving nothing in her own tone or choice of words to raise Betty's suspicions as she folded her hand about the woolen key chain Betty pressed into her palm—the same sort of key chain that Juliana had filched from the backpack in the ruins.

TWENTY-ONE

LOLA HAD BRACED HERSELF for quick, suspicious interest when Naomi found out about the visit to Betty. She hadn't expected approval.

"That's wonderful!" The inevitable pitcher appeared, filled with a rosy liquid, tall glasses for herself and Lola, short ones for the girls. Pink lemonade, Lola thought.

"Pomegranate juice," Naomi announced. "I poured your glass and mine separately."

Lola forced a smile that threatened to turn into a grimace at the bite of vodka. She took tiny sips and contemplated the possibility that Naomi stayed pleasantly sloshed all the time. Maybe she kept a Nalgene bottle of innocuous-looking juice at her desk at work to get through the days. She wondered what necessitated Naomi's habit. Just another statistic in the woeful tally of reservation alcoholism? On-the-job stress? Self-administered therapy for the trauma of her family's eviction from their land? Problems with Gar? Lola could imagine herself driven to drink—at least a few stiff ones, if not a chronic problem—if Charlie had announced such a pompous nickname.

"Why is seeing Betty so wonderful?"

Naomi spoke past a dry cough. "If you want to know about the mine, Betty's the one."

Lola started to explain that they'd just happened across Betty when they were out exploring, then considered that Naomi didn't seem to care. "We ended up at one of the trading posts after we saw her." At the trading post, she'd longingly fingered a rug whose deep red coloring reminded her of the similar garnet strands in carpets from the Baloch region along the Pakistan-Afghanistan border. Then she'd read the five-figure price tag and contented herself with buying a postcard for Jan. "I thought maybe we could visit the mine, but it doesn't look like they let people in."

Though Lola had barely touched her juice, Naomi's glass was nearly empty. Her eyes glittered. "Good thing. What if something else blew up while you and the girls were there?"

Lola remembered her own involuntary reaction when she'd seen the truck. She shivered. Had Naomi divined her own unease and tweaked it? And if so, to what end?

But Naomi's face was all concern. "Are you cold? Would you like a sweater?" She wore another silk shirt, this one sleeveless. Her biceps shifted, a quick strain against taut skin as she lifted her glass and drained it.

Lola blinked. "Are you a climber?"

"How'd you know?"

Lola ducked her head to hide a blush. There'd been a dalliance in Wyoming, one that had come entirely too close to full-blown infidelity. He'd been a climber. She'd been an idiot. Still, those arms…

She held her own arm next to Naomi's and flexed. Nothing happened. "My muscles are like overcooked pasta. You've got guns. But

145

I thought climbing wasn't allowed on the reservation." Signs at the cliff houses had announced as much.

"It's not. Too many people clambering all over sacred sites." Naomi poured another glass. "I learned to climb in college, of all places. Dartmouth had a mountaineering club."

College was a long time ago, Lola thought. Obviously Naomi had kept up. "Where do you go now?"

"Oh, Flagstaff, Sedona, Hualapai Wall. Arizona's lousy with good spots. Thomas comes with me sometimes. I taught him. You know how it goes—get kids doing something physical, something that they like, and they stay away from drugs. It his case, it worked. That's how he got that scar, though, taking a bad tumble early on. Now he's probably better than I am. You can see that he's in great shape."

Lola, awash in guilty memories, didn't want to think any more about climbers and how good they were and what great shape they were in. "Did you hear anything about that note?" she said. "Do they have any idea about who might have sent it?"

Naomi took another sip of juice and choked. Long spasms wracked her body. "Sorry. Went down the wrong way. Anyway, no idea as to the sender."

"I don't suppose there's any chance it was some sort of prank." Even to herself, the idea was ridiculous. Lola wished she'd never suggested Charlie as some sort of undercover bodyguard. "How's it working out?" she asked. "With Charlie."

She waited for Naomi's return to her earlier insistence that the precaution was unnecessary. Naomi didn't oblige.

"Not nearly as bad as I expected. He's very good at being unobtrusive—he's there all the time, but not hovering over my shoulder. He's in his element, of course, in the courts. And the police are in and out of the building all the time, what with various cases, so he chats them up. Watching him work, it made me think of the immense amount of good he could do if only he were working for the Blackfeet."

Slash.

Lola checked an impulse to pat herself down, to see whether Naomi's latest jab had drawn actual blood. She tried to come up with a suitable response, one that didn't involve profanity. Rescue came in the form of a glimpse of motion through the window. It was Valentine, moving faster than Lola would have thought possible given his wide belly and short legs. Bub and the girls trailed behind. They'd braided the horse's mane and tail and tied off their efforts with bright scraps of fabric from Naomi's sewing room, which fluttered merrily as Valentine made his escape.

"The pony's running away," Lola said.

Naomi's shrug indicated routine. "He'll come back. He always does. This is where he gets fed."

"Will you still climb with Thomas?" Lola couldn't stop herself from poking back at Naomi. Climbing involved absolute trust in one's partner. Naomi had bristled when Lola implied Thomas might have written the note, but Lola wondered whether she, too, might harbor doubts about her ward.

"Why wouldn't I?" Naomi's words dared a response.

Reminding herself that her husband would be spending the next several days with Naomi, Lola tried yet another change of subject. "Speaking of Dartmouth." She reached for an orange in a fruit bowl so artfully arranged that she felt guilty disturbing it. She dug a thumbnail into the skin and circled the orange, pulling the peel away and tugging the fruit into sections. She wanted something in her stomach to counteract the alcohol. "Your family was still living on the mesa when you went to college, yes?"

Naomi nodded, and Lola thought of Betty's hogan. Even if Naomi's parents had lived in a standard BIA bungalow, life on the mesa would have been isolated, spartan. "College must have been quite a change."

"You mean running water? Electricity? Yeah, I even had to wear shoes to class."

Every time Lola thought she could relax around her sister-in-law, Naomi took another slice out of her with that verbal knife. The hell with this, Lola thought. She was tired of being nice for Charlie's sake. "I just don't know how you square it all."

"Square what?"

Lola took a defiant swig of her juice and held out her glass for more. "This." She ran her hand over the granite countertop and waggled her glass, which matched all the other glassware in the cupboard, nothing like the collection of jelly glasses she and Charlie had amassed over the years.

"That." She pointed through the window toward the shade house with its stonework fireplace. "The new Silverado. The Prius. All of it." Let Naomi take all the potshots she wanted. It was time for Lola to establish her willingness to fire back with a howitzer.

Naomi's lips thinned. "Gar and I have worked hard for what we have. We're not ostentatious about it."

No, Lola thought. They weren't. From the outside, the hogan looked modest. Their luxuries—the top-of-the-line kitchen, the fancy sewing machine, the central AC rather than a rattling window unit—were hidden indoors or otherwise disguised.

"And," said Naomi, "we give back."

"How, exactly?" She wanted to hear how Naomi would explain it.

"We look out for the people's interests. Me, in the court system, ensuring our people get a fair shake, not like in the whiteman courts. And Gar's work at the mine. The tribe deserves its fair share of the profits made from our land. We're role models. You know how it is. So many kids end up pregnant, drugging, dropping out. Or if they avoid those things and make it through college, they leave their people and work in cities. Or"—the invisible knife carved away another chunk of Lola's psyche—"even towns nearby. But we came back."

Lola bit into a section of orange, welcoming the spray of bitterness against the lingering sweetness of pomegranate, and swallowed. "Edgar didn't come back. He left his reservation and came to yours instead."

"Still. He's working for Indian people, not white people." A swing of machete, no finesse at all.

Lola had had just enough alcohol to refuse to concede the point. "If he's working with the corporations, he's dancing cheek-to-cheek with white people. Especially if the mine's involved. That kind of money has a way of being seductive."

Naomi's glass hit the countertop so hard it shattered. Shards of glass sparkled amid the spreading pool of pink. Lola reached for a towel. Footsteps sounded outside.

"Are you accusing my husband of cheating the people? He'd do anything for them," Naomi hissed just before the girls burst into the kitchen, hot and dusty and bursting with the news that they'd recaptured Valentine.

Lola threw the towel atop the mess on the counter and slid everything into the trash can while Naomi tended to the girls. She thought of how, the first night they'd met, Naomi had mentioned the possibility of a provocateur, someone on the inside, as the bomber. Edgar would do anything for the people, she'd said.

Lola hadn't accused Edgar of anything. But she wondered if she should.

TWENTY-TWO

SHIZHÉ'É COMES TO ME again that night, as he has every night since he died. Since he was murdered. Despite the reassurance I'd been given: *That one. That was an accident.*

This time, he's got company, their outlines wavering, merging and then parting, like smoke from two cigarettes. The truck driver. You think one is bad? Try two. It should have been twice as bad, but it seemed four or even five times worse. Before, with *Shizhé'é* working on me, it felt like I had something lodged in my throat. It wouldn't go away no matter how hard I coughed. Now I barely have any air at all. It's as though each one has reached a ghostly hand down my windpipe and taken hold of a lung, squeezing, squeezing.

I gasp for breath as *Shizhé'é* drifts around the guest room in Edgar and Naomi's house, walking in that bent-kneed way that made him look like an old man long before his time. Korea, was all he ever said about it. Grenade. That blast didn't kill him. But mine did. Now he takes hold of the sheet that covers my trembling body, rubs it between thumb and forefinger. It takes all of my will not to look toward the nightstand, topped by the legal pad that holds my instructions for the next action. Not that he'd understand them. They're in English, not Navajo, and although *Shizhé'é* spoke a broken English well enough when he wanted to, I'm not sure he ever learned to write much beyond grade-school level. Besides, they're in a sort of code. The words when I received them echoed in my head: *Everybody honors the Code Talkers, calls them heroes, even though all of their service was on behalf of a government that hadn't yet given them the right to vote. And everybody laments the fact that they're dying out. But they're not disappearing, not at all. What we're doing here, we're the new Code Talkers. And we're not doing this for the whiteman government. It's for our people. We're the true heroes.*

Words that might have heartened *Shizhé'é*. He'd been willing to die for a government that never respected him. Maybe if he'd known our aims, he'd have thought his own death worth it, accidental though it was. So why don't I want him to see what we're doing?

He comes closer still, somehow whole again, even though I know there wasn't nearly enough of him left to half-fill the best casket the funeral home had to offer.

"Fancy," he says. "How you like sleeping on silk sheets?"

"I don't think they're silk." Somehow, I force the words. I stretch my neck, gulp at air gone syrupy. A molecule or two of oxygen finds its way to me. "Cotton. They've got what they call a high thread count. Makes them feel really smooth." Gar and Naomi tell me about things like this. Around the rez, the fact that they know this shit gets them called apples—red on the outside, white inside. Don't think they don't know it. Both of them went to some Ivy League school. I didn't even know what Ivy League was before they explained it to me.

"Money," Edgar said over Naomi's burbling laugh. "It means money."

It was hell, they said. Sitting side by side with kids who spent their summer vacations backpacking across Europe, the gear they carried on their backs worth the equivalent of a few months' salary on the rez. Kids who said things like *Are you a real Indian?* And *Do you have a horse?* Who called Gar *Chief* and Naomi that most disgusting of sexual insults, *Squaw.*

"You just called me a cunt," she'd tell them. "Now go fuck yourselves." Then she'd sit back and watch those boys go a whiter shade of pale. That's the thing I love about her. Naomi doesn't believe in going along to get along. Me, I've said those sorts of things beneath my breath lots of times. Naomi, she says them loud and proud.

"Well?" *Shizhé'é* dropped the sheet. He was waiting for something. I can't see his companion anymore but can feel him inside me, raking anew at my lungs with clawlike fingers.

"It wasn't supposed to happen that way," I said past the rattle in my throat. "None of it was." Same thing I told him every night.

"But it did," he said. Same reply he made every night. "And I'm still dead."

His companion floated beside him. "And so am I."

TWENTY-THREE

LOLA AWOKE THE NEXT day to blinding sunlight and silence.

She fumbled on the nightstand for her phone, held it close to her face, and squinted. Eight in the morning. She heard a swish, not enough time to brace herself, and Bub whomped onto her chest, forcing the air from her lungs, bathing her face and hands with his tongue. "Go bother somebody else," she managed when she got her breath back. She shoved him aside and made her way to the bathroom, where she splashed water on her face and scrubbed at her teeth with her toothbrush. She padded barefoot into an empty kitchen. Two sticky notes hung from a cupboard above the coffeepot, whose contents were fast going to sludge. Lola poured and drank anyway, and, once her eyes had refocused, examined the notes. *Back to work with Naomi*, said one in Charlie's handwriting. It was Saturday, but the attacks would mandate seven-day work weeks until the bomber was captured.

Getting an early start, said the other in tall, back-slanted scrawl. *Watch the girls? I owe you. Suggested outing—Antelope Canyon. I*

153

booked you on a tour at ten. It's about an hour and a half away. The note was signed with a slashing *N*. Lola figured the "I owe you" was the closest thing she'd get to an acknowledgment, let alone an apology, from Naomi for the previous night's strain.

She reached for an apple, further unbalancing the fruit bowl's perfect arrangement. A stack of textbooks sat beside it. Poli Sci. Criminal Justice. Chemistry. So Thomas was back from wherever he'd been. Sleeping in? Lola bit into the apple and stepped to the window. His car was gone, though. Maybe he'd accompanied Naomi and Charlie. There was no sign—or sound—of the girls. "Why aren't you with them?" Lola asked Bub around a bite of apple. "If you left them alone while they went for a ride on that pony, you're in trouble." The chunk of apple stuck in her throat. The remark had been a lighthearted rebuke, but it occurred to her that the girls could have crept from the quiet house, and that she had no way of knowing where they might be. She tossed the apple core into the sink, sprinted down the hall to the girls' room, and flung open the door. Two forms stirred in the twin beds. Lola sagged against the wall. "Wake up, sleepyheads," she said, her voice shaky.

"No," came an indistinct voice from the lump beneath the covers on Margaret's bed. Although Margaret had inherited her father's talent for instantaneous deep sleep, she lacked his ability to go from near-coma to instant wakefulness. Mornings were a contest of wills between Lola and Margaret, mother sometimes carrying daughter's limp form to the breakfast table. There, she'd dump Margaret into a chair, insert a spoon into her hand, and remind her, several times, that the bowl of cereal before her was not a decoration.

Lola looked to Bub for help. Margaret was much more likely to arise, sometimes even cheerfully, after Bub's exuberant ministrations. But Bub cringed against the bedroom's far wall, ears flat against his head. He curled his lip and refused to move when Lola called to him.

"A lot of good you are. Come on, girls. We need to get a move on if we're going to go to Antelope Canyon today."

"Don' want to." Margaret would have objected to a trip to Disneyland if it were suggested first thing in the morning.

"Too bad. Hey, Juliana." Lola raised her voice. "You too. Both of you, up and dressed and in the kitchen in five." Lola yanked the covers from Margaret and reached over and did the same to Juliana, who responded by rolling onto her stomach and pulling her pillow over her head. Lola turned to the dresser and found clothes for Margaret, then lowered herself to her hands and knees and rooted under the bed for Margaret's sneakers. Her hand closed around one. She pulled it toward her. Something brushed the back of her hand. The sneaker emerged into the light, just as the tarantula emerged from the sneaker.

————

Later, Charlie would swear he'd heard the shriek all the way in Gaitero.

"Windows shattered," he said. "Eardrums burst. People ran for cover. Everybody grabbed their cellphones and dialed 911."

Lola rubbed at her hand as though she could still feel the bristly touch against her flesh. "It's not funny," she said. "And poor Bub."

The dog, his wiser instincts undone by the sound of her scream, had rushed to her defense, snapping at the creature as it raised its forelegs. Now his snout was swollen to twice its normal size, flesh stretched tight around the angry wound. Worse than the bite, Naomi had earlier informed Lola as she held a handkerchief dipped in vinegar to Bub's nose, were the tiny sharp hairs the spiders hurled in defense. "They're like needles. We'll never find them all. They'll

155

work their way out eventually. We'll give him a Benadryl to help with the itching. That'll make him sleep, too. That should help."

Lola had nodded, faking a calm she in no way felt. It was all she could do to keep her gaze fixed on Bub instead of letting it roam the kitchen, darting into corners and under the edges of cabinets, places that might shelter more lurking arachnids. The trip to Antelope Canyon had been abandoned. She'd called Naomi and Charlie as soon as she'd gotten herself, the girls, and Bub out of the room, slamming the door tight and, for good measure, blocking the opening beneath it with rolled-up towels.

Now Naomi directed Lola to hold the vinegar-soaked cloth to Bub's face before she and Charlie hotfooted it back to her office, Naomi barely concealing her annoyance. "Edgar's on his way home," she said. "He'll take care of the spider. He knows how."

The bedroom door stayed shut, and the girls remained in their pajamas, until Edgar stomped into the house and disappeared into the girls' bedroom with a Tupperware container and a sheet of paper in his hand. He returned some moments later with the tarantula in the container and the paper held tight across it. Lola shrank from the sight.

"Don't worry," Edgar said. Bub growled as he passed. "I'm going to release it outdoors."

"Outdoors" covered a lot of territory, Lola thought. Edgar probably meant the yard. Lola would have preferred the next county.

"Here's the thing," she said to Charlie as they lay together at the end of the interminable day. "The door to the girls' room was closed when I went to wake them up."

"So?"

"So how did that thing get in there? The window's really high. And tarantulas are ground spiders." Lola had spent much of the afternoon in the shade house, scrolling through spider websites on her phone as the girls rode back and forth on Valentine, interrupting her research with occasional entreaties to widen their range.

"Don't even think about it," Lola had said, scanning the ground around the pony's hooves for hairy, skittering creatures. Her own feet were tucked up in the chair.

"What are you saying?" Charlie asked now. The words slow, the question reluctant.

Lola stalled her answer. "Did you go in there last night?"

"Only to kiss them good night. And that was early."

"And you closed the door behind you, right?"

His head brushed hers in a nod. "So you think…?"

Lola thought of how Charlie and Edgar had walked into the house after dinner the previous evening, heads close together for a moment, then thrown back in shared laughter, the years of tension between them dissolving noticeably by the day. Tread carefully, she warned herself.

"I'm not saying anything. Not for sure. I just think we should consider the possibility that somebody put that damn thing in there."

———

Lola lay awake a long time after Charlie fell asleep on the far side of the bed, his back a hard plank of rejection. His words looped back through her head. "I don't believe this. You're accusing my brother."

"I didn't accuse anyone. I just said—"

"Who else could it be? Naomi didn't want to deal with it when she came back."

Lola thought of the textbooks on the counter. "Thomas was here sometime yesterday. He left some of his things."

"And now you're accusing a boy. Someone who's like a son to my brother."

Not a boy, Lola thought. She put Thomas at about twenty, a grown man. That guessed-at age was nearly all she knew about him. He was like a shadow, flitting in and out of the house, his face seemingly set in a permanent scowl, the scar across his cheekbone an emphatic underscore to his mood. He only seemed to soften in Juliana's presence.

"Juliana worships him." Charlie's voice echoed her own thoughts. "He'd never do anything that would hurt her."

The tarantula had been in Margaret's shoe, not Juliana's, Lola thought. Every time she closed her eyes, she saw again its striped forelegs raised high in preparation to strike, heard Bub's wail of pain. Imagined the creature's jaws sunk instead in Margaret's soft skin. She fought an impulse to leave Charlie alone in the bed, tiptoe down the hall to the girls' room, crawl into bed with her sleeping daughter and wrap her arms tight around her, shielding her against the danger that, despite Charlie's protests, she felt closing in on her family.

TWENTY-FOUR

WITH SOME SATISFACTION, LOLA surveyed the lunch she'd packed. Sandwiches, fruit, and two gallons of water. She was getting the hang of the desert.

Naomi quirked a perfectly plucked eyebrow. "Sure that'll be enough?" A moment later, she flashed a grin, showing her chipped tooth to charming advantage. Lola took that as a good sign. Maybe she could make an ally of Naomi after all, enlist her in softening Edgar's opposition to her presence in his brother's life. "I'm so glad you're going to Antelope Canyon," Naomi said now. "I was afraid, after you canceled yesterday, that you'd never get there."

Tourists like Lola couldn't go wandering off into the celebrated slot canyon on their own. Navajo-run tour companies led people through the canyon's two access points, Upper and Lower. Lola was lucky, Naomi told her, that spots for her and the girls were available again. "This time of year, it's so hot that not as many people go. Plus, it can be a little dicey because of flash floods during summer cloudbursts. But there's no rain in the forecast, and besides, the guides have a good weather eye. You'll be fine. You've got your camera, right?"

Lola held up her phone, ignoring the flicker of disdain across Naomi's face. The woman probably had a Leica with a pro's array of lenses, she thought.

"You'll be gone all day," Naomi said. "And Gar and I will probably be working into the night. Sorry that Charlie's stuck with me." So am I, Lola thought as Naomi rattled on. "There's a quiche in the refrigerator for dinner. Just help yourself when you get back."

A quiche? Lola couldn't remember the last time she'd seen one on a menu, let alone heard of anyone baking one. She shook her head at yet another example of Naomi's effortless perfection. She shook it again at Bub, hovering beside her. He was sleepy from the Benadryl, nose still swollen, though not to the previous day's clownish proportions. "You're staying here today." She couldn't, in good conscience, leave the dog alone in the truck during the tour, even in the unlikely event she found a shady place to park. She carried a tiny thermometer clipped to her bookbag, which she'd left sitting in the shade house the previous day; when she'd retrieved it, the mercury had measured 107.

Bub threw himself down in a corner of the kitchen and shot accusing glances at her as she marshaled the girls through their breakfast. Even her offering, made after Naomi left for work, of the breakfast plates to lick clean failed to win Bub's approval. He polished the plates but stalked away as soon as he'd finished, refusing to come when she called a goodbye to him—not unlike the way Charlie had departed earlier that morning, turning his head so that her kiss brushed his cheek instead of his lips.

Edgar, as usual, left without acknowledging the forced cheeriness of her goodbye. Just as well she hadn't seen Thomas that morning,

Lola thought. "Just one more male who'd have been mad at me," she muttered as she held the truck's back door open for the girls.

It felt strange not to have Bub beside her, Lola thought as she set off in the usual cloud of red dust, venting her annoyance with a quick stomp of the gas pedal. Let Charlie spend yet another day in an air-conditioned office with his sister-in-law on what was supposed to have been his honeymoon. Lola had every intention of taunting him at the end of the day with photographs of what would have been a romantic outing to Antelope Canyon—as romantic as an outing could be with two youngsters in tow.

"I'll show you," she whispered, a mantra usually applied to rival reporters, recalcitrant sources, and editors who wielded a red pen too freely for her taste. But never, until this minute, at her husband.

———

Charlie often commented on Lola's ability to nurse a grudge. It was, she'd always say in response, what fueled her ability to out-report other journalists. Beat her once on a story, and never again. Now bitter thoughts typically reserved for competing reporters twisted like snakes, jabbing at her with poisoned fangs as she drove toward the canyon. She'd always taken Charlie's loyalty for granted. If anyone in Magpie had questioned their relationship—and Lola was sure there'd been plenty of that—he'd never let on. But now the questions came from Gar, the person who, after Margaret and Lola, meant the most to him. And Lola was questioning that person in return, putting herself in the way of Charlie's renewed relationship with his only brother. What if Charlie felt he had to choose between them? And if he did, whom would he choose?

Lola's eyes flitted to the rearview mirror and fastened on Margaret, her trump card. So there, she thought. But then, Margaret was blood, as was Edgar. Not just any blood, but Blackfeet blood, precious in that it conferred tribal enrollment.

Lola rubbed at her damnably white forehead, trying to erase such thoughts. Their arrival at the canyon provided welcome distraction, and any lingering anxiety leached away with her first glimpse of the cleft in the smooth rock of the desert, so narrow she could have stepped across it.

"Here." The guide leading their group gestured toward an opening, barely wider. Metal steps led down into blackness. "You were good to get an early start," he said. "Later in the day, even this time of year, it will be crowded. And the upper canyon will be worse. Tourists can't seem to get it into their heads just how hot the days are here. We should have the lower canyon mostly to ourselves, though." Lola couldn't imagine anyone foolish enough to endure the jolting ride across the desert in the blaze of midday sun. Ten in the morning and already the mercury nudged three digits. The temperature fell apace with her descent down five flights of stairs—some barely more than ladders—into the slot canyon. She'd hesitated at the top, fearing a repeat of the vertigo she'd felt on the ladder at the cliff houses. But the canyon walls hugged her tight, and the darkness below cloaked any awareness of just how far she was from the canyon floor.

"Oh," she breathed as she reached the bottom, tilting her head back to trace the winding blue thread of sky visible far above the canyon floor. Her feet sank in sand soft as talcum powder. Rock walls, striped red and yellow and gold, wound sinuously up and away. Lola stretched her arms, flattening one hand against the wall to the left, the other against the opposite wall, letting the cool soak into her palms.

"This way." The guide led them to the left.

"What's back there?" Lola pointed right. The canyon meandered away into gloom.

"Lake Powell, eventually." He led the group ahead. Camera clicks, alternating with gasps of wonder, marked their progress. Lola heard low conversations in German. French. Even in their multinational enthusiasm, people spoke with the hushed reverence usually reserved for cathedrals.

Lola had heard of the reservation's famed Canyon de Chelly and Chaco Canyon. She'd decided to put off those trips until Charlie could accompany them. And she'd easily persuaded him that at some point on their honeymoon, they owed it to Margaret to leave the Navajo Nation for a side trip to the Grand Canyon, only about three hours away. Somehow, she'd missed any reference to Antelope Canyon. Now, as the guide led the group farther into the canyon and she stood alone in awe, she was glad she'd arrived with no preconceived notions. She listened from a distance as the guide talked on and on, explaining the geologic forces that had created the fifty-foot-deep gouge in the earth, and the sobering reality of the flash floods that occasionally coursed through it, rising high between the narrow walls, capturing people unawares, drowning them as they scrabbled for nonexistent purchase on the smooth, inward-sloping canyon walls. Juliana and Margaret stood rapt before him, taking in every word.

Lola drifted backward, letting a hand trail over the rock, imagining she could feel the stripes beneath her fingertips. She wanted to experience the canyon on her own. She reached the ladders. The sound of the guide's lecture, the girls' high-voiced questions, faded. The narrow fissure beyond beckoned. Lola stepped into the darkness. There was a dampness to it, welcome after days in the desiccating heat. She inhaled, imagining she could catch the scent of faraway Lake Powell.

A hand clapped across her mouth; another grabbed her wrist and jerked her farther in. A voice hissed into her ear.

"Not a fucking word."

————

Lola tried to scream anyway.

Only a whimper escaped. Her captor yanked her against him, his arm like an iron bar across her chest. She kicked against his shins and stomped at his feet. He wrapped one of his legs around hers. Lola realized he'd wedged himself into the claustrophobic space, the walls holding him upright no matter how she struggled. She had no hope of knocking him off balance, of staggering free into the main canyon where the guide and the girls and the other tourists ambled, ignorant of her desperate struggle. She bit at the wide hand over her mouth. His fingers smashed her lips against her teeth. She tasted her own blood. Her heart slammed against her ribs, so hard that she thought her captor must feel it.

"Listen to me. Are you listening?" The voice spectral, unrecognizable.

Lola tried a yes, and a few other words besides. The hand clenched still tighter over her mouth. She settled for a ghost of a nod. She wrenched her head against his grip, trying for the slightest glimpse of his face. Look first at the eyes, Charlie always told her. The color, the shape. Too many bad actors got away because their petrified victims couldn't provide a decent description. He didn't want Lola ever to find herself in that position. She would laugh at him when he said such things. Now his words rang in her head. But she couldn't move. The man's grip was too strong.

Her mind flashed on the possibilities. Did this person want to rob her? Rape her? With people only a few yards away? She'd heard of such

164

things, women pulled into stairwells, doorways, their disbelief that something could happen in so public a place working to an assailant's advantage.

Her terror expanded beyond the personal with the man's next words. "You don't belong here. You and your man and your white child. The spider? Just a warning. It will get worse. Not just for you and yours, but for everyone. You think you know about bombs. Not firsthand, you don't. Get out before you learn."

Lola's brain seemed cleaved in two, one side all silent screaming panic, the other ticking off things to remember. He knew about the tarantula. It hadn't just wandered into the girls' room by accident. He'd been in the house.

Lola moved her head a millimeter.

"Tell anyone, especially that cop husband of yours, and your little girl … You understand?"

Lola stiffened. Anger shouldered fear aside. Anger, and a kind of despair. The man in Wyoming who'd wanted to hurt her had endangered Margaret, too. She'd sworn to Charlie—and, more important, to herself—that she'd never risk her child's safety again. And now this asshole was putting her back in that place.

If you touch her, I will kill you, she said into his hand. No sound emerged.

He seemed to be waiting for assent. Lola granted him another head-twitch.

"Now go. Get out of Arizona."

The hand gone from her mouth. A sharp shove to her back.

She stumbled into a shaft of sunlight. Fell to her hands and knees in the powdery sand. Her head spun. With freedom, fear returned, the knowledge of what could have been—her neck snapped, her breath choked off, the divide between life and death a matter of moments—coursing through her body in shuddering waves.

A voice wound its way around the canyon's walls and found her. "Mom?"

"Oh, no," Lola whispered. He was still in there, and the girls were coming close. She pushed herself to her feet. Wiped her hand across her mouth. It came away streaked with red. She licked swollen lips, ran shaking hands through her hair, dusted the sand from her knees. Staggered toward the sound of her daughter's voice.

"Margaret, wait." The words came out in a croak.

Margaret and Juliana rounded the corner at a trot, the guide following at a sensible walk. "Thought we'd lost you," he called. "You don't want to go back that way. It's full of rattlesnakes. And a little ways in, it drops off about twenty feet."

Lola ranked rattlesnakes with tarantulas, but at the moment thought she might have welcomed an honest jab from a creature simply trying to protect its space rather than a human who'd gone out of his way to threaten her. She spread her arms, trying to stop the girls with a hug, thankful for the canyon's dim light. Margaret dodged away, suspicion in her eyes. "Mom? What's wrong?"

Behind her, Juliana. "It stinks in here."

Lola wondered if she'd peed herself in fear. She sniffed but could smell only the scent of the man's hand across her face. She shifted her legs. Her pants were dry. "Caves smell funny," she managed. "This place is more like a cave than a canyon." She turned toward the blackness of the cleft. She cleared her throat, raised her voice, and spoke toward it. "I think the heat got to me for a minute. Nothing's wrong. Not a single thing."

166

TWENTY-FIVE

THE SHADOWS WAVERED BEFORE the opening in the rocks, blocking my escape. Teeth flashed in skull-like grins, bright in the cool dimness. My lungs constricted.

"Leave me alone." I squeezed out more words. "There's no killing this time. You saw it. I just tried to scare her. She's fine."

As soon as I'd heard about the trip to Antelope Canyon, I made my plan. I had to drive like hell to get there ahead of them, scared to death she'd recognize my car when I passed them on the road. I tipped the guide extra to let me in without a tour. "I'll be a while," I told him. Then added another couple of bills.

Even then, it almost didn't happen. But she made the mistake of wandering away from everyone else.

They say criminals get a taste for it, the power they have over their victims. That the tangible fear, the begging, brings on a rush, one that makes it easier the next time, seduces you into upping the ante. Maybe that first time, you just give someone a scare. Hurt them a little the next, more still the time after that. Until finally you find yourself with your hands around someone's neck, a wild surge within as the writhing beneath you stops.

Maybe.

I don't see it. When I grabbed her and pulled her into that crevice, she trembled so hard in my grip that I thought she'd shake right out of it. I had to bite my tongue to keep from apologizing to her. And the things I did say, about her child. If someone had threatened Juliana that way, I'd have killed him. I could feel the same impulse in her, the way the trembling stopped and her body tensed at my words. Her jaw clenched against my hand covering her mouth.

"Forgive me," I wanted to say as I shoved her back into the main part of the canyon. Then I fell to my knees in the sandy soil and threw up.

Juliana's voice reached me a few moments later. "It stinks in here."

Now they'll find me, I thought. Which, to be honest, would have been a relief. I waited for the woman to denounce me, for the guide to call the police. In jail, I'd be safe. Nobody could make me do anything. Maybe all this craziness would fizzle out. No more killings.

Then, the guide. "That's funny. These look like coyote tracks. Two pairs. Let's get out of here." I'd always loved the fact that only Navajo guides staffed our sacred places. Now I could have used a white guide who didn't share our belief about Coyote.

Somehow, *Shizhé'é* and the truck driver had gotten behind me. I heard them back there, deeper in the rocks, chortling and jostling for position, anticipating my humiliation, so excited that they loosed their hold on my lungs. I sucked in oxygen, the first full breaths I'd taken in too long.

Then the voices outside faded. *Shizhé'é* and the truck driver gabbled their disappointment. I fled up the ladder, gaining strength with every step away from them, sprinted to my car, and drove home as fast as that junk heap would take me. Because just in case this wasn't enough to scare her off, there was one more thing I had to do.

TWENTY-SIX

"Too fast, Mom. Mom!"

"And too hot, Auntie Lola."

The girls' voices glanced off Lola's consciousness and slid away. She gripped the steering wheel tighter in sweating hands, stomped the accelerator, and watched the needle quiver past ninety, ninety-five, frantic to gain distance. She swerved around an elephantine RV, cutting back into her lane in time to miss an oncoming pickup by inches. Horns blared. Copper dust filled the cab. Lola sucked it in, grateful for the grit on her tongue, for the heat that blazed against her skin, for any sensation that reminded her she was alive and safe, free of the harrowing moments in the canyon.

"Please, Mom?"

The tearful words pinged somewhere deep within her brain. Margaret had inherited her mother's imperious and brusque manner. She was a child who employed demands instead of requests, one who would eyeball a dish of ice cream as it liquefied on the counter, refusing to ask for it, waiting for someone to bestow it upon her.

She'd mastered *thank you* early, but *please* was a work in progress. As for tears, Lola had seen her child's chubby hand red and swollen with a bee sting, her bare foot sliced open by broken glass, her whole body bruised by a fall from Spot, without releasing the moisture that glistened in her eyes. Before the moment's import fully hit, Margaret screamed, "Please!"

Lola worked clutch and brake so abruptly that the truck skidded across the road and spun back before lurching to a stop on the shoulder. A final mushroom cloud of dust rose, cloaking the passing vehicles. One of them backfired. Lola jumped. A glimpse in the rearview mirror of the two staring faces in the back seat convinced her not to turn around and face the girls. Terror fled, or at least receded. Shame flooded the space it had occupied. She fought for words to explain her inexcusable behavior.

"The sun." Then why hadn't she simply turned on the air-conditioning? "Something spooked me," she wanted to say. But she'd already frightened the girls badly enough. She hawked up a gob of dust and spat through the window, rolled up the windows, and belatedly turned on the air. She reached for one of the gallon bottles of water, unscrewed the cap, drank directly from it, and ordered her voice to behave.

"The truck. I think there's something wrong with the wiring. I couldn't work the windows, couldn't make it slow down. Thank God I finally got it stopped. I'm so sorry I scared you. I was scared, too. Are you all right?"

She finally turned, but looked only at Juliana, knowing that if she met Margaret's eyes, they would radiate a single message, a word Margaret had learned while still a toddler: *Bullshit*.

Juliana made a motion that could have been a nod. The girl's front teeth caught her lower lip. Doubt shone through the red dust filming her brown skin. "My dad's truck is brand new. How could something be wrong with it?"

Lola threw some praise her way. "That's a very smart question, Juliana. We'll let your dad know about it as soon he comes home tonight. And I'm going to drive slowly the rest of the way home." Give them a task, she told herself. Make them allies. And then distract them with the thought of something enjoyable.

"I want you girls to pay very, very close attention to the sound the engine makes. Your ears are younger and sharper than mine. The air-conditioning seems to be working again, but if you hear the engine rev the least little bit, I want you to holler and let me know. Okay? When we get to town, I'll stop at the gas station and ask someone to look at it while we get ice cream." *And the minute I'm back in cell range, I'll call 911.*

The man's voice echoed in her ears: *Tell anyone, especially that cop husband of yours, and your little girl ... You understand?* Lola understood. She should tell Charlie. But Charlie would insist upon action. He'd think he could keep them safe. Lola couldn't afford to take a chance he'd be wrong.

"Ice cream would be nice," Juliana allowed. Lola caught the movement of Margaret's head signaling grudging and belated assent. She gave silent thanks to the Creator she wasn't sure she believed in, adding an apology for the string of lies she'd just uttered. At least her next words, she thought, would be the truth.

"Just think how happy Bub will be to see us when we get home."

Margaret's nod became more emphatic.

Lola kept her promise, driving at barely more than a crawl, hoping the girls didn't notice how often she scanned the rearview mirror for any signs that the attacker they didn't know about might have pursued them. And she lightly goosed the engine a couple of times, just to give the girls something to do, tapping the brakes when they yelled a warning, issuing fulsome reassurances that whatever had ailed the truck seemed to have been only a momentary problem. Her efforts at soothing them had the benefit of easing her own pulsing tension, so that when they arrived home, hands sticky from dripping ice-cream cones, she was just as dumbfounded as the girls to find that Bub was gone.

———

Lola paced the kitchen, oblivious to the efforts of everyone in the household to calm her.

Charlie followed close behind, the flat of his hand at her back as though to steady her. She twisted away. The girls pored over a map of the reservation, drawing X's over sites they thought might appeal to a dog. "Anywhere with water," Juliana said knowledgeably. Margaret scowled at the map, searching for nonexistent bits of blue. "That's hardly anywhere at all." Thomas's car coughed in the distance. He'd volunteered to drive the local roads. Edgar put a hand over his free ear and spoke into his telephone. "Border collie. Three legs. Can't miss him." And Naomi offered a tall glass of her special lemonade. Lola waved it away with a chopping motion.

"I want to stay clear-headed."

Naomi cut her eyes toward Edgar. Lola rolled her own in response. How was it possible that Edgar remained oblivious to his wife's drinking? Or, at the very least, that Naomi believed him oblivious? Edgar said a few more words into the phone, clicked it off, and turned to them. "I've called all of the neighbors, at least the ones who have reception." Lola knew that wouldn't be many. Cellphone reception was a joke on most of the vast and empty reservation, while landlines, quickly becoming a thing of the past in other parts of the country, had never been installed at all in many parts of the Navajo Nation.

"Nobody's seen him," said Edgar. "Not alive and not—"

Lola flung up her hands to stop the words he'd been about to utter. She couldn't bear even the brief thought of Bub's limp carcass beside the road, a victim of one of the trucks from the mine, whose relentless stream of traffic had barely slowed despite the bombing.

"I know." Edgar acknowledged her fear. "But it's a possibility we have to consider. Along with coyotes, rattlesnakes, things like that."

"We have those in Montana, too," Lola reminded him. "As well as plenty of trucks. And somehow he's managed to keep himself from getting killed. I never should have left him alone."

Edgar's face telegraphed what he knew better than to say. *He's just a dog.*

Lola stopped pacing, braced her hands against the counter, and addressed his unspoken logic. "You have to understand. He's more than just a pet. I owe him—" Her voice caught. Bub had twice saved her life, once by attacking a man who'd tried to kill her, and again by leading Charlie to a trailer where she'd been held at gunpoint. She'd been pregnant with Margaret then, even though she hadn't known it, so Bub in fact had saved both of them. And in Wyoming, the man who'd threatened Lola had nearly killed Bub. The dog had lost his leg as a result of the first incident. The second had made him even more fiercely protective of her, a feeling the third incident did nothing to dispel. It was a feeling Lola returned with equal intensity.

"You owe him what?"

Everything, Lola wanted to say. But she knew he wouldn't understand. Edgar didn't wait for her answer. "He probably just ran off."

"Maybe. If someone came home and left the door open, he might have tried to find us ... " Lola began. But even as Edgar began to shake his head, she added, "No. He would never do that. He'd wait forever, right where I left him. There's only one way we're going to find him."

Naomi lifted the glass she'd prepared for Lola and drank deep. "And what's that?"

"When we find the person who took him."

Lola stared directly into Edgar's eyes as she said it, an act of impermissible rudeness. Maybe he was just being polite when he looked away, but she didn't think so.

TWENTY-SEVEN

"I don't believe this. First the spider. Now the dog. It's obvious you think Eddie had something to do with this. Is there no end to the evil you'll accuse my family of?"

Charlie's fury was no less fearsome for being of necessity sotto voce. They sat upright in bed, an acre or so of sheets between them. Even in the gentle glow of the bedside lamp, she could see the muscles in his face stretched taut, the skin whitening around his lips.

"I didn't accuse anybody of anything. Jesus, Charlie. You say you want me to be a badass reporter, but only if you approve. You don't want me questioning anything that makes you uncomfortable."

"You looked right at my brother. You might as well have pointed your finger at him. In the middle of this bombing mess, the man came home from work to help you. Just like with the spider."

"Hush." Lola glanced at the wall shared with the girls' room. Margaret, her daughter who never cried, who even in the midst of Lola's wild drive earlier had only hiccupped a brief sob, had wept for nearly an hour before falling into an exhausted sleep, her body convulsing against Lola's, heedless of her mother's whispered reassurances. "We'll find him, Margaret. We won't leave this place until we do. We will not go home without him. I promise you."

Below her own words lurked those of the man in the canyon. *Get out.* But they couldn't leave now. Dread pressed tight against her chest. "I promise," she managed again.

Now she tried to summon that same feigned certainty as she faced Charlie's wrath. "I'm not accusing anyone. Truly." Even to her own ears, she sounded insincere. "But Bub didn't run away. You know him."

Naomi's sewing machine hummed in the next room. Naomi had said she sewed to relax. Given the level of tension in the house, Lola figured Naomi would be sewing all night.

"I thought I knew you." Charlie's words fell like blows. Lola twisted away.

"I thought you put family first." She bent double.

"Except when you don't."

She put her hands over her ears. That last, the worst, with its reminder of the previous year, when she'd pursued the story that put both herself and Margaret in danger. Now she was back in that same dark place, with the morning's explicit threat to Margaret's safety.

Tell anybody about this, and . . .

Tell anybody. The only person she wanted to tell was Charlie. *Tell anybody about this, especially that cop husband . . .*

The only person she didn't dare tell was Charlie.

Look at me, her eyes begged him. Force me to tell.

But in his anger he turned away, announcing concern for his brother. "He's working late tonight, to make up for the hours he lost today. All of us—Naomi, Edgar, and me—came running home when you called us. We've got two men dead, people working around the clock to keep it happening again, and you want us to drop everything and look for a goddamn dog. Get a grip, Lola. Bad enough you think Eddie let the dog get away. I'm surprised you're not accusing someone in my family of being the bomber."

The thought that Gar or Naomi might be the bomber indeed had crossed her mind, based on Charlie's own oft-spoken mantra. *Ninety-nine percent of the time, the simplest explanation is the right one*, he liked to say. *The person closest to the victim is usually your perp.*

But in this case, the victims were so widely disparate—a Navajo elder who hated the mine, a young truck driver who worked for it—as to rule out the usual cast of friends and relatives. Unless, Lola thought. Unless you substituted "case" for "victim." The person closest to the case would be the one they needed to seek, the case being the mine, or things representing it. And who'd been affected by the mine?

Lola thought of Betty Begay, alone in her hogan, her sly smile barely perceptible in the darkness, her words a whisper. "Maybe little Betty big bomber." But even though Lola knew better than to rule anybody out, she couldn't overcome her own antipathy to viewing an elder, and such a likable elder at that, as a suspect, although she and Charlie had each had far too many encounters with entirely likeable perps. But Betty didn't drive. She'd have had to enlist someone's help to put the bombs in place.

Another of Charlie's sayings: *Get a partner, get caught.* He frequently pointed to Timothy McVeigh, whose co-conspirator in the Oklahoma City bombing, Terry Nichols, blabbed the details of the plot to his large and dysfunctional family. It had made fine fodder for conviction at the men's trials. It had to be someone capable of working alone.

Lola jumped as Charlie voiced her own train of thought. "What about Naomi? Have you homed in on her already? She's as angry about the mine as anyone I've seen."

Privately, Lola thought that Naomi should be considered, for that very reason. On the other hand, she couldn't quite picture Naomi's manicured hands wound in a tangle of detonation cord, those slender fingers packing nails and scrap metal into a container that later would be blown apart. She said as much to Charlie.

"But you have thought of her. Christ, Lola. You're worrying this one like a dog with a bone."

"You said it yourself. It's what I do."

When it came to stories, she never quite trusted other reporters to do as good a job on a story as she would, sure that they'd miss key details, forget to interview that one last source who would tie everything together. It was a tendency that went beyond newspaper stories, with Lola unable to stop herself from hounding Charlie for details of criminal investigations that he was, by law, unable to give her. On those occasions, he'd drive her crazy by pinching his fingers together and drawing them across his smiling lips, mimicking a zipper. Maybe he made the gesture again now. But he'd turned his back on her so she couldn't tell. For sure, there was no tolerant humor in his voice when he spoke again.

"Drop it, Lola. I know I encouraged you to work on a story here. But you're not, and you're not a cop. So there's no reason for you to be involved."

Until the incident in the canyon, Lola would have agreed with him, albeit begrudgingly. But I am involved, she thought now. *Dammit, Charlie, look at me.*

He switched off the lamp, falling asleep before the heat of anger had dissipated from him. Lola feared for his dreams. For that matter, she feared her own waking thoughts as she lay wide-eyed and tense, the possibilities continuing to run a treadmill in her mind.

The man who'd accosted her in the canyon that morning had spoken of the bombings. He'd also known about the spider. Lola's thoughts had gone first to Edgar, but he'd been at work when she was in the canyon, something that would be easy enough to verify. Still, there remained the discomfort of Edgar's ongoing hostility toward her, his continual mention of her whiteness, just as the man in the canyon had made a point of it. And Edgar, having grown up on the ranch with Charlie, would know how to blow things up. Stumps and such, although Charlie hinted that as boys, they weren't above practicing their detonative talents on lesser targets like ground hornets. "Dirt clods thirty feet high," he'd said with satisfaction. "No more stung feet."

Her thoughts roamed to Thomas. Despite Juliana's obvious affection for him, there was something dark and secretive about Thomas. Somebody had driven away from the house in the middle of the night, just hours before the truck bombing. And—Lola sat upright as though jerked by strings, her hand across her mouth to stifle her gasp. She thought back to that first meeting with Thomas, the hilarity caused to everyone but Lola and Charlie by his car's explosive backfiring. He'd carried a bookbag that day. More recently, though, there'd been the books stacked alone on the kitchen island. She hadn't seen Thomas with a bookbag since that first meeting—which was the evening before they'd discovered that bookbag in the cliff houses.

She wished she'd paid more attention to the bag Thomas had carried. Still, as much as she hated to admit it, Charlie's point about Thomas's youth was well taken. Bomb making required a level of sophistication usually not acquired during one's teenage years.

She let her mind wander still farther afield. There was that environmental writer. What was his name? Something bland, white-bread. Jim Andersen. He'd made the pilgrimage to Betty Begay, heard the tale of the betrayal of the mesa dwellers. Add that human wreckage to the ravishment of the environment and you could have motive, especially when it came to greenies of a certain bent. Along with ability, given Anderson's time in the military. Lola thought that if she found out the man had been a bomb expert, he'd rival Thomas for the Number One Suspect spot. But…

"Occam's razor," she whispered. Reining her wild theories back in. Every time she strayed from that principle, she got into trouble. "Simplest is best."

At which point, her mind circled back to where she'd started, with suspicions that lacked a shred of evidence beyond a prickling of skin, a chill in the blood whenever he turned her way. "Edgar," Lola hissed into the darkness. "Gar."

The thought muscled its way into the buzzing space in her brain already occupied by the man in the canyon, Bub's disappearance, and now Charlie's anger, a toxic stew that made focus impossible. Lola knew sleep would be her best weapon. She dug around in her Dopp kit for a sleeping pill, only to remember that she'd tossed the empty container before she'd left home. The long-unused bottle of painkillers rattled promisingly. She clicked on her phone's flashlight and squinted at the label: *May cause drowsiness.*

"Good enough," she said. She swallowed one dry and awaited the approaching blackout.

———

The sun sneaked between the blinds, striping the sheet that draped Lola and Charlie and the wide space between them. Lola watched its progress with eyes bloodshot from the long night. Even with the pill, deep sleep had eluded her. Whenever she'd drifted toward it, the words of her tormenter in Antelope Canyon whooped like emergency sirens. *Get out.* Or Margaret might get hurt.

She'd spent much of the night in the weird restiveness where bad dreams mingled with a worse reality. Daylight brought true wakefulness. She lay silent, mulling her choices. She knew that despite Charlie's avowed nostalgia for her previous brashness, if she put Margaret in danger again, their marriage might be over. She couldn't blame him. If the roles were reversed, she'd have felt the same way. But Margaret was already in danger—the tarantula in her shoe, the threat from Canyon Man, and now the dog kidnapped. Somehow, given what the man in the canyon had said, they were all related to the bombings.

And if Gar was involved, then they were all in danger, perhaps Charlie most of all. Lola edged closer to her sleeping husband, curling against his broad back, breathing in his scent. She was, he'd often remarked, the least demonstrative woman he'd ever been with. "Those others," he'd said, shrugging away her queries as to just how many others, "it's like they wanted to brand me. Hanging on me whenever we were out in public. Always leaving things of theirs at my place, staking out their turf. Bringing me home to their mom. Well. You know how it is on the rez. See a girl once, you're going steady; twice, you're engaged." Lola had winced, wondering how many girls Charlie had been "engaged" to before he'd moved in with a white woman.

Early on, she'd been self-conscious about her visible status as an outsider. Every time a pretty Blackfeet woman so much as smiled a hello at Charlie, she'd wondered if the woman had been one of those hanging on him before she'd stumbled into his life as a potential witness in a murder case. But then the woman in question would turn the same welcoming smile on her without the slightest change detectable even by Lola's hypersensitive radar, and as the months passed, she'd relax to the point where she could josh right back with the aunties about the sexual superiority of Indian men. She'd gotten so relaxed, in fact, that Edgar's hostility had come as a surprise.

And then, the words of Canyon Man: *You and your white child.* She pressed herself closer still to Charlie, forcing herself back into those moments of icy terror, trying to recall any twinge of recognition. But all she could remember was the utter strength of the man, the hand hard across her mouth, his lips to her ears, the foul words.

Lola jerked as her brain fastened on a detail. He'd been clean-shaven. There. That was something. And he'd bent his head to hers. So he was taller. Another thing. Two things, she thought ruefully, that probably applied to half the men on the Navajo Nation. But not Gar, who though clean-shaven was shorter than she was and possibly, as much as she hated to admit it, even a few pounds lighter. Thomas, though . . . He and Edgar didn't seem particularly close. But that might be by design.

Lola would make any queries about Thomas—about any of them—carefully, carefully. Nothing she said or did from this moment out could raise suspicions that she was looking into things. She'd announce to anyone who would listen that they planned on leaving—in a few days. The search for Bub made a good excuse for the delay.

Get out, Canyon Man had said.

Whoever he was, he'd know she'd ignored his order. He might make another run at her. Which, despite the danger, meant she'd have another chance to identify him.

"Come on," she whispered, trying to psych herself into a bravado she in no way felt. "I'm waiting for you."

TWENTY-EIGHT

I GRABBED A CHUNK of lamb from Naomi's refrigerator and held it out to the dog.

He hustled toward me and I backed away, through the kitchen, out the door, to the car. At the last moment, with his nose a millimeter from the meat, teeth bared to snatch it from my hand, he hesitated. It was almost as though he knew what was going on.

I moved fast, grabbing his collar and hauling him toward the rear door I'd left open. With only three legs, his balance was off. He half-fell onto the back seat and I shoved him the rest of the way in and slammed the car door behind him. He made a leap for it when I got in, but I managed to block his escape with my body. Shut my own door and locked it, just for good measure. He went crazy then, jumping around and barking, nipping at my arm as I worked the shift so that I nearly went off the road a few times. Fast as I was driving, that would have been a disaster.

When we finally stopped, it took me forever to wrestle him to a point where I could duct-tape his legs—with only three of them, it was like tying up a calf after roping it—and then wind the tape around his muzzle, too. He rolled his eyes around until his gaze found mine, the blue eye cold as steel.

"I'm sorry, buddy," I said. "Real sorry." But for what I had to do, he needed to be still. I couldn't afford anything else going wrong. I threw him over my shoulder so I couldn't see that accusing stare. He quivered and groaned against me until I released him from his suffering.

Afterward, I drove back home in the dark. For the final time that day, I almost crashed, wrenching the wheel hard to the right when two coyotes sauntered across the road in front of me. The car spun out and came to a stop facing them. They'd stopped in the middle of the road, staring straight at me, square in the beam of the headlights.

But their eyes were flat and dark, not throwing the light back at me. The sound of breathy laughter filled the night.

And no wonder. Because when I finally got back to the house, I found that my scheme had only served to make the woman even more determined to stick around. What I'd done to that dog—it was all for nothing.

TWENTY-NINE

LOLA TOOK ADVANTAGE OF her sleeplessness and managed to be the first one up. She fortified herself with a mug of coffee and had started on a second before Gar sauntered into the kitchen. She watched his gaze sweep the room, assuring himself that no one else was there. He gathered himself for some sort of pronouncement, straightening his shoulders, running a hand through his pompadour. Lola swallowed, set down the cup, and beat him to the punch.

"You know," she said just as he opened his mouth to speak, "it seems crazy for us to stay here while you and Naomi are in the midst of your investigation. It's nice to be able to help with Juliana, but in the long run, it just seems like we're in the way." Any more sugar in her voice and her teeth would have dissolved, she thought. She raised her mug to hide her expression and peered at him over the rim.

"Well. You might just be right." Spoken expansively, the sort of tone he might have used with the mine supervisors, matching their gestures and mannerisms as well as their suits and ties, saving the quiet, questioning tones of Indian-speak for time with his family, his friends.

The mug inched down. "Of course," Lola said, "we'll want to hang around a few more days in case the dog shows up." Gar jerked, as though a fisherman had snagged an errant fly between his shoulders blades and pulled hard, thinking he'd snagged a big one. Lola imagined herself digging around in the sugar canister and shoveling another scoopful into her delivery. "I hope I'm not insulting you by focusing on the dog when you're dealing with such important issues. But you know how kids are. And you know how it hurts when you see them hurting. I won't be able to concentrate on anything else until we find him—or until I've found a way to explain to Margaret that we can't find him."

Despite herself, her voice hardened on that last phrase. She'd find Bub, one way or the other. And then she'd get herself and her family out of Arizona. For once, she wouldn't complain about Charlie's speeding.

Gar gave a single, slow nod. His eyes narrowed. "I get that."

Lola figured his lie was at least equal to hers. Which meant that she probably wasn't fooling him. She gulped her coffee and declared her intention to go for a run. Despite her sleepless night, she was going to have to be on high alert as she moved through the day. She'd need a plan. A run always helped her focus. She laced on her running shoes, grabbed her water bottle, and headed out the door.

———

A half-hour later, fighting a stitch in her side, she had at least the beginnings of a plan. She'd let her speed creep up as the ideas came to her, and as a result had gone farther than she'd intended before turning around. For a few blessed, long-striding moments, heart pounding and arms pumping, the memory of the man in the canyon had receded.

Now it reasserted itself with the force of a fist to the jaw. What if he were shadowing her, watching to see if and when she complied with his order to leave? The house was far behind her, well out of sight. The desert rolled away in all directions, all rock and scrub, gathering itself to radiate the day's heat with the intensity of a stovetop coil. Lola slowed to a walk. She twisted and scanned the road behind her. There were, of course, no footprints on the pavement, but even if she veered to the side of the road, she'd be running on rock, leaving no sign that she'd passed. If someone took it into his mind to snatch her from this lonely spot, there'd be nothing to show she'd ever been there.

She turned and sprinted for the house, a good three miles away. By the time it showed itself, a squat dark hexagon against a sky fast losing dawn's rosy glow, sweat stung her eyes and blurred her vision, and cut meandering tracks through the dust on her arms. She swiped the back of her hand across her eyes, adding grit to the salty mix. Her breath came in ragged gasps. A scalding knife jabbed at her ribs. She forced herself to a jog, then a walk, and shoved to one side all thoughts of Canyon Man.

"The plan," she reminded herself. Her hands moved restlessly in the air, sketching the circles and arrows she would have drawn in her notebook if she'd been working at home. But in this place, it seemed better not to put anything on paper. She had to do it in her mind. She imagined a bull's-eye pattern, with the Conrad Coal mine at its center, asterisks beside it representing the elder and the truck driver. Gar represented the innermost circle, working as closely with the mine supervisors as he did. Naomi, Thomas, and Betty Begay were dashed circles a little farther out, the dashes indicating that Lola thought they had motive but not the means. Beyond them, a wide circle labeled Jim Andersen, the environmental activist. Start with him first, Lola told herself. Rule out the least likely.

She extracted the phone from the pouch Velcroed around her upper arm and texted the number she'd entered into it after he'd given her his card: *Meet today? Noon? 1? I have Q's re mine.* She looked at the time on the phone. Six thirty. There was a chance she might not even hear from him that day, which would mean twenty-four hours wasted on an already-truncated timetable. Even as she wondered whether to fill the day with a follow-up visit with Betty, the phone buzzed with a response. Lola smiled at the laconic reply. *Noon. Tuba City museum. C U then.* She tucked the phone back into its holder and ground the heel of her hand against the pain in her side. He'd even given her the excuse she needed—a museum visit—for another excursion.

———

Naomi hovered by the front door in full silk-shirted, designer-jeaned armor as Lola approached.

"I'm glad you're back. I need to go in early today. You can take the girls again, yes?" Maintaining the fiction that Lola had a choice in the matter. "We'll be late tonight, too. I didn't have time to put together a dinner. You'll have to take the girls out. Here." She thrust her hand toward Lola, greenbacks fanned within it.

Lola recoiled. "For God's sake, Naomi. It's not like we're paupers," she said before tact could intervene. She tried to backtrack. "Really. We'll be fine. Maybe I'll even cook something here."

"Sure. Okay. Fine." Naomi's words were clipped, rushed; her movements abrupt. Red veins mapped the whites of her eyes. Lola at first had thought Naomi's hair was still wet from the shower, but she realized it was unwashed, its hasty combing obvious in the oily tracks along the woman's scalp. She wondered if Naomi's appearance was a result of early morning imbibing or, maybe, an inexplicable stab at going cold turkey.

She put a hand on Naomi's arm, then yanked it away, fearing she'd leave grubby fingerprints on the smooth expanse of white. "Are you all right?"

Naomi stared at her arm, then Lola's hand. "You need a shower," she said.

"Yes."

Charlie stalked into the kitchen, stopping just long enough to fill a go-cup with coffee, and brushed past Lola with the barest suggestion of a kiss. "I'll just go start the car." The door banged behind him, just short of a slam.

Naomi hesitated. "Edgar's already gone in. I can stay until you're done with your shower. The girls—"

Lola wondered how many years it had been since Naomi feared to leave Juliana alone even for the few minutes it took to take a shower. Margaret had been self-sufficient enough for such indulgences for quite some time. She started to say as much. Canyon Man whispered in her ear, *Your little girl.* Maybe something had left Naomi equally unsettled.

Lola took Naomi's hand in her own, damn the dirt, and squeezed it, hoping to convey steadiness, reassurance, all the things that apparently were not going to be part of anyone's day. "Thanks," she said. "I'll be quick."

———

She was grateful for Jim Andersen's suggestion that they meet at the museum, the better to make it appear that they'd run into one another by accident. Little girls had big mouths, as Lola had learned.

She saw him across the room when she entered the building, hexagonal like so much other reservation architecture that harkened to hogans. He started toward her, then checked himself at the sight of Margaret and Juliana. Lola pointedly ignored him as she wandered slowly past exhibits on Code Talkers, sheepherding, and weaving, letting the girls get a little farther ahead with each display. Given the town's name, she'd expected something about a brass band and felt foolish to read that the name derived from that of Tuuvi, a Hopi leader.

Finally, when the girls had disappeared around a corner, she nodded and Andersen approached, standing with her before the sheep exhibit.

"What's this about?"

Right to the point. Lola appreciated that. Problem was, she couldn't be equally straightforward in her reply. What was she supposed to say? *Are you the bomber?*

"You know a lot about the mine," she countered.

"Some. I've been writing about this stuff for a few years now."

Lola pushed back against a rush of envy so intense it felt like pain. Years before, she, too, had had the luxury of specializing in a single subject, of soaking up enough expertise to be able to write authoritatively. In her case, that subject had been the conflict in Afghanistan. She reminded herself, as always when the old regrets tugged at her, that without the job in Montana, there'd be no Charlie and no Margaret. And no Bub. Anger moved in, welcome and focusing, giving useless nostalgia the heave-ho.

"These bombings. Have you ever seen anything like them in the other places you've been?" She sneaked a glance away from the exhibit and ruled him out of at least one scenario. Standing side by side, she was about the same height as Andersen, who had the emaciated look of a truly accomplished runner. A second later, she upgraded his athletic ability farther still; a tattoo on his calf, just visible below the hem of his frayed cargo shorts, showed the Ironman logo with a series of check marks beneath it. When it came to endurance, Lola thought, Jim Andersen could kick her ass several times over. But he wasn't the musclebound individual who'd wrestled her into the crevice in Antelope Canyon.

His hair swung as he shook his head. "I've written about all sorts of civil disobedience. Protesters chaining themselves to the White House fence over the Keystone XL pipeline. First Nations people holding Healing Walks up at the tar sands. Folks sitting by the railroad tracks in Montana to stop coal trains, or lying across the road to stop oversize truck shipments of equipment to the oil patch in North Dakota. But this business of blowing up people takes it to a whole new level. Hell, even ELF burned empty buildings. This is some cold shit."

He sounded sincere. But so would any half-decent criminal trying to cover his tracks, Lola thought. "So you don't think ELF or somebody like that is behind it?"

The hair swung in wider arcs, the denial more emphatic. His eyes briefly met hers. "I know those guys." He held up his hand. "Don't ask me to put you in touch with them. I won't. But I can tell you that they're freaking out, afraid it's going to get pinned on them. The FBI's already been sniffing around. ELF wants this solved just as badly as the mine people do."

Lola couldn't help herself. The more he talked, the more his status as a suspect diminished, at least in her mind. "Hey, I forgot to ask you the other day," she said, trying to keep her voice light as though the thought had just occurred to her. "Where were you stationed in Iraq? I did a couple of fill-in stints in Baghdad when our regular correspondent was on leave. Maybe I ran into you there."

He didn't even blink at the news that she'd been in Iraq. So he'd Googled her, then, before their meeting, just as she had him. Now he fleshed out the scant information she'd found online about his military career.

"Doubtful, especially if you were in the field. I was a fobbit, sitting on my ass on a forward operating base, writing press releases. I wasn't even high enough up on the food chain to warrant talking to reporters like you. I just put the right words into the mouths of the guys who did that."

"Ah." No explosives training, then. She'd hunt around some more on Google, see if she could find a reference to his status as a public information officer. After all, as the old newspaper saying went, *If your mother says she loves you, check it out.* But Jim Andersen was probably off the List. Maybe he still had his uses, though. "Any idea who did this?"

His smile was as knowing as Lola's, in response, was rueful. "Writing a story?"

She spread her hands. "Off the clock. On my honeymoon, as a matter of fact, such as it is. More to the point, I couldn't get anybody to bite on a freelance piece. But my in-laws are pretty deep into the investigation. My husband's helping out some. The sooner they're done, the sooner I get him back."

"Yeah, sure." Andersen's knowing look radiated skepticism. He was, Lola decided, more of a kindred spirit than she'd first imagined. In her experience, most environmental activists—most activists of any stripe, for that matter—tended toward tiresomeness in their earnest espousals of their causes. Andersen's sardonic attitude was a refreshing antidote. He knew she was trying to play him for information. But his next words were free of sarcasm, spoken with an intensity so fierce that Lola stepped back.

"Listen. I've got no earthly clue who might be behind this. And believe me, I've been looking. But one thing's for sure."

"What's that?"

"Mom!" "Auntie Lola!" The girls rounded the corner at a run, their default speed. "Come see," Margaret commanded. "There's more stuff outside." The desk clerk turned away from her computer and glared.

Lola held her finger to her lips, as much to warn Jim as the girls. Because she already knew what he was going to say.

He said it anyway. "He's going to do it again."

THIRTY

Next up, Betty Begay, this time without subterfuge. Well, maybe a little subterfuge.

"She might have seen Bub," Lola told the girls by way of explanation for another trip to Betty's hogan. "Or talked to somebody who's seen him. She knows the area better than anybody, and she seems to know everybody on the rez. Right, Juliana?"

"Everybody," Juliana agreed with solemn certainty. "I want you to find your dog, Auntie Lola. I like him."

Through the windshield, the desert peeled away on either side of the dividing line of black asphalt. The road ran straight to the horizon. With Juliana's statement, it blurred and wavered. Lola blinked her eyes and cleared her throat. "Me, too." She chanced a glance in the rearview mirror. Margaret stared out her window, jaw set, her stoic silence even more frightening than her tears. Lola had thought to focus the girls during the long ride up the mesa by urging them to scan their surroundings for signs of the dog. She realized Margaret had been doing that all along. She reached back and wrapped her hand around Margaret's ankle, trying to convey reassurance.

The mine's entrance reared before them, bristling with additional *No Trespassing* signs. The protesters stood at a farther remove than before. On this day, there were only three, none Navajo. Jim Andersen's ilk, Lola figured. When they saw Lola's truck, they lifted their signs halfheartedly, then dropped them back down in the dust.

A few yards away, a contingent of tribal policemen had joined the two white security guards Lola noticed on her first trip past the mine. On impulse, she swung the truck toward the mine entrance. The tribal policemen stayed put. The white guys stalked toward the pickup, footsteps heavy with purpose. Even in Montana, the malls had the occasional private security guard, usually a kid in a cheap uniform, sometimes even a handgun riding awkwardly to one side of a belly going too fast to blubber. But these men looked fit and hard, their uniform shirts the sort of lightweight material perfected in the desert wars, stubby Uzis held across their bodies, only a single motion required to bring them into firing position. Lola couldn't see their eyes behind their wraparound glasses but she imagined them trained laser-like upon her as she slowed to a stop, leaving her hands on the wheel where they could see them. Thank God for the girls, she thought, their presence making her seem less of a threat. An idea had just come to her, the sort of illogical impulse that sometimes actually panned out.

One of the men twirled a finger at her. His partner stayed put, raising his gun just enough to make sure Lola saw the gesture. She lowered her window. Time to tap-dance.

"Morning." Lola pasted a smile across her face.

"Afternoon," he corrected her. "State your business here."

Asshole, Lola thought. She pegged him as a former security contractor from one of the wars, missing his six-figure salary from Iraq, hiring himself out as corporate protection for nearly the same amount.

"I'm here to see Jeff Kerns."

Keeping his gaze—at least as best as she could tell behind those mirrored lenses—trained upon Lola, the man jerked his head at his companion. "Says she's here to see Kerns. She on the list?"

The second man shifted his gun to the crook of one arm and flipped up a notebook dangling from a lanyard around his neck. "Name?"

Lola raised her voice. "Lola Wicks. I'm not on your list."

"Then what the fuck are you doing here?" said Asshole No. 1.

Game on, thought Lola. She'd spent too many years jousting with the legions of self-important people, usually men, who'd tried over the years to stop her from getting whatever bit of information she sought. They looked at her, saw female, and went immediately to intimidation. Sometimes, Lola had to stop herself from yawning in their faces as one after another tried the tiresome tactic. Her smile was genuine. She was starting to enjoy herself.

"I'm here to see Jeff Kerns," she said again.

"And you're not on the list," said Asshole No. 2. "So turn the fuck around and drive away."

"Mr. Kerns isn't going to like hearing about the language you used in front of two children."

Asshole No. 1 took a step toward her, squaring his shoulders. Trying to *loom*, as they so often did, Lola thought. Problem was, she had the advantage of Edgar's truck, quite a bit larger than her own. She gazed down upon him. "Call him. Tell him Lola Wicks is here to see him."

"And who the f—I mean, who the heck is Lola Wicks?"

Score one for me, Lola thought. He wouldn't curse again, at least not in front of the girls, who leaned forward in their seats, training twin judgmental scowls upon him.

"I'm an investigative reporter," she said, and started counting beats. One … two … three …

No. 1 permitted himself a bark of a laugh. "Jeff Kerns don't talk to no reporters. You get on out of here now."

Four … five … "And I'm Edgar Laurendeau's sister-in-law."

No. 1 didn't get it. "Yeah, big fu—honkin' deal. I don't know any Edgar Laurendeau. Gary, you got any Edgar Laurendeaus on your list?"

One of the tribal cops stepped to No. 2's side and whispered something. Lola sat back and enjoyed the speed with which No. 2's expression went from arrogant to uncertain. His voice dropped a couple of decibels. "Uh, we might want to give the front office a call," he said to No. 1. "Laurendeau's kind of a big shot."

The information took a while to work its way into No. 1's testosterone-addled brain. Lola goosed it along. "Kind of," she said. "He works for the mine you're supposed to be protecting. I'll bet he knows your names, even if you don't know his. Wonder how it's going to go for you when he finds out you've hassled me?" She hoped Edgar didn't hear about any of this until after she'd gotten a chance to talk to Kerns.

No. 2 turned his back on them and muttered into a cellphone. He turned around and clipped the phone into a belt holster and waved his arm toward her. "Come on in. Sorry for all the trouble."

"Oh, you will be," Lola promised, flashing a final smile at No. 1. "See you later—at least, if you've still got a job by the time I leave here."

They would, she knew. But two could play the intimidation game. And it worked especially well when it came from a direction they didn't expect. She gave the truck a little extra gas, scattering pebbles as the towering, barbed-wire-topped gates of Conrad Coal swung open to admit her.

———————

Conrad Coal's on-site headquarters was exactly the sort of utilitarian building Lola would have expected at a mine: aluminum outside and plastic and linoleum within, surfaces easy to wipe clean or hose down. All of which must have been done frequently.

Its interior, given the rugged mission of its workers, was surprisingly bright, with only the lightest film of red dust that Lola supposed even the most assiduous of cleaning crews could never completely eradicate. A young woman, Hopi by the look of the lengthy last name on her badge, led them down a hallway air-conditioned to a level of frigidity that necessitated the sweater thrown over her shoulders.

"I don't want to be here," Margaret announced. The young woman stopped.

"Is everything all right?" she asked in a pronounced accent. Both the Navajo and Hopi nations had aggressive language preservation programs, meaning young people were more likely to have been raised in bilingual households.

Margaret assumed a feet-planted, arms-akimbo stance that Lola knew all too well. "This isn't helping me find my dog."

The woman cast a glance down the hallway as though expecting to see a dog emerge from one of a row of closed doors. "Excuse us," Lola said. She hurried to Margaret and pulled her a few steps away. Juliana stood between them and their escort, shifting from one foot to another.

Lola knelt before Margaret and took her face between her hands, forcing her daughter to look her in the eye. "I'm going to talk to a man here about the bombings," she said, pitching her voice so that Juliana and their guide wouldn't hear.

"Don't care about the bombings—" Margaret began.

Lola lowered her voice still farther and articulated an idea she wasn't sure that she herself understood. "Somehow I think it's all connected. I think somebody is afraid we'll—I don't know. That we'll find out too much about the bombings, maybe. I think they want to scare us. I think they took Bub because they want us to go home. And that's why I'm not going home, Margaret. Because I won't leave here without him." *Dear God*, she thought as she tossed one frightening adult concept after another at her daughter, *she's only seven.* "Oh, honey. I know this all sounds crazy. Just give me a few minutes with this man and we'll go talk to Mrs. Begay about Bub." She dropped her hands.

But Margaret's eyes, gray like her own and in this moment hard as polished granite, held Lola's. She gave a decisive nod that would have done credit to a general sending troops into battle. Her little chin came up and she brandished a book that Lola had handed to her on the way out of the car. "I'm sorry, Mommy." She cut her eyes toward the receptionist to make sure the woman was listening. "Juliana and I can read this book while we're waiting for you. I'm excited to see what it says!"

She infused her voice with a cheeriness that sent waves of both pride and fear through Lola. If a seven-year-old could dissemble so readily, what challenges would a teenage Margaret present? A few minutes later, she got an idea.

THIRTY-ONE

Kerns's office came as a shock after the hallway's sterility. Their guide's improbable high heels clicked a farewell down the tiles. Lola and the girls found themselves standing on carpet—industrial-strength indoor-outdoor, but a carpet nonetheless—in an anteroom with faux-leather chairs in each corner. Magazines with titles like *Coal Age* and *Coal International* littered a coffee table.

Kerns himself stood before them, extending a hand to Lola, who remembered just before taking it to switch to a whiteman-style handshake, returning his boss-man squeeze with her own take-that crunch. He acknowledged it with a flash of teeth that could have been a smile. Or not. "They can wait out here," he said, gesturing toward the girls.

"I want to stay with my mommy." Margaret's voice, so confident moments before, had gone all little-girl whiney.

Lola stopped herself from rolling her eyes. "Come along, you two," she said, striding through the door to the inner office before Kerns had time to object. A blast of arctic air stopped her. The hallway they'd just left seemed tropical in retrospect. Lola clasped her hands behind her back to hide the goose bumps rising along her arms and pretended to study the large photos of scarred earth that took up most of the wall space in the office.

"Some of our mines," Kerns said, pointing from one to the next. "Chile ... Venezuela ... the Philippines ... and, of course, here. Would you like my jacket?" He was already shrugging out of a blazer of summer-weight wool. Lola thought he could have worn houndstooth in comfort.

"No, thank you." She settled herself in front of his desk, a mahogany number whose size and strength recalled a helipad. The rest of the office was a model of squared-off corners and bare surfaces, but a mess of paperwork buried Kerns's desk, the stacks so high in some places that they blocked Lola's view of a couple of framed photos. Over the years, she had honed the reporter's skill of reading upside down, something she'd often demonstrated to Margaret, who'd then tried it herself on her grade-school readers. Lola scanned the sheets on the desk but saw mostly graphs and numbers, the sorts of things she'd have to study at length to make sense of. She blew out her breath in annoyance, then smoothed her expression when Margaret caught her gaze.

"Do you have a couple of pieces of scrap paper? The girls like to draw. That'll keep them busy while we talk."

Kerns walked to a printer across the room. Lola craned her neck for a closer look at the papers on his desk. All carried the company's logo. He returned with two sheets of printer paper. Lola extracted two pens from her shirt pocket; she tried not to carry a purse. "Maybe some magazines to put under the paper," she said. "This carpet is so thick, it'll be hard to draw on."

The muscles in Kerns's face tightened briefly. "Here." He handed her some copies of Conrad Coal's annual report, its cover as glossy and professional as any magazine, the contents quite a bit thicker than most. Margaret and Juliana crouched at Lola's feet and put pen to paper. Rather than sitting behind the desk, Kerns took the chair next to hers. "What brings you here, Ms. Wicks? Surely your brother-in-law didn't send you."

"He doesn't know I'm here," Lola said. There. Let him think he had something to hold over her. Especially because it was true.

"Which brings me back to my original question." His fingers drummed at the chair's arms, their well-tended cuticles bespeaking a manicurist. His scalp showed pink through his stylish stubble. A man like Kerns, Lola thought, didn't go at his hair with fingernail scissors, the way she maintained hers. He used a barber, or more likely a stylist. She wondered where on the reservation he found a stylist, and how often he had to go to maintain the just-short-of-shaved look. She'd read somewhere that men with shaved heads—the white-collar version, maybe, of the security guards' wraparound shades and Uzis—projected more masculinity than baldies or even men with luxuriant Kennedyesque pompadours. Like Gar.

"You probably know I'm a reporter," she said. Maybe he did, maybe he didn't. But even if he didn't, he'd find out soon enough. It might as well be from her. "I'm putting together a proposal for a story on your situation here. It's no secret Conrad Coal has a lot of enemies. But"—she laid on the standard blandishment—"you've got lots of friends, too. You said it yourself at the community meeting. You're a huge employer hereabouts. From what people tell me"—and by people, Lola meant Google—"Conrad Coal pays even better than government jobs. That's saying something."

She paused again, to give Kerns time to preen.

He took the bait. "If Conrad Coal shut down, the Navajo Reservation would go from being one of the country's richest to the poorest. Like that one up in South Dakota everybody likes to use as an example? What's it called?"

"Pine Ridge," Lola said. The reservation in South Dakota's southwest corner was routinely trotted out as embodying all the ills of Indian Country, the poverty, the alcoholism, the tribal infighting. But every so often, its people flexed their muscle, say, voting in a unified Democratic bloc that swung a crucial U.S. Senate race away from a sure Republican win. Which, unfortunately for the reservation's Oglala Lakota residents, did not reap the usual pork that might have gone to a white voting district that delivered such a treasured prize.

"So whoever's doing this is hurting his own people as much as he's hurting us," Kerns finished.

"You're sure, then, that the bomber is tribal?"

He'd spoken with a level of certainty that eluded everyone else with whom Lola had discussed the bombing. She made a mental note.

"Who else would it be?" When Kerns went for sincerity, his eyebrows pushed wrinkles into the pink expanse of skin above them.

"ELF, for starters."

Kerns's forehead smoothed. "Those idiots. Not a chance. We've had somebody inside them for years. Other than everybody being afraid the feds will hang these bombings on them, I haven't heard any chatter about this, and believe me, we would."

Lola took a moment to appreciate the casual revelation that Conrad Coal could afford to pay people for the years-long undertaking of undercover infiltration, a luxury affordable by the government only in the direst circumstances. A shame, she found herself thinking, that McVeigh hadn't directed his wrath at a coal mine. Maybe he'd have been stopped before he blew 168 people into oblivion. "No ELF, then," she said. "But you still haven't told me why you think the bomber is tribal."

"Stands to reason," he said. Condescension crept into his tone. "All those demonstrators, yammering about how we're exploiting them. You'd think we were evil incarnate."

"You said it yourself." Lola troweled it on thicker still. "People would starve if they lost their jobs at the mine." They wouldn't, of course. They'd lived for centuries in one of the world's harshest climates and no doubt would manage just fine decades hence, when the Conrad Coal finally exhausted the earth beneath it.

"Tell that to those people from the mesa. You can't talk reason to them. God knows, your brother-in-law has tried. No better friend to Conrad Coal—and by extension, to his people—than Edgar Laurendeau. Look here." He took one of the photos from the desk and handed it to Lola. It was a classic grip-and-grin, Edgar and Kerns shaking hands, smiling for the camera. "That's from last year. He's accepting a check for one hundred thousand dollars in engineering scholarships for tribal members, so the Navajo can send kids to school to learn how to run mines, not just work in them. Now you tell me. Does that sound like exploitation?"

Margaret leaned harder against Lola's leg. "It's very generous," Lola murmured. "You know these aren't his people, don't you?"

Kerns layered superiority with disbelief. "What do you mean? He's a lawyer for the tribe. And his wife—half her family is in tribal government."

Lola leaned back and prepared to enjoy herself. "He's tribal, all right. But not Navajo. He's Blackfeet. From Montana."

An entirely predictable array of expressions crossed Kerns's face, starting and ending with *what the hell?* She imagined the years of careful cultivation, the bowing and scraping, the scholarships awarded and ballfields paid for, the dinners and drinks and junkets, all to ensure the good faith of "their" Indian who now turned out to be somebody else's Indian. Maybe. "Looks like he's thrown his lot in with the Navajo," Kerns blustered.

"You'd better hope so." Lola kept reminding herself not to smile. Few things were more enjoyable than watching someone find out that money didn't buy everything, or, as in this case, might have bought the wrong thing. Of course, there's no saying Edgar had been bought. He'd probably say, if confronted, that every legal path he'd smoothed for Conrad Coal had benefited the reservations. See: jobs, scholarships, ballfields. Still, such coziness always made Lola squirm. It was nice to watch someone else be the squirmee.

"Mommy." Margaret rapped Lola on the knee with her pen. "I have to go to the bathroom."

The relief on Kerns's face was unseemly. "It's down the hall and around the corner. I'll show you out. We're about done here, aren't we?"

"No." Margaret was already on her feet. She took Kerns's hand and pulled him from his chair. "She doesn't know where it is. You show me. Juliana will come, too. Mommy, you stay here."

Kerns's dazed expression showed he wasn't used to taking orders from a seven-year-old. He didn't realize that, given the chance, Margaret could probably twist the Queen of England to do her bidding. He dutifully followed Margaret to the door. She cast a glance over her shoulder to Lola, and then at the desk. If she'd known how to wink, Lola thought, she probably would have. Lola waited until she heard the outer door shut before holding her phone over the papers on Kerns's desk and clicking the camera like crazy.

THIRTY-TWO

Any lingering elation from the small victory in Kerns's office vanished as the truck climbed the mesa to Betty Begay's hogan. Lola wrestled it around switchbacks, appreciative of the V8 engine that responded with a roar and surge of power whenever she touched toe to gas pedal.

Something was off about Kerns, but she couldn't put her finger on it. He was so insistent upon pinning the bombings on someone from the tribe. But if the tribe—or even just an individual—was turning on the company, that could only hurt the mine's business. Shareholders tended to get the vapors about matters that affected the bottom line. In Lola's experience, companies took pains to avoid anything that might bring that reaction. Yet Kerns appeared to have done just that. Lola had scooped up the annual reports along with the girls' drawings when she'd left the office, and she resolved to study them when she got home that night.

She reached down and touched a hand to the gallon jugs of water crowding the passenger seat. They'd been icy when she'd retrieved them from the refrigerated case at Bashas'. In her time with Kerns, they'd gone lukewarm. Lola shrugged. They'd be just short of hot after sitting for days in Betty's little hogan. But they'd provide the elder's morning tea—Lola had also picked up some Lipton, after seeing a box beside the tabletop camp stove in the shade hut outside the hogan—and even a precious wash-up. The truck rounded the final curve with a growl, and Lola let it drift to a stop. The hogan stood silent, no wisps curling from the smoke hole. No Betty at work in the shade house.

Juliana scrambled to extricate herself from the seat belt. "Maybe she's somewhere with the sheep, waiting in the shade until it's cooler before they come home." Just then, a sheep wandered around the corner of the hogan, followed by another.

"Oh, hell." Lola flung herself from the truck and raced Juliana to the blanket covering the hogan's doorway. If something had happened to Betty, she didn't want the girls to see. She veered left, as proper, upon entering and stopped, waiting for her eyes to adjust. "Mrs. Begay?" The hogan seemed empty, its few objects in their place, the chair empty, blankets drawn across the sleeping pallet of sheepskins. Lola took another step. Something beneath the blankets. A body, unmoving. Lola forced herself forward and held her hand in front of Betty Begay's inert lips. She sighed at the puff of air upon her fingers, and fell back at the words that issued loud and clear from Betty's mouth.

"I'm not dead."

Lola responded with some words that demanded an apology. Then she choked out a "Sorry" and crouched beside the pallet. "Are you all right?"

Betty's eyes opened, startling Lola almost as much as her words. "I'm fine. You go away now."

Huh, thought Lola. Although she knew there were vast differences among tribes, members of each one she'd encountered so far reflexively offered food and drink to visitors. "I'll just bring the water in," she said, moving fast toward the doorway before Betty could object. The girls stood just outside in full sunlight, arms wrapped around one another.

"She's here," Lola reassured them. "I think she might be a little bit sick, though. Why don't you girls look after the sheep?" Even though she had no idea how one looked after sheep. But maybe Juliana did. The ache for Bub gnawed at her afresh. As far as she knew, he'd never herded a single sheep in his life. But the skill was bred into him. He'd have found a way to help.

Lola staggered twice between truck and hogan with a gallon jug of water in each hand and another under each arm. Back inside, she poured some water into a cup and knelt beside Betty again. She slid her arm under Betty's shoulders and eased her into a sitting position. Betty lay limp as an old cloth, and nearly as light, against her. Lola held the cup to her lips. Betty turned her head away. "You go away," she said again, the strength in her voice startling Lola anew.

"If I leave, I'm only going to call a doctor."

"I'm not sick."

"All evidence to the contrary."

Betty stiffened at the rudeness. "I'm not sick. I'm dying."

"Please." Lola offered the cup again. "Just a sip." She tilted the cup so that it wet Betty's lips. She could have sworn she saw a quick flicker of tongue against the moisture, but in the daylong twilight inside the hogan, it was impossible to tell. "Are you ... do you have ...?" Lola fished for a way to ask if Betty had some sort of bad disease. Cancer, probably. But she'd said she wasn't sick. Lola had known elderly people, and not just Indians, who'd set their minds against their stubborn bodies and achieved death. Her own grandmother, after her grandfather died, had announced she was done with the business of life. "What's the point? They're all gone. Him, my sisters, my friends."

"I'm still here," a teenage Lola had protested, twining her fingers with her grandmother's, feeling the bird-fragile bones, the papery skin. Her grandmother's eyelids slid closed and she lay back against her pillow. She and Lola had the same long jaw, and it quivered as she spoke. "You'll be fine. You're strong, like me. You put your strength into living. I'm using mine for this now." Her hand tightened around Lola's. Her chest rose and fell almost imperceptibly, a little more slowly each time Lola went to see her. "Not much longer," a nurse said on one of Lola's final visits. "A few days now."

"How is she doing this?"

The nurse had the quick gestures and overly bright voice of the perpetually overworked, keeping herself revved up for the next crisis. She went still a moment. When she spoke, the words came slowly. "Damned if I know. I've seen it before, every few years. They're barely breathing by the end. It's like they slow everything down, maybe starve their organs of oxygen, until everything just stops. You ask me, they're the lucky ones. They get to call the shots."

Lola wondered if Betty had reached a similar decision and, if so, why. The woman had seemed in almost embarrassingly good health for her age, sturdy and energetic. "Mrs. Begay," she said. "Look at me." She sat down the cup and put a finger beneath Betty's chin and forced her head around. Betty's eyes briefly met hers before she jerked her head from Lola's hand.

No, thought Lola. Something else was going on. When her grandmother had set about dying, she'd become almost preternaturally calm, her eyes trained unblinking on something in the distance, maybe whatever her view of the hereafter happened to be. With a quick stab of regret, Lola realized she'd never asked what that was.

But in that quick communion with Betty, the woman's eyes had radiated anguish, along with something else. Lola wrapped her other arm around Betty and cradled her as she would a child, rocking gently and whispering, "It'll be all right. We'll help you. Whatever it is, we'll protect you."

Betty's body jerked in her arms. Lola could have sworn she heard Betty's trademark skeptical "Hmph."

Well deserved, she thought. Because the other emotion she'd read in Betty's eyes was terror, so overwhelming that the woman now saw death as preferable to life. And without knowing what had so frightened her, Lola had no idea how to protect her.

THIRTY-THREE

I HAD TO TALK to someone. Someone else. Because this has to stop.

So I went to *Shimá*. Brought tobacco and water and some of those Fig Newtons she likes. Sat with her under the shade house for a long time, talking about sheep and the weather and all of the usual things as the sky went from white to pale blue and then purple, the buttes standing up like sentries against it. She lit a fire and rolled a new cigarette, long and slender, her fingers nimble from the weaving. I pulled a stick from the fire and held it out. She put the cigarette to her lips and bent her head to it, the flame briefly illuminating her face, her eyes sharp and knowing upon me. The cigarette's tip flared. I looked away and shivered, hoping she'd attribute my shudder to the cold. Temperatures drop fast in the desert when the sun goes down. "Can I bring you a blanket, *Shimá*? Maybe some tea? Or would you like to go inside?"

"No blanket. Tea is good. We'll stay out here and watch *So' Dine'é*," she said of the Star People. She pointed with her chin to the sky. "Few months yet until *Áltse Álts'oosi* comes." The constellation heralded winter, striding across the sky, bow at the ready, an arrow nocked in its string. I hadn't found out until junior high, reading some whiteman science textbook, that he had another name, Orion. He carries a bow, too. But where Orion is a hunter, stalking prey across the sky, *Áltse Álts'oosi*, the Slender Man, is a protector, going before the children, making sure no harm awaits them. I thought of the implications of *Shimá* speaking of him rather than the other, more benign, stars and constellations. Was there any way to think of my actions as helping to protect our people? Because that's what I've been told. Maybe *Shimá* would tell me the same thing.

I heated water on the stove and brewed the tea a long time, the way she likes, adding plenty of sugar, and wondered yet again at the way her teeth shine white and strong in her mouth even though she's drunk her tea that way for as long as I've known her. I brought it to her and she took a sip and nodded, letting me know I'd fixed it just right, stirring in sugar until the liquid was the consistency of syrup. She slurped in satisfaction.

"Young man like you," she said. "You should be down in the valley, finding some girl and breaking her heart. Or maybe she breaks yours. Hah!" Her shoulders shook. She was pleased with herself. "But instead, you're up here, with this old lady."

I didn't say anything. It was dark, but I could feel her gaze jabbing at me like a pissed-off rattlesnake, striking again and again. Her next words ran like cold poison through my veins. "Maybe you're here about the mine. I think so."

"I—" I couldn't imagine how to start.

She waited. So I told her.

No. She didn't think of me as a protector.

———

213

What had I been thinking? That *Shimá* would raise her hand in absolution like Father O'Callahan used to do, back when my family still went to church? Tell me it wasn't my fault? Or give me the backbone to return and say "No more?"

Here's what hadn't occurred to me: that she would wither before me as the words poured from my mouth, nearly disappearing beneath the flood of the unthinkable. That by the time I finally stopped, too late, her own breath came in rasps.

"*Shimá*," I said. I bent over her. "Oh, *Shimá*."

She reached a shaking hand toward me, her fear more frightening than anger, than tears. She'd never needed help from anyone. She was the one people went to for help, who then turned and marched upon the coal company on their behalf, who spoke truth at council meetings before a crowd riven by the competing needs of honoring the land and feeding their children. She could handle anything until I handed her this. I folded my hands around hers, pulled her to her feet. She nearly fell. I lifted her like a child, a near-weightless bundle of flesh and bone within the sack of her clothing. I carried her to the pallet in the hogan and laid her gently upon the soft sheepskins and pulled the woolen blankets over her.

"I'm so sorry, *Shimá*," I said again and again. "I'm so sorry."

The enormity of what I'd done hadn't occurred to me, not until the words left my body and lodged in hers. Now she knew. And knowing left her with a choice: tell someone, and see some of the people she loved most dearly sent to jail. Not just jail, but hard time in a federal prison. But to stay silent was to see more people dead.

Before, that choice had been mine. I had cringed from it, and turned to *Shimá* instead. Dumped that sack-of-cement burden right on her bent shoulders. Now she lay panting and shaking on her pallet, overwhelmed, suffocating beneath the weight of this new knowledge.

Which left only one thing to do—the thing I should have done on my own, without this cowardly attempt to find someone to share the responsibility with me. I bent over *Shimá* and touched my lips to her ear. "No one else is going to die," I said. "I promise."

I sat back and waited for her breathing to ease, the shuddering to stop. If anything, it intensified. I understood. *Shizhé'é* and the truck driver had her in their grip and would not loosen their lethal hold until I made good on my words.

THIRTY-FOUR

BETTY'S CONDITION LEFT LOLA so unsettled that she forgot about the likely consequences of her visit to Kerns. Those consequences awaited in the form of Edgar on the front step, arms folded upon his chest, legs spread wide. Classic testosterone stance, Lola thought.

She slid Conrad Coal's annual report and a sheaf of other papers beneath the front seat as the girls scampered past him into the house, then climbed the steps to confront him. She mirrored his own body language and rejected the courtesy of a smile.

"Edgar."

"Lola. Busy day?"

"Good day. Productive." Let him chew on that one awhile, she thought. She wondered what Kerns had told him about their conversation.

"I don't appreciate you using my name to go someplace you had no business being."

"I had every business being there."

216

"Then why not make an appointment, like a normal person? Why just barge in?"

Rather than concede the point, Lola waited. It didn't take long.

"Because you're doing a story. A story! How dare you take advantage of our hospitality that way. Charlie told me you were a workaholic. I didn't realize that extended to your honeymoon."

Lola made her voice silky. "Not a story. Just a freelance proposal. You know how it is, trying to make it on the crap salaries in this part of the world. Oh, that's right. You don't." She let her eyes drift to the shade house with its stone fireplace and fountain, the late-model truck that in Lola's part of the world would have been called a Cowboy Cadillac. She shifted a little so that she stood in the stream of chilled air leaking from the half-open door and gave an exaggerated, appreciative shiver.

Bitch, said Edgar's eyes.

You have no idea, said Lola's.

"What are you two doing out here in the heat?" Naomi materialized in the doorway, perfection in another hand-tailored silk shirt. Her impeccable cool stopped at her eyes, where suspicion and worry did battle.

Lola played her trump card, laying down the ultimate distraction. "Oh, good. I'm glad you're out here where the girls can't hear. I was just about to tell, um, Gar about Betty Begay. I'm really concerned about her."

"What about her?" Edgar and Naomi spoke in unison.

Lola brushed past them into the house. Thomas sat at the counter, bent over his books. He didn't look up.

"We saw her today."

A textbook crashed to the floor. Lola jumped. Thomas's muttered "sorry" was barely audible.

"What were you doing there?"

217

Lola decided she was better off ignoring Edgar's question. "There's something wrong. She's pretty sick. At first, I thought she was—" Mindful of the fact that just because the girls were out of sight didn't mean they weren't listening somewhere, she switched course. "I thought she'd fainted."

Naomi crossed to the pantry and retrieved two empty milk jugs. She stuck one beneath the faucet and turned on the water. "I'll go up there. If she needs help, I can bring her to a doctor."

"I don't think she'll go. She chased me out of there pretty assertively."

"Because it was you." Lola read Edgar loud and clear: Not one of us.

"Wait." Thomas rose from the floor with textbook in hand. He spoke so rarely that Lola looked at Edgar before she realized where the command had come from. Even Naomi turned to stare. The water filled the jug and gurgled over the top.

"I was up there just yesterday. She seemed, uh, she seemed okay." Thomas reached past Naomi and turned off the water.

"Okay, how? Did she seem dizzy? Sick in any way? What did you two do? Describe her condition for me."

Lola pictured Naomi in a courtroom, firing questions at a witness. They seemed innocuous enough, but Thomas flinched as though she'd asked whether he'd committed a crime.

"We drank tea. Looked at the stars. Shared a smoke." He capped the jug and hoisted it onto the counter without looking at her.

"She was smoking? She seemed short of breath," Lola offered. "Maybe that's why."

"She's been smoking since before I was born. The woman has titanium lungs. Gar, have you seen my keys?" Naomi grabbed her purse and a light jacket. "Thomas, could you please fill that other bottle? Thanks."

"I can do you one better." Thomas took the keys from Gar. "I'll drive up and check on her. You two are so busy with everything else. Mind if I take the Prius? It'll get me there quicker than that beater of mine."

Naomi nodded. "Of course. But I should go with you."

"Look. I just saw her. Who better to judge any change between then and now?" He turned away again, filling the second jug. "It would probably just be a waste of your time, anyway. Lola here doesn't know her the way we do, can't read her the way we can. She's probably mistaken."

Naomi sagged onto a stool. "Maybe. I hope you're right."

"No. She really was sick—" Lola began.

She stopped. Her eyes narrowed. Thomas's skepticism about her was all it had took to change Naomi's mind about going to the mesa. She got that. What she didn't understand was why Thomas didn't want Naomi going up there.

———

Lola waited until past midnight before she retrieved the headlamp she'd stashed under her pillow. She positioned it on her forehead, adjusted the band for comfort, and cast an apprehensive glance at Charlie's sleeping form. Not that she needed to bother. She could probably bend over him and shine the thing directly upon his face without waking him. Just once, she thought, she'd like him to suffer a night of insomnia, if for no other reason than to get some sympathy on the too-frequent mornings when she stumbled groggy into the kitchen after hours of tossing and turning.

This would not be that night. Charlie's breath came deep and regular. Lola slipped from bed and tiptoed through the house, stopping every few steps to listen for sounds of wakefulness—a restless turning, a muffled voice, the whir of Naomi's sewing machine. But the quiet was absolute. Once outside, she moved quickly, wary of lurking tarantulas.

On the way home from Betty Begay's hogan, she'd stopped at a library and used the public computer to print the photos she'd snapped of the documents on Jeffrey Kerns's desk, stashing the printouts under the truck's seat along with Conrad Coal's annual reports. The opening and closing of the truck's door echoed like shots in the darkness. She stood beside the truck awhile, waiting for the front door to be flung open, for the wash of light across the yard that would illuminate the damning papers in her arms, for a flood of the accusatory questions. But the house lay calm amid the velvety darkness. Maybe they thought it was Thomas, returning in the silent Prius. Which he might do at any minute, she reminded herself. Still, she stood a moment, acknowledging the sequined sky, unabashed in its showiness. A coyote wailed. Lola hastened back indoors.

She spread the papers across the bedroom floor and switched on her headlamp, hoping that the rows of numbers she'd glimpsed would magically have transformed themselves into the reassuring familiarity of text. She shuffled through the papers. No such conversion had occurred. The numbers sat smug in their rows, as comprehensible to Lola as the Navajo words that rattled from the truck's radio whenever she turned it on. In college, she had majored in English, and, with the fervor of a phobic, avoided any courses requiring math. She'd done her share of municipal budget stories over the years, each one a cause for heartburn during the writing, with strong drink afterward. She sighed, pulled off a highlighter's cap with her teeth, and chewed on it as she ran her eyes down the lines of numbers.

She looked again, and read more slowly. Fifteen minutes in, her absorption was complete. An hour later, yellow lines striped the pages.

Lola felt around for the annual report she'd taken from the office. She could have found the same information online. But the hard copy was so much easier on the eyes and—Hallelujah!—comprised more words than numbers. Lola flipped the pages and wielded her marker with the same alacrity with which she'd attacked the charts.

The next time she checked the clock, another hour had passed. She switched off the headlamp. Gray light oozed through the blinds. Lola slid headlamp, papers, and highlighter beneath the bed. Charlie would be awake soon. Maybe she could sneak in a little sleep before he arose.

But even as she squeezed her eyes shut, the numbers swam before them, telling the same story no matter how many different ways she looked at them. Conrad Coal may have been one of the world's richest companies, a fact repeated ad nauseam in the rosy language of the annual report, but the Arizona mine appeared to be hemorrhaging cash. The report gave no inkling of that, but the papers on Kerns's desk had told a story that even Lola could understand. Those numbers would surely show up in the next year's report, and even if Conrad Coal's shareholders weren't yet aware of them, workers at the mine almost surely were. Things like that had a way of getting around. The big bosses might try to keep it to themselves, but inevitably a secretary would copy some charts for one of them, or collate some papers, and then she'd say something to her brother, who drove a truck for the mine, and he'd talk to his uncle, who was a supervisor, and the next thing you knew, the invisible lines of gossip that wrapped the reservation like a spiderweb would be humming, practically lighting up the night with their intensity.

All of which made Lola wonder why anyone would try, to the point of murder, to shut down a mine that was probably going to close anyway?

THIRTY-FIVE

HER PLAN WAS TO impress Charlie with this new information, to woo the cop in him with a tidbit he'd heretofore lacked.

He rose first, tiptoeing from the room without the usual moth's wing of a kiss to her cheek. She feigned sleep until he returned to the bedroom with an insulated go-cup of coffee that he meant to put on her nightstand, a tradition that she publicly ascribed to true love but, in private, acknowledged was more likely proof of a strong survival instinct on Charlie's part. Lola Before Coffee, he'd often said, was the equivalent of a primed nuke, set for destruction. His job was to deactivate the threat with the pre-emptive morning ritual, which she usually accepted with mumbled thanks. Today, she startled him by leaping from bed and snatching the cup from his hands, putting her mouth to its lid and swallowing half the contents in a single gulp.

"Careful—" he began.

"Gahhhh." She fanned her mouth. "That's hot."

"Fresh," he said. "Not like usual." Some days, the go-cup sat there for as long as an hour before Lola stirred.

"I want you to look at something."

"Good morning to you, too." His clipped tone let her know that he hadn't forgotten her suspicions of his family, and that the resentment lingered.

"Knock it off. This is important." She thrust the sheaf of papers at him, pointing to one highlighted line after another, outlining her conclusions. "The place is going broke. The way it's bleeding money, they're going to have to shut it down before this shows up in next year's annual report. So why don't they just say so? If whoever is doing these bombings knew that, they'd probably stop and nobody else would get killed. Edgar has to know about this. Find out what he has to say about it."

Charlie opened his hand. The papers fluttered to the floor. "Find out." He mimicked her voice. "Whatever happened to 'please'?"

"Please find out." Next he'd be comparing her to Margaret. Which he'd done before, more often than she'd have liked. "Look. Your brother has worked with these people a long time. Either he knows what the deal is, or he can get them to tell him. Maybe they can make an announcement. Stop this craziness. And whomever has Bub can let him go and we can go home."

Charlie kicked at the mess of papers on the floor. "Christ, Lola. My brother already has his issues with you. Now you want me to go to him with your crackpot theory and, oh by the way, presto change-o, you've solved the bombings! White girl swoops in to save the great Navajo Nation." His mouth twisted around the last sentence as though he'd bitten into something sour.

Lola stepped back. Never in all their years together, and in their few but intense fights, had Charlie referenced the color of her skin. Something drained from her, some small bit of trust. "I can't believe you said that." Her voice was an alien thing, riding a quiet, cold emotion welling up from the place where it had been stored away since her days overseas, when the only person she could rely upon was herself.

Charlie had the good grace to look abashed. "I didn't mean— what I meant was, that's how Edgar would see it."

Lola moved around the room, pulling up the covers on the bed, stepping into her clothes, running her fingers over her head in a futile effort to untangle her curls, her actions dictated by the same icy being that seemed to have taken over both body and brain. "Whatever." She stopped and looked somewhere past him, training her eyes on a bit of the wall over his shoulder. She picked up a set of keys from the dresser and flung them toward him.

He caught them reflexively, stepping backward to deal with the force of their trajectory.

"Those are your brother's car keys. I'll take our truck today," Lola said. "You take the girls. Naomi can get herself a new bodyguard for the day." Not giving him a choice. "I've got some things I need to do."

———————

She slipped out the back door and into the truck. As soon as the motor caught, the front door opened. Lola trod the gas and watched as Charlie, arms folded across his chest, went small in the rearview mirror.

She checked her headlong rush on the outskirts of Gaitero. It wouldn't do to get stopped for speeding; besides, the mine offices wouldn't be open for another couple of hours. Still, Kerns had the look of a guy who arrived early and stayed late, giving his subordinates heartburn and avoiding the home front in the process. She wondered, briefly, what life in the Arizona desert was like for Mrs. Kerns, or if she was one of those wives who stayed at home in, say, Indiana while her husband moved up mining's corporate ladder via stints in unappealing locales like Mongolia and eastern Wyoming. Lola steered the truck past a Burger King and pulled into a café next door. Inside, she ordered wheat toast and scrambled eggs, reluctantly shaking her head to questions about bacon or sausage. *Go healthy*, the chilly inner voice advised her. *And double up on the protein, not to mention the coffee.* She'd need her strength and her wits, both. And for as long as possible, she'd have to keep Naomi and Edgar from finding out what she was up to. The protesters outside the mine entrance were sure to notice a truck with Montana tags passing through the gates, driven by a woman who in no way appeared to be a mine worker.

Lola doused her eggs with hot sauce and a liberal shake of pepper. She forked them up with her left hand and flipped open her notebook to jot down questions, an exercise that took but a moment. There was only one real question, the same one she'd posed to Charlie. *WTF?* she wrote before turning her full attention to breakfast. Which, more or less, is what she asked Kerns after rolling through the gates of Conrad Coal with a flippant wave to the security guards, trying hard not to let her middle finger wag higher than the others.

Kerns was on the phone, his back to her, when she waltzed into his office. He swiveled in his chair, bristling as though she'd flipped him off instead. "I'll have to call you back," he said into the phone, and hung up. Despite the office's walk-in freezer temperature, sweat slicked his forehead. Lola fell into a chair and recited her planned spiel, the one that featured the damning figures she'd memorized.

"Where'd you get these numbers?" Kerns was on his feet.

Lola lifted a shoulder. "Doesn't matter where." He'd figure it out fast enough, she knew, remember that he'd left her alone in the office after being hoodwinked by a couple of schoolgirls in mismatched playclothes. His desktop, this morning, was a vast empty plain but for the photos and a vacant in-box. A woman with a blank, Botoxed expression looked out of one of the photos, her graying hair disguised by blonde highlights and angled in the de rigueur bob of the middle-age woman.

"Bet your wife will be glad when you're out of here. How much longer do you think you'll be staying, anyway? Under the circumstances."

Kerns's fingers performed a quick dance on the desk's glassy surface. "What if I told you your numbers were wrong? Which they are. I hope you're not thinking about publishing this sort of nonsense. We'll sue you quicker than you can say anthracite. Is your little pissant newspaper going to pay for a lawyer to defend you against the resources of Conrad Coal?"

Lola lolled back in her chair and propped one ankle on her knee, letting him see the grungy running shoes that had left dusty prints across his carpet. Technically, the fact that he was standing gave him the advantage. But he was sweating and she wasn't. She grinned up at him. "Believe me, Mr. Kerns. When—and notice that I'm not saying *if*—I publish something, it'll be suit-proof." The grin and the cocky words hid the confusion rising fast within her. She tried to maintain her tone while giving it voice. "But I have to say, I'm puzzled by one thing. I should think it would be to your advantage to let this be known." She sketched her theory of the bomber backing off once the mine's precarious financial standing was known. It took only a few sentences, but by the time she finished, his face was purple. The fingertip performance went from tango to mazurka.

"You don't understand a goddamn thing. Get out of my office."

Lola unfolded herself from the chair in a series of leisurely movements designed to disguise the fact that she was now officially stumped. She opted for honesty.

"I don't get it."

Kerns came around from behind the desk like a stone hurled from a slingshot. Despite her vow to hold her ground, Lola took a quick step back.

He strode past her. "What about 'get out' don't you understand?" He yanked open the door to the outer office. "Celeste. Call security if Miss Wicks's ass isn't walking through your door by the time I count three. One—"

"I'm going, I'm going." Lola was in the outer office before he got to "two."

Behind her, the phone rang. Kerns barked a greeting into it, followed quickly by "My God." And then, "Where was Anna? Oh, thank the good lord." Celeste hovered in the doorway, her wide-eyed expression mirroring Lola's own. Lola edged back into the inner sanctum. Kerns called to Celeste, "Tell the guys to bring my car around. And a second car to follow me. I want two men with me and two behind. Some asshole just bombed my house."

He finally noticed Lola. "You. Out. Now."

Lola got out. But not so quickly that she didn't catch a glimpse, over her shoulder, of Kerns reaching yet again for the phone.

"Get me Gar Laurendeau," he said.

Celeste reached around Lola and slammed the office door in her face.

THIRTY-SIX

ONCE AGAIN, THE COLUMN of greasy black smoke, the wailing sirens, the agitated chatter in Diné on KTNN.

A line of cars idled in the heat, lookie-loos gathering, but not too close, at the entrance to the gated development where Kerns lived. People left their cars and held phones high, dodging the late-arriving news crews with their unwieldy equipment balanced on their shoulders. The news vans, rooftop satellites fully extended, pulled off the road and formed what Lola knew would be an hours-long encampment.

Lola coasted past, for once entirely lacking in envy. The reporters would sit in the hot sun, waiting for absolutely nothing of substance. Maybe tribal police and that slab-jawed FBI man would stage a news conference late in the day, where they'd say all the usual things. "All avenues being pursued." "Extraordinary cooperation among law enforcement agencies." "No. We can't reveal any details that will jeopardize an active investigation. No, we can't comment on that, either. No, no suspects have been identified. Sorry, folks. That's all for now." Lola mouthed the phrases to herself, knowing she'd see something very much like them as soon as stories started going up online. With any luck, she'd glean more information back at the house.

Charlie and Edgar were in the shade house when she arrived, facing one another in chairs pulled to one side of the table, elbows on knees, sweating glasses in hand. Edgar's head jerked when she appeared. A look passed across his face. The girls sat at the table, listlessly shaking a Yahtzee cup. The men turned toward Lola, glances flicking between them, wondering who should be the one to tell her.

She saved them the trouble. "I already know. I drove by the site on my way back. It's a cluster."

"Back from where?" Frost edged Charlie's words. But at least they appeared to be on speaking terms again. Lola kissed the top of Margaret's head and ignored his entirely justified suspicion. "Who's winning?"

Margaret thrust her lips at Juliana. "She is. For now." It wouldn't matter to Margaret that Juliana had two years on her. Margaret played to win, even against her parents, and the only thing that made her angrier than losing was when someone threw the game her way.

"Careful, Juliana," Lola said. "She cheats." Which Margaret did, without compunction, whenever she deemed herself losing badly enough. Lola dodged her daughter's halfhearted swat, pulled up a chair beside Charlie, reached for his glass, and took a long swig. Lemonade again. She wished, mightily, for a cold beer. She was sick of Naomi's teetotaler fiction. She handed the glass back to Charlie. "They said nobody was hurt this time."

"Could have been, though."

"Was anyone in the house?"

"His wife goes to Phoenix every Tuesday with some of the other wives." This, from Edgar. "They shop for clothes, go to fancy restaurants, that sort of thing." He left the subtext—*the sort of thing nobody here can afford to do*—unspoken.

The notion distracted Lola. "That's a long way to go for shopping." And where, she wondered, would the women wear the good clothing they bought? Lola imagined linen sheaths, strappy sandals that showed off pedicured toes, maybe some humorous straw hats against the sun. She juxtaposed the image in her mind with the cheap cotton blouses and loose slacks that seemed standard reservation wear for women of a certain age. She pushed away the thought that sooner rather than later, she'd find herself in that category.

"Where's Thomas?"

From Charlie's expression, Lola knew he'd divined the reasoning behind her question.

"Should be on his way," Edgar said. "No matter what he's doing, he usually manages to show up when it's time to eat."

No matter what he's up to, indeed, Lola thought.

"There's more," Charlie said. He looked at his brother.

Edgar knotted his hands together. Veins pushed against the skin of his forearms. "Apparently today was just a prelude."

At the table, the girls made no pretense of not listening. Lola thought of how she'd burdened Margaret with her own fears. Let her hear, she thought. At this point, the more she knows, the better. Lola didn't want to frighten her child any more than she already had. But neither did she want to brush off Margaret's concerns.

"Charlie?" she said, when neither man spoke for a few moments.

"This is off the record," he warned.

Lola narrowed her eyes to let him know the insult had registered. After trying unsuccessfully, early in their relationship, to avoid talking about their jobs with one another, they'd fallen back on an agreement that anything either told the other—about crimes being investigated, in Charlie's case, or written about, in Lola's—was privileged information, not to be shared without explicit approval. Lola didn't appreciate the reminder. But Charlie was waiting for some sort of acknowledgment.

"Goes without saying."

"Somebody left a warning in the house."

"How? Where?" said Lola. "I can't imagine anything there survived. I couldn't actually see the place, but that was one heck of a cloud of smoke. It looked like enough for three houses."

Charlie's mouth twitched. "In the freezer." In his world, people were forever stashing things in freezers—money, whether illicitly gained or not, drugs, jewelry—in the belief that the refrigerator would survive a fire. Which, in this case, was apparently true.

"Well?" Lola didn't appreciate the way they kept drawing it out, teasing her with details but withholding the actual information. They'd been tag-teaming the narrative, so she turned to Edgar, awaiting the next installment. He studied his drink, swirling his glass so that the ice clinked against the sides.

"It was something to the effect that he'd gotten off easy," he finally said. "'You weren't here this time. But you could have been. And the next time, you will be.'"

"'Next time,'" Lola repeated.

"Right."

"Sounds like a promise."

"Exactly."

"Sounds like the note left for Naomi," she added. *And it sounds like what Canyon Man said to me.* But she kept that part to herself. She took a breath and avoided Charlie's eyes. "There doesn't have to be another bombing. The mine's probably going to shut down anyway. Listen to what I've found out." This time, she recounted the numbers to Edgar, the list coming more easily with repetition, and ended on a bit of a flourish, telling him what he surely already knew.

"The mine's a goner. All you need to do is publicize that, and the bombings stop. I tried to talk to Kerns about it this morning, but he's not having any of it. I don't get it. Anyhow, maybe he'll change his mind now. It could save his life."

"Where'd you get those numbers?" Edgar said, and Lola finally saw a resemblance between the brothers. She had only seen Charlie angry, truly furious, a handful of times, and she remembered each nearly to the day and hour. She'd remember Edgar, too, when this date rolled around the following year. Was it because she'd gotten the numbers? Or because Kerns had concealed them even from him?

"It doesn't matter. They're accurate."

Charlie half-rose from his seat. To go to his wife, or his brother?

Lola held her breath. Charlie glanced over his shoulder and sank back in his seat. A teasing citrus scent reached her a moment before the rustle of silk. A cool hand dropped to her shoulder. "Lola. You're back. And you've been busy."

Lola took the fresh glass of lemonade that Naomi offered. "How much of that did you hear?"

Naomi spoke to Lola but looked at her husband. "Enough. Interesting theory. If it's true, it makes sense. Gar? Maybe you could use your influence with Kerns to get him to listen to reason."

Edgar, raging moments before, turned tame in the presence of his wife. "Sure. Great idea."

Lola choked on her so-called lemonade. "Went down the wrong way," she said by way of explanation.

The shade house's dimness, usually so inviting, on this day felt claustrophobic. She checked an impulse to move everyone out of the shadows and into the sun, with its pitiless glare on falsehood, evasion. She glared at her feet instead of Edgar. Her shoes' mesh fabric was worn and faded, and her little toe poked through on the left one. She needed a new pair. Lola vowed to start watching sales when she got home. Her own feet felt large and clumsy next to Naomi's slender sandaled ones. She thought about feet and shoes until her flush of anger at Edgar had subsided enough for her to trust her voice.

"Kerns will probably take it better coming from you than from me," she said.

"Not just Kerns," Edgar replied. "I got a call just before I came home. Conrad Coal's flying in a bunch of the muckety-mucks from headquarters, day after tomorrow. The tribe's called another meeting then, to update people on the investigation and on new security precautions. The Conrad execs will be there to talk about the company's role. Kerns wants me in on it, too."

Naomi moved to stand behind him. She kneaded his shoulders and dug her knuckles against the base of his neck. "God, you're tense," she said. It was the first time Lola had seen Naomi touch her husband.

Edgar's head lolled back and he closed his eyes. "Think about it," he said. "Two of our tribal members dead. The mine likely to shut down—either permanently, if Lola's right, or at least temporarily because of this goddamn crazy bomber. Think what that's going to mean around here. All those jobs lost."

Naomi murmured soothing phrases, barely audible. Lola caught only a few words. "Survived for centuries without it . . . will again." A coughing fit interrupted her soliloquy. She turned away, resuming when her body stopped its convulsions. "Tough people . . . Strong."

Lola turned away. She felt as though she were observing a private moment. Charlie caught her eye and inclined his head toward the house. They slipped into the kitchen. The girls had preceded them. They sat on stools at the island, twisting and turning in dramatic boredom.

"I'm hungry," said Margaret. Who was always hungry.

"I want to ride Valentine," said Juliana.

"Me, too." Riding took precedent even over food in Margaret's rigid hierarchy. "We can look for Bub," she added.

Charlie started to shake his head. "The bombing today—" he began.

Lola cut him off. The girls' world had been disrupted enough. "I'll go with you," she said. "But not now, not while it's so hot. Wait until after dinner"—Margaret's imminent protest vanished—"and I'll go for a run with you while you ride Valentine."

Much hilarity ensued at the notion that Lola could keep up with Valentine. She let the girls take their shots, relieved to hear Margaret's familiar chortle for the first time since Bub had gone missing. "We can race," she added. She allowed that Valentine had the edge for a short distance, but she'd trained herself to jog for miles while the pony appeared to do little besides doze all day in the corral, waking only to stuff his fuzzy face with more hay. "You watch. I'll cover more ground than he does," she said to hoots from the peanut gallery.

Behind her, Naomi busied herself with a simple dinner of hamburgers and salad, although Lola suspected these would be the best hamburgers she'd ever eaten. She allowed herself to luxuriate in the brief normalcy afforded by the scene. Normal, that is, considering that a man's house had been blown to bits, and that her dog was still out there somewhere, waiting for her to find him.

THIRTY-SEVEN

"Lola." Charlie poked his head around the bedroom door as though seeking permission to enter.

"Charlie." Nothing in her tone granted it. She twisted to fasten her sports bra, pulled a singlet over her head, and wriggled into her running shorts. With no other way to ignore Charlie, she propped a heel on a chair and bent toward her knee, doing the stretches she usually ignored. Behind her, she heard the door close. Maybe he'd gone. Good, she thought. Let him sweat awhile longer.

"I was out of line this morning." So he hadn't left.

"No shit," she said after the silence had stretched awhile. She switched legs and remembered why she didn't do stretches. "Ow."

"I'm sorry."

"Huh." She abandoned the chair, stood on one leg, and reached behind and grabbed the other toe, pulling it toward her butt. She wobbled and nearly fell. Charlie caught her. She waited for him to let her go. He didn't. He pulled her close and whispered the one phrase guaranteed to make her melt.

"I was wrong."

"You sure as hell were."

His arms tightened around her. He pressed his cheek against hers. "This thing is making us both crazy. Listen. It isn't my case. It's not your story. But we're both wrapped up in it. Let's say we figure it out together."

She turned in his arms, inhaling the tinge of sage that clung to him. His hand slid under her shirt. "Those stretches. They're not doing you any good. I know how to loosen you up."

And so help her, he did.

———

The edges of the bluffs had gone blurred and violet, dissolving into the deeper blue of sky, when the girls set out on Valentine. Lola strode alongside, thinking about the iPad she'd ordered online for Charlie after he'd slipped smiling from the room, and trying not to think at all about the way the order had diminished her already-anemic checking account to the low three figures. The pony flattened his ears, tossed his head, and mouthed the bit, broadcasting his unhappiness at this late-breaking excursion. But Juliana and Margaret drummed sneakered heels so insistently against his generously padded sides that he finally broke into a jolting trot.

"Not too far!" Charlie called, behind them. "It's getting dark."

Lola lifted an arm and waved acknowledgment. "Geez, you two," she said to the girls as she kept pace with them. She put a hand on Valentine's neck, dancing away when he turned his head and snatched at her with his yellow teeth. "I'm not even breaking a sweat here."

"Forget about him," Margaret ordered. "We're supposed to be looking for Bub." She raised her voice. "Bub! Bub!"

Lola knew it helped Margaret to feel that she was taking action, however futile, to find Bub. But she felt obligated to inject a bit of reality into the evening. Besides, they only had about twenty minutes before true night fell. "Honey, don't you think if he were this close, he'd have come back to the house?"

Margaret sat behind Juliana, one hand on her cousin's shoulders, perfectly balanced, barely holding on. "Maybe he's hurt. Maybe he's lying somewhere and we can't see him."

If he was, Lola thought, then he'd have died of thirst that first day. She kept that thought to herself.

"Maybe," Margaret continued, "his collar got caught on something. Maybe he's stuck someplace, like back in those rocks." She pointed toward a cleft in a low butte. "We should go look there." She slid her arm around Juliana's waist and kicked Valentine as hard as she could. He rocked into a canter.

Lola sprinted to keep up. "No way are you two going in there," she called between gasps. "That pony's too fat to fit. Let me check it out. You guys circle around while I'm in there. I'll be back in five. And then we're going home." Already she could barely see the desert floor beneath her feet. If Bub was in there—and she was sure he wasn't—it would be a challenge to see him. Not to mention rattlesnakes and spiders and whatever else might inhabit such a space.

She looked over her shoulder. The girls had put some distance between them, but she could see their heads turned back toward her. "You're supposed to be looking for the dog, not at me." They turned back and cantered away. Good, thought Lola. That way they wouldn't realize just how cursory her check would be. The rocks loomed before her, releasing the day's heat. But the opening, when she edged into it, was cool by virtue of having been in the shade all day. The sudden chill, the narrow walls, reminded her of the day in Antelope

Canyon. A long shudder ran through her. Her breath came short. She inhaled, counting to five. Then exhaled. Another count of five. "Settle down," she told herself. She raised her voice for the benefit of the girls. "Bub! Hey, Bub! You in here?"

"Yeah," a low voice answered. "Right here."

The blow to the back of her head cut off her scream before it ever left her throat.

THIRTY-EIGHT

THIS IS THE LAST THING.

That's what I was promised. Along with, *It buys us the final bit of time we need.*

For what? I wanted to ask. But I knew better. I'd have thought that blowing up the house was the end game. Even though it didn't quite work out the way it was supposed to. I guess I was wrong. Anyway, I wanted to say that there's no *us*, not anymore. Even if I end up in a whiteman lockup. It's what I deserve. But I need some time to figure out how to end this. And I have to admit that getting that reporter out of the way helps me as much as it helps the plan. When I saw her jogging off into the desert just as I got out of the car, I crept along after her, dodging behind the scrub, ducking into an opening in the rocks when she and the girls stopped to talk. I could hear their voices but couldn't make out the words. And even though I knew they couldn't hear me either, I held my own breath against the wheeze that threatened to escape. I'd hoped that once *Shizhé'é* divined my plan, he and the truck driver would loose their hold on me. The better I could function, the quicker I could put an end to things. But they only grabbed me tighter, bony fingers wrapped around my windpipe, the surprisingly corporeal weight of their ethereal bodies collapsing my chest. My lips fell open despite my clenched jaw. I sucked in air, the relief so sweet that it took me a moment to become aware of the receding hoofbeats—and the approaching footsteps. Oh, sweet, sweet stroke of luck. I whispered a swift apology for what I was about to do and drew my fist back.

The hardest thing was hearing the girls, their voices high and sharp with fear.

"Mom?"

"Auntie Lola?"

I tried to block them out as I dragged the inert form through the twists and turns of the narrow track through the rocks. Juliana probably knew that the split went all the way through the butte, but I doubted she would venture into it in the darkness, and by the time the adults were summoned, I'd be gone. I tightened my grip beneath the woman's arms and gave a final jerk that freed us both from the confines of the rock. Then I bent my knees, stooped, and heaved mightily, balancing her across my shoulders, the way I might have done an injured sheep. Except that a sheep's legs didn't dangle nearly to the ground. And sheep generally froze with fear once you'd hoisted them, didn't moan and stir the way she was beginning to do. Shit. I hurried back toward the house, being careful to step only on bare rock, watching the house light up, window by window, as I approached. The girls' voices sounded again, this time followed by deeper adult replies. Valentine emerged into the spill of light from the front door; Naomi,

Edgar, and Charlie stood silhouetted within it, concern evident in their rigid stances. The girls slid from the pony's back and ran to them. A touching scene, if I hadn't known the cause. If I hadn't *been* the cause. I peered through the darkness, straining to see the lift of elbow, cellphone to ear. The woman stirred again, more forcefully this time. She was coming around. I readjusted her on my shoulders, tightened my grip. When I looked up, Naomi, Edgar, and Charlie were following the girls back out into the darkness.

I took my chance, moving as quickly as I could toward the car. I dumped the woman on the ground and stripped my T-shirt from my body, took the hem in my teeth, and tore it into strips. I tied her hands first. Her eyes flickered as I stuffed the gag into her mouth. I followed the gag with a blindfold before she got a glimpse of me. She kicked at me, bucking beneath me like a horse as I sat on her legs to tie her ankles. I considered. I took my last strip, ran it between the ties on her wrists and ankles, and pulled it tight. I couldn't have her bouncing around like that, making noise, alerting someone to her presence.

By the time the panicked foursome arrived back at the house, she was in the trunk and I was in the kitchen, an expression of horror and words of shock and dismay at the ready, ignoring the mocking laughter of those two unseen beings.

THIRTY-NINE

LIKE HE DIDN'T THINK she'd figure out who he was. Lola's fury surpassed even the slicing pain in her head.

She'd faded in and out for a bit, but came to for good when the car started moving after an inexplicable delay. She jounced around in the trunk, hog-tied, unable to brace herself against the jolt from each fresh pothole. The car alone would have told her, its motor rattling and coughing, an amped-up version of its asthmatic driver. Oh, she'd heard that too, the way he'd labored for breath as he bound her, the same wheeze she'd heard beside her at the kitchen island on the nights he'd joined them for whatever perfect meal Naomi had prepared. She jerked against her bindings, but each fresh struggle only pulled them tighter, her back arching in torment. Yet the physical agony was nothing compared to the panicky sensation caused by the wad of cloth in her mouth. She drew in stale air, not enough, through her nose. Her lungs burned. Her heart slammed against them. Before she'd gone to Afghanistan, so many years earlier, she'd undergone training for reporters headed to war zones where kidnapping was a real possibility.

Be the gray man, she remembered. Her instructor, a former member of the British special forces, hadn't appreciated her question as to whether being a beige woman would do. She didn't feel gray now. She felt scarlet with rage and terror. She rubbed the side of her face against the hot metal floor of the trunk, trying to loosen the blindfold as well as the tie that held the gag in place, succeeding only in removing a layer of skin from her cheek.

Lola vowed to herself that the minute she got free of the car and her bindings, she would do her damnedest to hurt or even kill her captor, with her bare hands if necessary. And she would have, clenching her fists in preparation as soon as the car stopped, had not the creak of the opening trunk been followed by the press of a cold steel circle against her temple.

She knew that feeling. She froze. Her captor worked one-handed to cut her bonds, freeing first her feet and then her hands and then, blessedly, the cloth holding the gag in place. Lola spat it out and gulped air. The gun stayed pressed to her head all the while. A hand grasped her arm, pulling her from the trunk. Lola clambered out and stood swaying. The gun dug deeper into her temple.

She awaited release from the blindfold. It didn't come. She flexed her fingers. Maybe she could get the gun away. She would, she swore, shoot with a smile. "Sonofabitch," she started to say.

"Shut up." The voice was hoarse, muffled, as though her captor, too, wore a gag of some sort, or at least a bandana around the face in an unnecessary attempt to at disguise.

"Forget it," she said. "I know who you are. You might as well take this damn blindfold off."

The gun slid from her temple, traced her jawline, and stopped at the back of her neck. "Move. Now."

Lola slid a foot forward, half expecting to find open air beneath it. Maybe she would be walked off a cliff, so that it would look as if she'd fallen to her death from some high place. But why leave on the blindfold, a sure sign that a fall was no accident? The ground remained firm beneath her feet. She took another step.

"Keep going."

Her feet made slight scraping noises in the fine layer of sand atop the rock. She moved another few steps.

"Stop. Take hold of this."

Her fingers were folded around a vertical railing of some sort. It was cold. The gun stayed firmly against her neck. Her other arm was guided toward a similar railing. A kick to her calf sent her forward.

"Start climbing."

———

"What the—?"

The gun tapped against Lola's skull. "No talking. Get going. Up."

She lifted a foot, felt a rung. They were at the cliff houses, or someplace like it.

"No fucking way." The words escaped before Lola could stop them. Under the best of circumstances—in daylight, surrounded by her family, and able to see—the ladder had been torture. She thought of the lizard that had skittered past that day. What if tarantulas lurked in the heights, coming out in the cool of night? She'd read that they were ground spiders, but what if that was wrong?

The gun poked at her again, this time in the soft flesh of her throat. "Do I sound like I'm kidding?"

A traitorous foot landed on the first rung. Her biceps bulged, pulling her upward. She achieved a few steps, then stopped. Cold steel lay briefly against her ankle. "Good job. Keep it up. I'm right behind you."

Lola strained to see through the cloth binding her eyes. At least she couldn't look down. Or up. Or anywhere. She climbed faster; or, at least, not as slowly.

"Better." The voice floated past her ears. Lola couldn't imagine the purpose of this nighttime climb. There was a gun. Why not just shoot her? The gears within her aching head whirred and clicked, the answer coming more slowly than she would have liked. When it arrived, it provided cold comfort. A shooting was a clear-cut murder. With ballistics, it would be entirely too easy to trace. Her brain spun back to its original fear. Maybe the blindfold would be yanked just before the shove from the cliff's edge. She hesitated on the ladder.

"Keep moving!" The cold steel jabbed at her ankle, threatening to push her off balance. Lola picked up the pace again. If she was going to fall to her death, it wasn't going to be from this damn ladder. At least, once they arrived at the top, she might have a chance to outwit her captor in some way—if indeed a faked fall was the plan. But even that didn't make sense. What could possibly explain Lola's presence at the ruins in the middle of the night? Why would she vanish on the girls? None of it made sense. Lola's head pounded afresh. Her throat was dry and raw from the gag, and her wrists and ankles burned from where she'd pulled against her restraints. She slid her hand up the ladder and grabbed air. "God!" she yelled before regaining her grip. They'd come to the top sooner than she would have liked. She should have thought of some sort of plan before they got there, she thought as she half-crawled, half-fell onto the ledge. She pulled herself farther from the cliff edge and cautiously stood, backing away as she heard her captor leap nimbly onto the ledge.

"Stay there."

An unnecessary command. Lola remembered the ledge as a curved place, with deadly drops on three sides. Obedience seemed advisable. She heard something drop to the ground, then rustling, clinking sounds. "Now what?" she muttered.

A metallic buzz answered her, a sound she usually associated with the shop table in their garage in Montana, where Charlie fiddled with various projects, most of them mysterious to Lola. It sounded like the little saw Charlie used to prune the larger tree branches, limbs—she recalled uneasily—about the girth of her own. Given how easily Charlie's saw sliced through wood, she could only imagine the effect the buzzing implement might have on flesh and bone. Stories flashed through her head, real and fictional, of murder victims cut into manageable pieces, the better to dispose of them. She wondered if the rustling sounds had been black plastic garbage bags in which to dispose of her dismembered body.

"Wait," she said.

"Shut up. I'm in a hurry. If I read the signals right, you're afraid of heights."

"No," Lola said. "You read them wrong. I'm fine." She thought of her halting progress up the ladder, her quavering voice, and tried to think of any other way they could be read. "You can't blame me for being nervous. Under the circumstances."

"Right. That's why you've got your back plastered to the wall."

Indeed, as the saw buzzed, Lola had inched backward across the ledge, somehow safely maneuvering herself against one of the cliff houses, its seven-hundred-year-old adobe bricks still giving off the heat of the day's sun. She tried to make her objection more believable. "That's because you've got that gun—and that saw. No way do I want to be near you."

"I don't have time for talk." The voice still indistinct. She wasn't corrected about the saw, which meant she'd been right. *Dammit.*

"It doesn't matter. We're almost done here." The saw went back to work, buzzing louder as it bit into something.

Now, thought Lola. It would take only a few long, loping steps, a hard shove. She'd have to plant her hands hard, then pull back fast before she tumbled over, too. She'd be free. She took one step. Two. She imagined the yawning chasm and halted. Laughter rose above the sound of the saw. The noise stopped, replaced by a moment of silence, and then the clinking sounds again.

Action, however hesitant, hadn't worked. Maybe words would. "The tourists. They'll find me in the morning." Even to herself, Lola's protests had a flailing, desperate quality.

"No, they won't. The site is closed tomorrow. Security precaution for all the historic sites, because of the bombings. Now shut up and listen."

Lola's ears strained. Something cracked, so loud she jumped back against the wall. A faraway crash followed. It sounded for all the world as though the ladder had fallen. Which meant she was trapped with her captor.

But the words that followed spoke to the impossibility of that notion. "Time for me to go. Listen. I know you don't believe me, but I probably did you a favor. You'll be up here just long enough."

A long swishing sound mimicked the wind.

"*Hágoónee'.*"

The Diné word that people used for goodbye. Its truer meaning, Edgar had told her once, was closer to "That's settled, then." Lola supposed that whatever was happening, the meaning applied.

She waited for the next words. But they never came.

Lola counted to ten the slow way. One-thousand-one, one-thousand-two, one-thousand-three. She finished in a rush despite herself. Her fingers twitched. She did the count again, then tore at the blindfold, loosening it just enough to slide it above her eyes. She cast a glance around the ledge to assure herself that she was truly alone, then dropped to her hands and knees and crawled toward the cliff edge.

The ladder was gone. It looked as though it had been severed below the ring bolts that fastened it to the cliff, then pushed backward until it broke away far below of its own weight. But if the ladder was gone, where was her tormenter? She heard a hissing sound and drew back, afraid of rattlesnakes, doubly so after glimpsing something long and slithery just below. But the thing was all wrong for a snake, sliding down the face of the rock. A rope, moving fast through the ring that had once bolted the ladder to the wall. She remembered Naomi's words: *I taught him. You know how it goes—get kids doing something physical, something that they like, and they stay away from drugs. It his case, it worked.*

"A shame you didn't teach him not to kidnap people," Lola whispered now.

A form briefly bounced away from the cliff, darker than the starlit sky beyond. So he was belaying, or rappelling, or whatever they called it, his way down. She lay flat and inched forward on her belly. If she shook the rope, could she dislodge him, sending him tumbling to his death? And then what?

"One thing at a time," she told herself. Whatever he was up to, he needed to be stopped. Lola dragged herself another inch forward, whimpering. Vast space yawned mockingly ahead of her. She dug her fingers and feet against the rock, seeking nonexistent purchase, and forced herself to look down. Her head spun. She closed her eyes and ordered herself to focus. When she opened her eyes, she saw another flash of movement far below. He was nearly to the desert floor.

"Dammit!" Lola forgot about the height, almost—enough to reach one hand to the rope, yanking hard against its resistance. It flew hissing through her grasp, burning layers of skin from her palm. She clenched her teeth against the pain and pulled harder. The rope went loose.

"Yessss," she said. Maybe she'd dislodged the bastard. Then, "No!"

The rope whisked free. She drew her hand back and blew on it, sliding away from the edge all in the same movement. But not before she saw the figure far below, sprinting across the desert floor toward the car.

FORTY

LOLA SCRAMBLED BACKWARD, NOT rising to her feet until she'd put a few yards between herself and the edge, the ruins reassuringly at her back.

The walls were losing their heat. She leaned against the bricks, trying to soak up what was left. When she'd set out from the house, what seemed like hours ago now, the heat had been oppressive. But the temperature had done its nighttime dive. A breeze slid past. She revised her timeline of the increasing chill. She was in for a long, cold night—and then maybe a long hot morning before she somehow managed to attract the attention of someone looking for her, or even just passing by. The wind sliced at her again. Something alien rode it. Lola raised her head and sniffed a familiar odor. She inhaled more deeply.

"Dog shit?"

Even as she spoke, a scratching sound reached her. "Jesus Christ!" She leapt away from the wall. Anything could be in there. A rattlesnake, its scales dragging across the desert floor. One—or more—of those tarantulas. Rats, maybe. Lola removed herself with alacrity to the narrow strip of safety, the section of the ledge out from under the overhang, so spotlighted by the moon that she'd be able to see any approaching creature but still far enough from the edge as to keep her vertigo in check. She listened for the sound. There it was again, a frantic quality to it, this time accompanied by a whimper. She cocked her head. It came from beyond the cliff house. She tried to remember her visit there, visualized the site's layout. The kiva was back there.

Step by stiff-legged, ready-to-run step, she advanced upon it, fighting the impossible hope rising in her heart, booming like thunder against her ribs. She reached the kiva. Stood a moment to let her eyes adjust to the darkness. Dropped to her knees and looked down into it. Saw white against black, flashing like a miracle as Bub flung himself again and again at the kiva's wall.

His fur was rough, his ribs newly prominent. Lola sat on the floor of the kiva, her arms around him, twisting as his tongue polished her face. "Bub. Oh, Bub. How is it you're still alive?"

He answered with a yelp, turning away and looking up toward the lip of the kiva.

"Right. Let's get you out of here. That'll be the easy part. Then we have to figure out how to get ourselves down from this cliff. Or get somebody up here to get us down."

When Lola stood up, she could just see over the kiva's edge. She thought of Bub hurling himself at the walls for three days straight, handicapped by his missing leg, always falling short of the mark. When she ran her hands over his body, seeking injuries, he whimpered and trembled. Nothing seemed broken, but he must have been badly bruised. "How'd you get here, buddy?" Another thought struck her. "And how in hell are you still alive?" He could have survived three days without food, but lack of water, even in the cool of the kiva, should have killed him after the first day.

She shook her head and hoisted him in her arms and carried him to the kiva wall. Her foot struck something and she stumbled, nearly dropping him. Metal clanged. "Hold on." She put the dog down and felt around on the darkened floor. Her fingers encountered a familiar shape. A bowl, with a quarter-inch of water in the bottom. Lola crouched, swirling her fingers in the water, thinking hard. Maybe someone, too soft-hearted to kill Bub outright, had dumped him in the kiva to let him die there. Given the events of the past few hours, that someone must have been Thomas. But why, then, bring the dog water? What was the purpose of keeping him alive? And what was the purpose of leaving Lola stranded on the cliff? Bub leaned against her leg and whined.

"Sorry," she said. "First things first."

She hoisted him again. "Count of three," she said. "One, two—" Fifty pounds of dog careened skyward. Toenails scrabbled on adobe. Lola leaped and shoved at his butt. He disappeared over the lip of the kiva.

"One down," she said, breathing hard.

She reached up. The kiva's edge was about shoulder height. She put her hands on it, jumped, and pulled—and fell back. "Ow." Bub's head appeared over the edge. "Give me a minute," she said. She climbed to her feet and tried not to think about all the times she'd dismissed Charlie's suggestion that she join him in lifting weights.

"The running is great," he'd say. "But you want upper-body strength, too."

"Yeah, and I should eat more vegetables," Lola, a ravenous carnivore, had always responded.

"That too," would come the placid reply.

Now she wondered: Would it have hurt to have picked up a bar-bell now and then? She shook out her arms, backed up to the center of the kiva, took a running start, and leapt for the kiva's lip, this time getting her elbows onto the rim. She felt herself begin to slip, made a superhuman effort, and threw a knee over the edge. Another pull, and she lay gasping on the surface of the ledge, Bub prancing around her in paroxysms of canine joy.

"Don't look so happy. We're out. Now what?"

————————

Hours later, the rock spires began to emerge from the night, a deeper shade of black than the softening darkness. The first real suggestion of dawn was still a couple of hours away, but hints of light seeped into the landscape. Lola welcomed the promise of warmth, but she knew that with warmth would come thirst. She thought of the skim of water in the bowl, wondered how quickly it would become ap-pealing, then put the thought out of her mind. Besides, she wasn't sure if she could get herself out of the kiva a second time.

"Come on, Bub," she said. "Let's see how bad this is."

A ten-minute exploration of the ledge—staying as far from the drop as possible—told her that things were very bad indeed. The ledge was tucked into a bend in the wall. It arced like a giant C, curv-ing in a great shell to the very edge of the cliff, which plunged down as precipitously as the walls above climbed high. She had thought to find a way around, or maybe even a route up and over and back down the other side. She sat with her back against the wall of the cliff house and gazed out over the lightening desert. Bub lay beside her with his head in her lap. She stroked him, remembering the day when she'd clung to the ladder and watched the truck dissolve into a burst of flame and smoke. She'd been able to see the road from the ladder. So, logically, motorists on the road would be able to see her, especially given that Charlie and others had to be out looking for her. She calculated the distance to the road. A half-mile? More like a mile.

The trucks and cars on the faraway main road had been easy to spot, the sun glinting off their metallic surfaces. But would a lone person be so noticeable? Especially high above the road, where likely no one would expect her to be? Those looking for her would probably explore surfaces, gullies, canyons, washes. The places where someone might slip and fall, or—the thought would have occurred to Charlie—dispose of a body. Which brought her back to wondering why Thomas hadn't flat-out killed her.

Maybe he didn't have the stomach for it, Lola mused, the same way he apparently had no stomach for killing the dog. Or maybe he'd stranded Lola and Bub on the cliff in hopes that no one would find either of them, and they'd die a slow death there. Maybe he thought people would attribute that to natural causes. "No way." Lola addressed her own speculation aloud. Too many people knew about her fear of heights to imagine she'd have gone to the cliff houses on her own. And besides, there was the matter of the vandalized ladder. Maybe he'd just wanted her out of the way for a while. But why?

She thought, with a pang that bent her double, of Margaret's fear at her mother's disappearance. Impossible now to pretend that her family wasn't a target. Margaret would want Charlie to find her. But she'd also want him to stay close, afraid of losing him, too. And Charlie would see that terror, would want to reassure Margaret— but wouldn't dare bring her along with him on a search for fear of putting her in danger.

If—Lola's mind balked at the thought—no one found her within twenty-four hours, the next day's search would be disrupted by the tribal meeting, this time attended by mine executives several pay grades above Kerns, necessitating extra security. A moment later she was on her feet, shouting "No, no!" as Bub yelped beside her.

The meeting.

Thomas was going to bomb the meeting.

———————

"Help!"

The car crawled beetle-like along the blacktop far, far away, oblivious to Lola's gyrations on the ledge. She leapt and shouted, stripped her running tank over her head and flapped it above her. "Get me down from here!"

The car vanished around a curve. Lola collapsed in the dirt and put her shirt back on. It was inside-out. She didn't care. "Oh God, Bub. What are we going to do?" He leaned against her and licked her cheeks. She raised her head. The desert floor grew lighter by the moment, the reddish tone of the rocks emerging from the gray. She guessed it was about seven in the morning. The meeting was more than twenty-four hours away. But what if Thomas got spooked, did something ahead of time? Surely Edgar and the mine executives would be huddling today, planning strategy. Lola thought about Charlie's grief if his brother was killed just as they were beginning to reconnect.

And then there were the others. The faceless mine executives, all with families who'd grieve equally. Tribal officials and elders. The magnitude of Thomas's probable scheme washed over her like a splash of ice water. She dug her fingers into her palms as her brain clicked through the scenario. Now she was sure why Thomas hadn't simply killed her. After all, she'd be able to finger him as the bomber. But it wouldn't matter. "He's going to kill himself, too," she told Bub.

"He's going to kill them all. He just needs me out of the way long enough to do it."

Bub cocked his head and looked at her out of his blue eye.

"You're right. That's crazy," she said. It was crazy. She was imagining things. How could Thomas justify killing all of those people?

Even as she tried to push it away, the reality shoved back at her, urging her to her feet. She'd written too many stories overseas about fanatics. One last grand action. The sacrifice—the collateral damage, a term Lola had always despised—worth the result. Such an attack would guarantee that no corporation would ever again consider the Navajo Nation worthy of development.

The sun grew brighter still. The rocks glowed red. Lola cast a last look toward the useless motorists on the useless road and uttered the impossible.

"We're going to have to get down from here ourselves."

FORTY-ONE

Too many minutes later found her flat on her stomach, her chin resting on the edge of the cliff, her hands clutching the rock. Bub danced back and forth along the precipice, surefooted on his three legs, tail wagging in anticipation of action. Lola told him his delight was premature.

"Because that's just not going to happen," she said. Even though she knew it had to.

That being the barely perceptible trail zigzagging down the side of the cliff, the one the guide had pointed out the day of their tour. "Just imagine," he'd said. "They went up and down that every day. Whole families, little kids, moms with babies on their backs and pots on their head. Carrying big bundles of firewood, heavy jars of water, seeds for planting, and crops they'd harvested." At the time, her sweaty hands slipping along the ladder, Lola had thought its rungs none too reassuring. Now, as she studied the ladder's wreckage, it loomed in her memory like a grand sweeping staircase, the sort of thing she'd have descended without a second thought.

She glared at the pieces of ladder that mocked her from the desert floor. But the ladder's bottom half remained intact, held in place by other bolts. Lola's eyes narrowed. "All we have to do is make it that far," she said. Then half-laughed, half-sobbed at the notion. The ladder, with its solid rungs and firm side-rails, had nearly defeated her before. The trail—now she could see where it met the ledge, the slightest of indentations in the rock—mocked her.

"No," she said.

She closed her eyes and thought of Margaret, of Charlie. Imagined her child's velvety cheek against her own, Charlie's arms around both of them. What if they, too, got caught up in whatever Thomas was planning? She thought of all the times she'd spoken to Charlie about her suspicions involving his brother. She needed to get down, if for no other reason than to apologize. Her jaw tensed.

"Yes," she said.

———

She'd thought to crawl—something reassuring about being low to the ground, less likelihood of teetering over the edge. But the trail was simply too narrow, the pedestrian's version of what cyclists called a single-track, demanding one foot planted firmly in front of the other, not even room for both side-by-side. The first steps were the worst, her body swaying high above the cliff edge. She crouched, trying to hold onto the lip, but then her butt stuck out into thin air. "I can't do this," she said. She conjured her daughter's face. "Margaret," she said, and took a step.

"I can't," she said.

Then, "Charlie," and another step.

It was easier, just, after the first few steps, when the rock was waist high, then over her head. She pressed her chest and stomach against it, savoring its rough physicality, so reassuring as opposed to the terrifying expanse of air surrounding her. She'd started off staring fixedly at her feet, but it had proven too easy for her eyes to stray farther downward still, her gaze slipping over the edge just inches from her toes, plummeting to the desert floor. Her mind tugged at her to follow, to just lean out and let go. Now she trained her gaze on the cliff face, hands hard against it, and let her feet feel for the trail, an inch forward at a time. She sought a rhythm. Breathe. Slide. Breathe. Slide. She achieved maybe a foot before she stopped again.

Bub, bless him, seemed to be doing fine but wisely stayed far behind, although the occasional heaving sigh warned her that he'd have been happier scampering ahead. But there was no room to pass. Just as well, she thought. So much as the brush of fur against her calf might have sent her over the edge. The sun jumped above the horizon and shone full force, turning the cliff into a vast, vertical griddle. Sweat slicked her hairline and dampened her singlet against her back. Her own sigh echoed Bub's. Even if she made it down, there was no guarantee she'd be able to get to the police in time to stop Thomas.

Again, her mind sounded its siren call: Better, maybe, just to lean back, fall onto the air as though it were a cushion. That way, if her worst fears came true, she'd already be dead, no agony over the fate of her family. *Her family.*

"Margaret," she said through gritted teeth. Step.

"Charlie." Step.

———

Lola stared at the rock an inch in front of her face and thought of the water bowl in the kiva. How much had it held? Not even an inch, or a half-inch. Just enough to moisten the bottom of the bowl. Slicks of dog saliva atop it. Her throat convulsed. If someone had handed her the bowl at that moment, she'd have loosed a hand from its death grip on the rock, snatched the bowl away, and bent her face to it, slurping up the few drops that remained, dog spit and all. Even though she knew, as the mirage faded, that she'd have been obligated to share the bowl's paltry contents with Bub, panting a few feet behind her. Her head swam. Her stomach felt knotted down to the size of a walnut. A few hours earlier, she'd been hungry. Now hunger had vanished in the face of a monstrous thirst. She tried to remember the last time she'd had something to drink. At the house, certainly. Probably some of Naomi's high-test lemonade. At this moment, she'd have been grateful for straight vodka. Rotgut, even. Motor oil. Anything liquid.

Lola touched her tongue to cracked lips. Once, in Afghanistan, she'd gotten so dehydrated—refusing water during a long day of covering demonstrations so as not to have to pee in a place that offered no obvious opportunities—that when she'd finally returned to the safety of her hotel room, her urine was a scary dark orange and her head spun so that she'd clutched the sink to avoid falling off the toilet. She felt that way again now. She shook her head to clear it. It was one thing to fight the urge to leap into the abyss. It would be another to fall into it by accident or through her own carelessness.

"Help me," she murmured, to no deity in particular. A lizard appeared. Lola blinked. It blinked back. It sat on a protrusion of rock, perfect for a handhold. Its fingernail sliver of a tongue flicked out, then back. Its blue-striped tail switched. There was no way it was the same one she'd seen on her tour. Still. "Hey, buddy," said Lola.

It was, she reminded herself, a reptile, with a brain about the size of a dust mote. Still, its calm unperturbed presence seemed a blessing of sorts. It turned bright black eyes upon her. They reminded her of Betty Begay's before she'd gotten sick, serene and steady. I'm just fine here, it seemed to say. You are, too.

Lola replied as though it had spoken. "No, I'm not. Not at all. For starters, I could really use that little rock to hold on to. Do you mind?" She slid her hand along the rock toward it. The lizard obligingly skittered from its perch, spread its toes wide, and clung to a vertical section of wall. Lola grabbed at the rock with her right hand. It was the most secure handhold she'd had so far on her descent. She lifted her left hand, raised a finger, and tentatively stroked the lizard's back. It stretched out its neck and closed its eyes. "Thank you," said Lola.

The encounter somehow steadied her. Her next breaths shuddered a little less, her next steps slid a little farther. Then her toe encountered an obstacle. She nudged it. It didn't move. She inched her foot to one side. Air. She tried the other side. Vertical rock. She looked back toward the lizard, thinking to beseech its help again. It was gone. She kicked a little at the obstruction. Nothing.

She ground her forehead against the rock and cursed. To have gotten this far, however far it was, only to be blocked. She tried to imagine inching her way back up. Repeating that silly business of waving her shirt over her head in a hopeless attempt to attract attention. Surviving another night, then looking for the telltale roiling smoke that would signal the deaths of so many. The temptation to jump tugged at her yet again.

"Goddammit." She turned her head, millimeter by millimeter, to one side and chanced a glance down to see the obstruction.

It was the splintered end of the intact section of ladder, bolted firmly into place, leading downward to safety, shining as bright and precious in the sunlight as the goddamned yellow brick road.

FORTY-TWO

LOLA HIT THE GROUND about five minutes after Bub.

She'd beckoned to him from the ladder, thinking to carry him down, but he'd raced past her with a disdainful sniff, free at last to negotiate the trail at his own headlong speed. When she stepped from the last rung, he launched himself at her chest, knocking her to the ground, her laughter and his yapping mingling in a joyful chorus.

The exultation was brief. Lola lay flat, Bub on her chest, the sun shining above. Not straight down on them, but too close. She scrambled to her feet, earning an injured look from Bub as he fell to one side. She still had to get back to the road, and then to town, so that she could warn the police and FBI about Thomas's plans.

She bent and loosened the laces on her running shoes, easing the pressure on feet swollen and puffy from the heat. A mile, at most, to the main road. "Hell," she reassured Bub, "that's a sprint." Except that after the first few steps, she knew it wouldn't be. She was going on twelve hours with neither food nor water. The goose egg on the back of her head throbbed, competing for attention with her ferocious thirst. She'd been used to running in the relative cool of the morning, the sun slanting low and friendly across the desert. Now it launched a full-on assault from on high. And finally, because she'd set out on her run so close to nightfall the previous evening, she'd seen no need for a cap. She angled her head downward and traced a crooked, stumbling path down the dirt road leading away from the ruins. Her toe caught a rock. Her hands smacked the ground just seconds before her face. She lay still, spitting red dirt. Bub nosed at the back of her neck.

An hour earlier, she thought as she pushed herself up, she'd have given anything for a flat surface beneath her, blissfully extending in every direction. She'd made the mistake of relaxing her guard once she got on the ground. Potholes and rocks made the track more of a jeep trail than an actual road, and Lola wove her way among them at a trot, thinking back to the occasional races she'd run, always striving for a PB, or personal best, time. If there were such a thing as a personal worst, this was it, she thought. Her head swam. Bub, who usually raced ahead of her in long, low-to-the-ground zigzags, easily achieving five times her own distance, lurched behind her. Normally his missing leg, lost to that gunshot meant for Lola, was no impediment, but on this day the handicap was evident.

A sawhorse loomed before them. Lola stopped and leaned against it, marshaling what remained of her strength. A hand-lettered piece of posterboard flapped in the searing wind: *NO CLIFF HOUSE TOURS. CLOSED UNTIL FURTHER NOTICE.* She let her gaze slide past it to the beautiful ribbon of blacktop now only yards away. They'd made it. At least, this far. Next step: Flag down a ride.

As though in response to her thoughts, an approaching engine grumbled on the other side of a rise in the road. Lola jogged the final few steps to the road and lifted her arm in preparation. A truck topped the hill. The driver's head turned her way. The truck slowed.

Conrad Coal's logo adorned its side. She turned and walked back toward the road leading to the cliff houses, a woman and crippled dog trying to look purposeful in the middle of nowhere. She wasn't sure enough of Thomas's intentions to gamble on a truck that might end up a victim of a second bombing. The sound of the truck's engine faded. She turned and stared after it, wondering if her own foolish fears had damned the one chance she might have had.

She broke again into as much of a jog as she could approximate. When a car finally appeared, she simply moved to the center of the road and stopped, blocking its passage, not even bothering with the charade of flagging. The decrepit rez car wheezed to a stop. Regret and relief warred within her. She'd half-hoped for a tourist's shiny new SUV, one that could speed her to her destination. The car now before her hadn't sped anywhere in a very long while. But a tourist might not have stopped for her ragged, disreputable-looking self. Indian people generally were more apt to accept that anybody, anywhere, might be having a bad day.

Lola approached the car, reflecting that this was fast turning into the worst day of her life. She opened the back door without asking permission, squeezing herself next to a couple of aunties, pulling Bub onto her lap. An elder dozed in the front seat next to the driver, a middle-aged man who wore a Conrad Coal cap. No one spoke. But as she settled herself in the seat, the driver reached for a plastic water bottle in the console and handed it to her. Lola drank so fast that precious droplets ran down her chin and wetted her tank top. She swiped the back of her hand across it, then licked her hand. She forced herself to lower the bottle and pour some of its contents into her cupped hand for Bub.

"Thank you," she said when the bottle was empty. And then, "Gaitero. Please. As fast as you can. Do you know Gar Laurendeau's place?"

Charlie probably would be at the house, she thought. Or he might be with the tribal police, persuading them that his own anxiety about her disappearance in no way would prevent him from helping with their search. He'd take comfort from the known rituals, the cop talk, the bad coffee. But his first priority would have been Margaret, making sure she was safe with someone, almost certainly either Naomi or Edgar. Not, please God, Thomas. The possibility clutched at Lola's throat even as she rejected it. Charlie barely knew Thomas. In a situation this serious, only immediate family would do.

The car's rattling progress slowed as Lola pointed out the turnoff to Naomi and Edgar's. She pushed her foot against the floor, impossibly willing the driver to speed up the dirt lane to the house. She barely remembered to fling thanks over her shoulder as she and Bub staggered toward the front door.

Lola barely registered Naomi rising from a counter stool, her face a rictus of fear. Behind her, Thomas shrank into a corner.

Lola shot him a look of pure poison and dodged Naomi. "Margaret. Where is she?" Without waiting for an answer, she stumbled down the hall to the girls' bedroom and pushed through the door.

Margaret and Juliana lay on their beds, unread books propped on their stomachs. Margaret, the girl who almost never cried, shrieked and burst into tears. Lola waited until her daughter was cradled in her arms—and Bub wrapped in Margaret's—before sliding to the floor, muscles that had been taut with fear and exhaustion for eighteen hours finally relaxing into the reality that she was safe.

Naomi eased into the room.

"Charlie and Edgar are on their way. The police, too. But I'm thinking we should get you to the hospital so they can check you out."

Lola shook her head and clutched Margaret tighter. "I'm fine. I just need more water. Maybe some food. And—" She lifted a hand and studied its surface, rendered unfamiliar by layers of dirt, cross-hatched with scratches and scrapes. She bent her head to one side, sniffed, and recoiled. "Maybe a shower. And some clean clothes."

Naomi shook her head. The prosecutor in her spoke. "You have to do this. They'll need to document your injuries. Especially if you were—" She hesitated.

Lola's lips twitched in a half-smile of acknowledgment. Any woman would have had the same question. The possibility of rape hovered over even the most innocuous situations. "No," she said. "He just kidnapped me. He didn't do anything else." Except leave me to die, she thought.

Naomi sagged back into her chair. "Oh, thank God." She pulled open a drawer, fumbled with its contents, and brought out a schoolgirl's black-and-white marbled composition book and a pen. "The police should be here any minute. But maybe while it's still so fresh in your mind, you can give me a description of the guy. That's what they'll want first."

"No need," said Lola.

"But—" Naomi held up the composition book as though the very sight of it might cause Lola to change her mind. "It's really important. Given everything else going on around here, it's possible the person who took you is the bomber."

Margaret whimpered in her arms. Lola stroked her hair. "He is the bomber. I'm sure of it. And I don't need to give a description. I know who he is."

Margaret raised her head. Juliana, who'd lingered in a corner of the room, crept close. She had to have known, from the day Thomas's bookbag and its telltale key chain turned up at the cliff houses, that he was involved, maybe not in the bombings—she probably couldn't have brought herself to think that—but in something he shouldn't be. Lola cast a glance her way and braced herself to break a nine-year-old's heart.

Enough damage, she told herself. Juliana would find out soon enough, but she wouldn't find out from her. She eased Margaret from her lap, clambered to her feet, and gestured to Naomi to come close. She whispered into Naomi's ear and watched in fascination as the skin on Naomi's face, so smooth and brown, went as pale and mottled as that of a corpse.

FORTY-THREE

I WAS TIRED OF *Shizhé'é* and his companion, and their sick sense of humor.

They laughed and laughed, a rusted creaking sound that iced my veins, when Lola stumbled through the front door. Relief washed in behind the fear. Because a part of me, no matter the reassurances, thought she might die up there. Dehydrate before I could get more water up to her and the dog. Or fall in some crazy attempt to get down. Which somehow she'd managed to do without killing herself. Edgar was always talking smack about her, but the woman had earned my respect. And something else, too. She made me hope there was still a way that this could be stopped. Because it wasn't over yet.

Only one more thing. And your part is done now. So you can relax.

Relax? If I knew what that one more thing was, I could do my damnedest to stop it. But I had no idea. Maybe this woman, Lola, maybe she could figure it out. And maybe if I stayed closed to her, I could figure it out, too.

I waited for her to come out of the bedroom. She and Naomi and the girls had been in there a long time. At one point, I heard Naomi's voice raised high, but couldn't make out the words. A few minutes later, sirens. I went to the window. Edgar's white truck led a parade of Navajo Nation SUVs and black sedans, all of them moving so fast I could barely see the flashing lights through the cloud of dust.

I stood back as the door burst open, lifting my chin toward the bedroom. Charlie blew past, calling his wife's name.

Edgar stopped in front of me. Spread his hands wide. "I don't know what to say." His voice broke. Maybe *Shizhé'é* was after him, too? But no. His eyes filled.

"About what?" He couldn't possibly know.

"This will break Juliana's heart. All of ours." He leaned in for a hard, unexpected hug. I hugged him back, wanting to hold on, to postpone whatever was about to happen. Because I had a pretty good idea. *Shizhé'é* chuckled in my ear, raked his claws through my throat, wrapped his hands around my lungs and squeezed and squeezed.

Outside, car doors slammed. I fought for breath.

Edgar's arms fell away. He stepped back, his eyes dry, his voice even. "Tell me it's not true."

Heavy footsteps. Lights flashing on the walls. Cops and men in suits burst through the door. "FBI!" one of the suits shouted. So that explained the sedans.

A tribal cop, voice pitched gratifyingly low. "Thomas Benally? You have the right to remain silent … " Handcuffs bit into my wrists.

Those earlier words ringing in my ears, louder even than the ghostly cackling. *Your part in this is done.* Maybe my part was done. But it wasn't over.

FORTY-FOUR

THERE WAS THE HOSPITAL, the indignity of the bright lights and various assessments and the necessity for photos of her various injuries, surprisingly minor though they turned out to be.

Then the endless questions from police, Charlie hovering just outside the door, too much the cop to press for inclusion, too much the husband to go get some lunch, as suggested. Eventually, though, there was lunch, Lola ignoring the admonition to eat slowly, the result being that most of her Navajo taco came right back up just seconds after she reached the shelter of the bathroom.

"Another," she said when she made her shaky way back to the table. "And a milkshake. And a really big glass of water. In fact, you can just leave that pitcher right here."

And finally, a fistful of sleeping pills from the hospital. "You're exhausted, both physically and mentally," the doctor said. "These should get you through the first week. You think you'll sleep, but you won't. You're still wound up, and that's normal. The minute you close your eyes, it's all going to come back. Believe me, I've seen this before. Too many times." The doctor took off her glasses and rubbed her eyes. The skin beneath them was dark as a bruise. She was white, younger than Lola but looked older. Probably doing a residency at a reservation hospital, Lola thought, to satisfy the requirements of whatever government loan program had gotten her through medical school, counting the days until she could get herself to a big-city emergency room where, despite the nightly mayhem, at least there'd be the nearby consolation of bright lights and martini bars when she finished her thirty-six-hour shift. "Your body needs rest, and your brain needs it even more. Oh, and find a counselor."

The doctor had been right about the images. After a shower of unforgiveable length, given their desert locale, Lola dutifully swallowed one of the pills and let Charlie and Margaret tuck her into bed. Bub curled next to her, asleep before they'd even said their good nights, even though it was only midafternoon. "Want us to stay?" Charlie asked.

"I'll be fine." But she wasn't, finding herself back on the ladder, swaying blind and terrified as the gun rapped against her ankle, as soon as the door closed behind them. She rose up on her elbows, thinking to call out to Charlie, but her voice came out in a croak, fallout from all of the shouting atop the cliff. She waited for the pill to work. It didn't. She climbed out of bed and retrieved one of the painkillers from the container in her Dopp kit. She spent an entire millisecond worrying about the combination of sleeping pill and painkiller, then gulped it down, letting it pull her into a blackness even more enveloping than the fear.

————

"Lola. Lola."

The voice floated above her. A hand on her shoulder. "Lola." A shake. "It's been almost a day."

A familiar scent.

"Is that coffee?" The words emerged in a croak.

A chuckle. "Thought that might get your attention."

Her eyelids eased up by degrees. Then slammed back down. The desert sunlight streamed into the room. Homesickness wrapped Lola. Montana's mornings started gray and cool, easing a person mercifully into the day, nothing like this face-slap of glare and heat. She tried again, sitting up, slitting her eyes, and reaching for the cup. Charlie let her have it, but he kept his hands wrapped around hers lest she spill it. She sipped and sipped, and then, as it cooled, inhaled the rest in long gulps. "What time is it?"

"Nearly nine. The meeting with the mine honchos is at noon. I thought you might want to go."

"Where's Margaret?"

"She and Juliana are out with that pony."

Coffee splashed across the bedspread. Lola was on her feet, heading for the door. "Are you crazy?"

Charlie pulled her back. "Wait. I'm not crazy. They're not riding him anywhere. They're braiding his mane and tail or some such, trying to turn a desert plug into some sort of East Coast show pony. Naomi's with them."

Lola tried to free herself. "I was with them, and look what happened."

Charlie led her to a chair and eased her into it. "He's tied up to one of the shade house supports. Anybody wanted to snatch them, he'd have to come right up to the house." He let go of her, picked up the mug and set it on the nightstand, then stripped the coffee-soaked spread from the bed. "We'll need to wash this."

"Right. Sorry." Lola took a breath and tried to talk sense into herself. "Besides, they've still got Thomas, right? Where did they hold him? Is there a reservation jail or does he have to go to a federal prison while they prepare the charges?"

The spread slipped from Charlie's hands, pooling around his feet. He kicked it aside, knelt before her, and took her hands. "About that. Lola, what made you so sure it was Thomas who kidnapped you?"

Lola pulled away. "Why?"

"Seriously. I want to know."

"Talk to your cop friends. I told them yesterday. Again and again." She went over it anyway, the wheezing breath, the noisy car, the general size and shape of the man who'd clobbered her. She told him, at long last, about Canyon Man, trying not to see the effort it cost him to bite back a lecture. And the circumstantial stuff—the bookbag, the key chain, the way Thomas always seemed to be around whenever bad things happened. The way he came and went at night. "No doubt in my mind. None whatever."

"But you never saw the man who kidnapped you. Never saw his face. What about his voice? Did you recognize that?"

Lola pressed her back hard against the chair, away from her husband-turned-interrogator. In the brief time she'd known him, Thomas had barely said two words in her presence. She might not recognize his voice. But that didn't matter. Nor that she'd never seen her abductor's face. "I never needed to. I know it was him."

"Lola."

"Stop saying that." He almost never called her by name. It was unsettling. She tried to decipher his expression. The man could have played poker with the best. But something flickered at the corners of his eyes, pulled his mouth askew. Pity?

"Here's the thing. There's an alibi. I didn't want to tell you yesterday—you were upset enough as it is."

"What alibi?" Lola shoved herself out of the chair, forcing Charlie back on his heels.

He regained his balance and stood beside her. "He was here when you got kidnapped."

Lola paced away from him. "No, he wasn't. He was dragging me through the desert, forcing me up some stupid ladder. Hitting me. Holding a gun on me. Goddammit, Charlie. How can you even believe him when he says that? He wasn't here. He was with me."

Charlie's head wagged back and forth, regular as a metronome. "He was here. He got here not long after you went out with the girls."

Lola clenched her teeth, balled her hands into fists. "So he wasn't here when it actually happened. He had time to knock me out and grab me before he showed up at the house. That's why he let me sit in the car awhile, so that all of you could see him there. Some alibi. I can't believe the cops let him walk."

The look she'd seen before passed over his face again, lingering this time. "There's a witness. Someone was with him when you were taken up to the ruins. No matter how you look at it, the time frame doesn't work."

"What witness? Naomi? Edgar? They'd stick up for him no matter what. He's like family to them." *And I'm not.* She bit her lip to keep the bitter words from escaping.

"No. I'm the witness. It was me."

FORTY-FIVE

IT TOOK A WHILE for the adults back at the house to realize she was missing, Charlie said.

"The girls got scared, tried to find you on their own. They thought they'd be in trouble if they came back without you. Thomas came in before they got back. When it got dark, Naomi went out and started calling for them. They came back then. Crying. Shaking. Naomi tried to tell them you'd just gone on a longer run than you'd planned, but we all knew better."

Lola pictured Margaret's face and turned away from the image.

"Eddie called the cops. But we didn't want to wait for them."

Lola nodded. The police station was miles away. It was the curse of rural life, exacerbated by the reservation's vast empty stretches— help was never close.

"We all wanted to go out looking. Naomi and Eddie insisted. And no way was I going to sit at home. Margaret needed me, but—"

But I did, too, Lola thought. Charlie's poker face failed him yet again, his warring distress over his wife and daughter etching deep lines from mouth to chin.

"Where was Thomas?"

"He waited with the girls until the cops came." He held up his hand. "I already asked. The girls said he was with them the whole time."

When she was jouncing around in the back of his car.

"I came back when the cops got here. Edgar went back out with them. I wanted to go out again, too. But Margaret was near hysterical, not wanting me out of her sight. So I took the girls with me, and Thomas, too. It was a risk. We might have found you"—Lola watched him struggle with the word *dead* and lose the fight—"hurt, and I didn't want the girls to see that. But I knew you didn't trust him, and I didn't want him looking for you alone. Just in case."

By then, she would have been climbing the ladder.

"But." Lola's legs, still none too steady after the hours in bed, gave way. She sank into a chair. She took a moment to appreciate the fact that Charlie had taken her distrust of Thomas seriously—so seriously that his actions had ruled out Thomas as a suspect. She'd been so sure. Whoever had knocked her on the head and put her in the trunk had had to carry her across some distance of desert. Thomas was the right size. But so were a lot of other men. But. But.

"I know it's him," she said one last time. Her shaking voice betrayed the certainty of the words.

"No," said Charlie. "You don't. And give yourself a break. One thing I've learned is to give crime victims time. Right after an incident"—he lapsed into cop talk—"people are typically so traumatized they can't remember details except in bits and pieces. It'll come back to you gradually, more than you'd like it to. You'll feed that information to police, and it will help them."

Stop talking like a cop, Lola wanted to say. Be my husband. She didn't have to say it.

"You know what worries me more than anything?"

She stood and walked to the window and peered through the blinds, drawn against the sun. "That whoever did this is still out there?"

"That, too." He bent his head to hers. His lips moved against the tangle of her hair. "You were doing so well. Getting back to your old self. Kicking ass. Being obnoxious."

Lola leaned into his embrace. "I'm not obnoxious."

"Yes, you are. When you're onto something, you're like a runaway horse. Nothing can stop you. Don't lose that again."

Lola thought back to the hot darkness of the car trunk, the blind swaying trip up the ladder. The gun barrel grinding its perfect circle into the soft flesh beneath her jaw.

"I just want to go home." The words slipped unbidden, truer than any she'd ever spoken. She braced herself for his disappointment. But he only tightened his embrace, rocking her like a child.

"If that's what you want, you've got it. Now that we've got Bub back, there's no reason not to. You can keep in touch with the cops by phone. I want to go to the meeting. Eddie asked me to sit in. Said maybe that, because I'm not from here, I'd pick up on something that everyone else has missed. But we can pack the truck ahead of time so we can leave right afterward."

"No!" Maybe Thomas wasn't the bomber—although Lola wasn't prepared to accept that. But the meeting was still a target. "Surely you can see that."

"Lola, every tribal cop, every state trooper, every sheriff's deputy, every game warden, for God's sake, is going to be at that meeting. On the entire Navajo Nation, that meeting is the safest place we can be."

FORTY-SIX

ONCE AGAIN, A STANDING-ROOM-ONLY meeting, the best seats reserved for elders. Even Betty Begay was there, pale and shrunken, helped to her seat by a well-dressed woman Lola recognized from the photo in the hogan as her daughter.

Cops from various agencies, just as Charlie had promised, lined the walls and manned the metal detectors set up at all of the entrances to the gym. Lola's theory about Thomas might have fallen flat, but the authorities weren't taking any chances with the meeting, not with the bomber still at large. In the press corral, reporters tried to worm between the bulky TV cameras that had appropriated much of the first row, blocking the view for hapless latecomers. Good luck, Lola thought. She'd long had a theory that cameramen spent their downtime playing rugby, so adept were they with rough elbow jabs and toe-crushing missteps. "Oh, was that your foot?" Not apologizing, not ever.

Lola saw Thomas across the room. She stiffened. His gaze flicked her way and slid past. Coward, she thought.

"Ow, Mommy." She sat between the girls, holding their hands. She loosened her grip, hoping Juliana hadn't seen Thomas. Too late. Juliana jumped to her feet and waved. "Over here!"

Lola was glad when Thomas opted to stay put. She didn't trust herself not to kill him in front of a roomful of witnesses. Okay, killing him might have been an overreaction. Punch him, maybe. Right in his smug, not-in-jail face. She remained certain that somehow, he was involved. Maybe he had an accomplice. And with that thought, the memories—kept at bay by the night's sleeping pill/painkiller cocktail—asserted themselves yet again, circling her like feral creatures. She closed her eyes and tried to concentrate on the fact of *home*. The truck sat parked in the shade a couple of blocks away, windows cranked down, Bub snoozing in the front seat, his filled water dish on the floor. The gas tank was full, their duffel bags stacked atop one another next to Margaret's seat in the back. They'd be in the truck within the hour, Lola told herself, speeding home. For once, the thought of Charlie's balls-to-the-wall style of driving appealed to her.

Then she factored in Indian time and revised her estimate to two hours. Or even three. As impatient as she was to hit the road, she relished the idea of the Conrad Coal honchos fidgeting, looking at their chunky status watches, wondering about the apparent lack of urgency for the matter that had pulled them away from their Very Important Jobs.

This meeting involved a level of brass far shinier than that of Kerns. Given that one of their own, or at least his house, had been attacked, Kerns's overlords were on hand to try to soothe the restive crowd filling the gym. Lola had seen them earlier, three well-fed men in the inevitable suits, heading through the halls toward the classroom where Kerns and Edgar, with Charlie sitting in as a courtesy, would brief them on the most recent developments. Naomi would listen in as part of a tribal delegation. She'd swished out of the house that morning armored in a suit of her own, the skirt's linen pleats miraculously wrinkle-free, her legs gleaming in nylons, slender feet encased in pumps of buttery black leather that matched the briefcase swinging from her manicured hand. Just looking at her had made Lola's legs and feet itch. Her own wardrobe may have been short on style, if not lacking it entirely, but at least it allowed her to move in comfort.

She wondered how the executives would spin things when they came to the gym for their public presentation. Maybe, with more finesse than Kerns, they'd try to pin the blame on the tribe, all the while thankful that the bombings would give them an excuse to shut down a failing operation. The company might cut its losses if it were seen as shuttering the mine under threat of ecoterrorism, doing the responsible thing to protect its employees. That was the theory Lola had espoused to the cops and the FBI. They had, she'd noted with satisfaction, given it more credence than Charlie. Which didn't mean they'd bought it entirely.

"Mines fail all the time," one of them told her. "The gold, or silver, or coal—eventually it runs out. It's the nature of the business. You're from Montana. Ever been to Butte?"

Lola had, in fact, visited the city whose copper mine had once been known as the Richest Hill on Earth, and whose frenetic extraction operations had made it one of the biggest cities west of the Mississippi, drawing people from around the world desperate for the high wages that accompanied the dangerous and often deadly work of prying the copper free from the surrounding granite. But the mine finally went bust and Butte was now a fraction of its former size, its once-bustling streets empty but for windblown trash, the grand brick buildings moldering into decay. Now the only thing "biggest" about Butte was the toxic waste site in an old mining pit gouged into the side of a hill above town, its slowly rising waters owing their ghastly shade of green to a mix of heavy metals.

Butte in its heyday had featured death aplenty, with recalcitrant unions eternally at war with moguls whose gimlet gaze focused on profits, profits, profits, and damn those troublemakers in the way. But once the copper was exhausted, they'd simply pulled up stakes and moved elsewhere. Lola's mind ticked along, likening that situation to the one at hand. Apples and oranges, she told herself. Copper versus coal, 1900s versus the new millennium. Still. While it made sense for Conrad Coal to seize upon the face-saving opportunity for closing the mine due to the attacks, it made no sense whatsoever for anyone from the company to have instigated them. Which left her … "Square One," she murmured.

Yet again, she ran the possibilities.

———

Rule out Thomas, she commanded herself, even as her instincts balked. Cross him off the list and see who rises to the top.

Edgar … even though the reluctant, logical part of her brain told her it was just because she didn't like the man. Edgar had so transparently wanted her gone. But no matter how she took it into her hands and twisted and turned it, looking at it from every angle, Edgar's objections had been to her, not to the mine. Hurting the mine, after all, would hurt his own livelihood. Unless going after the mine was a twisted way to win Naomi's approval.

Lola rubbed the back of her head, still tender and swollen from the blow that had knocked her out. But the pain was between her eyes, the product of too many things making too little sense. Too many *buts*, she thought. She remembered the shade house conversation in which

Edgar had revealed that Naomi had pushed him to work for the mine. "Keep your enemies close," he said Naomi had advised him.

Then they'd argued idly about how the saying went: Was it friends close and enemies closer? Or the other way around? "Friends closer," Naomi had insisted with a Mona Lisa smile.

Naomi. Lola dutifully ran through the reasons even as she mentally checked Naomi off her list yet again. Motive: Sure—the mesa. Means: None that particularly distinguished her from the next person. Anyone could learn the basics of bomb making in just a few hours on the Internet, Lola knew. Successfully building one was an entirely different proposition. Besides, the person who'd accosted her in Antelope Canyon had been male, and the person who'd kidnapped her had been too, she thought. The old reminder, a favorite of editors—*assume makes an ass out of u and me*—nudged at her. She had no idea who'd hit her that night. But the strength required to haul her unconscious body across the desert and into a car required someone who was stronger and bigger than she was, and she wasn't a small woman.

Her suspicions returned insistently to Thomas even in the face of the most convincing evidence of all: Charlie's word. The car had to have been close by, as Thomas's had been. Maybe he did have an accomplice. Maybe he'd knocked her on the head, dragged her into the car, and then turned her over to someone else to take to the ruins while he went back to the house to establish his goddamn alibi, later going back out with Charlie and the girls while Edgar rode with the tribal police.

Naomi, according to Charlie, had stayed home to work the phones. Lola's mind, wandering freely, jerked to a halt. She tried to recall the voice of the person who'd urged her up the ladder. It had been low, throaty, indistinct, as though muffled by a bandana. But the person would have had to be strong enough to haul her out of the trunk. Lola's brain snagged on another memory. The person had loosened her bonds while she was still in the trunk. She'd climbed out by herself. And the person had never touched her with anything other than the gun. She had no idea whether the person who'd urged her so roughly up the ladder was male or female, short or tall, muscular or frail.

Again, her mind caught upon a detail. The person was strong, had rappelled down the side of the cliff before Lola could even make a futile grab at the rope. She went back over everything the person had said, searching for Naomi's voice, not finding it, seeking any gleanings of information.

There was the person in Antelope Canyon, the person she remained sure was Thomas. What had he said?

It will get worse.

Well, it hadn't, not really. Kerns's house was gone, but no one had died. And whoever had kidnapped her hadn't killed her. It seemed like they'd just wanted her out of the way for a while. But why? Nothing had happened while she was up there. And, gratifyingly, the FBI and local authorities had taken her concerns about the meeting seriously, adding the security at the gym. So nothing was likely to happen there, either.

Someone came out of a side door and whispered to one of the elders in the front row. The elder turned to the man next to her, and that man turned to the next, a message flying around the room like a game of telephone: The gathering before the public meeting was taking longer than expected. A few more minutes. Which Lola translated as at least another half hour.

She wished Charlie would come out. He was in there with Kerns and Kerns's bosses, with Edgar and some of the tribal cops, with the tribal president and some council members, and Naomi. Lola's body reacted to the notion before her mind fully grasped it, shoulders hunching as though against a blow, her breath coming fast.

Not the big meeting. The one before it, in a classroom without metal detectors. After all, everyone entering was a known quantity. All the executives of the hated mine in one place, along with Edgar who represented the mine, the tribal cops who investigated the crimes against it, and the tribal president and council members who supported its presence. A target-rich environment, as the saying went. *It will get worse.* Charlie was in there. As was Naomi, flashing that chipped-tooth smile as she'd left the house that morning with her briefcase swinging at the end of her arm, an arm whose blazer disguised its climbing-enhanced biceps. *I taught him. You know how it goes—get kids doing something physical.*

The thought of what that briefcase might contain, the wires and detonator and explosives layered beneath some innocuous papers, propelled Lola out of her seat, deaf to the cries of the girls, ignoring the surprised faces turning her way, shock giving way to annoyance as she shoved past the elders, threw an elbow of her own—hah!—at the cameraman who reached for her shouting, "Hey, what's going on?"

She fled the gym, sprinted down a dark hallway, banged on the classroom door. No time to wait for an answer. Twisted the knob, thankful that it gave. Flung herself into the room, slamming the door behind her, praying it was strong enough to contain a blast within. The room, a lab by the looks of it, was long and narrow—too much space between Lola and the group at the other end. Naomi stood at the head of one of the lab tables, her briefcase resting on its soapstone surface, her fingers at the latch. "Let me just show you—" she was saying. She straightened. "Lola?"

Edgar stood near Naomi, Charlie beside him. The mine guys, the cops, the council members, leaned over the table, waiting for whatever Naomi planned to reveal.

"A bomb," Lola said. Her voice shook. "There's a bomb in her briefcase. Get her away from it. Get yourselves away from it."

"Oh, Lola." Naomi's face went soft and fond. She turned to the rest of the room. "She's been through a terrible ordeal. Still in shock. She should have stayed in the hospital." She looked to the tribal cops. "Maybe you could help her." They began to move toward Lola, even as others stepped away from the table.

"No! Don't let her touch that briefcase!"

Naomi's head shook in slow motion. Her hair swung through the luminous air. Dust motes swirled prettily. Edgar stared at her. Charlie's head jerked. He looked a question toward Lola.

"Yes," she mouthed as the tribal cops closed in. "Really."

Charlie grabbed his brother and flung him aside, then went for Naomi as the room burst into sound and flames.

FORTY-SEVEN

The visiting room chair was plastic, the table steel, the window between Lola and Thomas badly scratched Plexiglas.

He picked up the phone on his side of the window and nodded toward hers. She lifted the receiver. Beside her, Edgar leaned close, his ear at the receiver's side.

They sat about midway down a row of booths, the dividers providing the barest minimum of privacy. Most of the chairs on Lola's side were populated by wives and girlfriends. At least that's what she surmised, given the abundance of special-occasion makeup, hairdos, and clothing, most of which was cut as low and slit as high as prison regulations allowed. Warring perfumes filled the air. Lola wondered if the women expected it to waft through the holes in the telephone receivers.

Most of the men on the other side of the Plexiglas were white and middle-aged, midsections spreading after so long away from the gym, hair finally going to gray after years of discreet touch-ups. Federal prison housed the big shots, the players, the guys whose minions had ended up in some hellhole of a common room in a state prison. Only a few brown faces punctuated the row. Natives, probably, given an inexplicable law that sent tribespeople convicted of felonies on reservations to federal instead of state prisons. Lola wondered if they put the guy who stabbed his cousin in a bar fight in the same cell with the insider trading honcho. Part of her hoped so.

"Hey." Thomas's face was rounder, the scar sunk in the yielding tissue surrounding it. All that starchy prison fare, Lola supposed. His voice, too, was softer than Lola remembered, clear of the asthmatic hitches she remembered. Lola fought an urge to smash the phone receiver against the glass. She said nothing at all.

Thomas tried again. "Thanks for coming to see me. I know Tucson is a long way from where you live."

An understatement, Lola thought. Tucson took the harsh environs of the Navajo Nation and went one better, from near-desert to the real thing, saguaros standing guard like something out of the cartoons she'd watched as a child. "I don't want to be here," she retorted. "I don't want to see you. I'd be happy never to see your face again. I just want to know how this all went down. Oh, and feel free to tell me about all the times you could have stopped it."

"Lola." Edgar's hand fell on her shoulder. Lola jerked away. "Hear him out," Edgar said.

"It's okay. She's right. I could have stopped it. But if I'd said anything, Naomi would have gone to jail. I kept trying to figure out how to tell someone without leading them to her, but I couldn't."

Lola's fingers tightened on the phone. "You didn't want Naomi to go to jail, but you were fine with her killing the elder and the truck driver and my husband—and herself, too. And it could have been even worse."

288

Charlie's last-minute lunge had knocked the briefcase under the table, whose heavy soapstone surface helped deflect the blast. Some council members had suffered grievous wounds, but Charlie and Naomi had been the only two fatalities.

"I didn't know—" Thomas began.

Lola cut him off. "You just said you did."

"No. Not all of it. I didn't know how it was going to end."

She spat the words at him. "How it didn't have to end. If only you'd spoken up. Don't forget. If you'd told someone, your precious Naomi would still be alive."

"Lola, please." Edgar's voice brought her back. She'd been his precious Naomi too, Lola reminded herself.

Thomas's voice burst loud through the receiver. "Nobody was supposed to die! It started with the billboard. Something big and symbolic, just to get their attention. No one was supposed to be out there that day. I set the ... the thing—"

"The bomb, you mean." Lola couldn't help herself.

"I set it down behind the billboard the night before. There was a timer."

"Who made it?"

"She did."

Lola thought of all the times she'd considered Naomi as the bomb-builder and had rejected the thought. Even now, her mind pushed back at the possibility.

"How? It's not like she was some kind of chemistry whiz."

A shadow of a smile twitched at one corner of Thomas's mouth. "The Internet."

"But—" Naomi would have been smart enough not to use her own laptop. Lola thought of all the confiscated computers on the reservation. Thomas supplied the answer.

"Down in Tempe. She'd look stuff up on the law school comput-ers when she went there to teach her class. She bought all the stuff there, too. Went from one store to another, getting a little here, a little there, not just in Tempe, but in the towns along the way." Ad-miration shaded his voice. "You know how she's a good cook? And she does—did—all that sewing?"

Lola glanced sharply at him, wondering if a slam at her own ob-vious lack of ability lay beneath the words. He continued, guileless. "She said it was just like cooking or sewing. Follow the recipe or the pattern, get the proportions right, and it works. She hid everything in the sewing room. She kept pressing the pedal on the sewing ma-chine when she was working on it so it would sound like she was making something to wear."

Lola thought of the old-fashioned skirt that surrounded the sewing machine table, of the late-night whirring that had disguised the assem-blage of explosives while she and Charlie—and Margaret and Juliana, for that matter—lay just feet away on either side of the room. Of the girls, going into the room to retrieve scraps of fabric to weave into Val-entine's mane. Her hand tightened on the receiver. "She could have killed us all," she said to Thomas. "Instead, she killed those people. How'd you square that with your conscience? What about the bomb in the middle of the road that killed the truck driver? The cops said who-ever set that one used a remote control. Who set it off? You or Naomi? Either way, you had to know it would kill someone."

He shook his head. "She said she was just going to blow a big hole in the road leading to the mine. Send another message. She swore to me she didn't mean to kill anyone. She said there was some sort of lag between when she dialed the number on the cellphone. She'd already sent the signal when the truck came along."

"Bullshit."

"Yeah. I thought so too, afterward. But it was too late then." *Ask me anything*, Thomas had written in the identical letters he'd sent to Lola and Edgar, telling them that he'd put their names on his visitors list. *I'll tell you. I owe you that much.*

Some sort of prison twelve-step program, Lola had surmised even as she'd hurried to her laptop to buy a plane ticket and rent a car. She'd arranged for a couple of aunties to come stay with Margaret at the house. If nothing else, the presence of these women, whose soft, large bodies so often shook with the laughter that sprang from an unending series of practical jokes, would likely bring a burst of warmth and cheer to the rooms whose silence echoed the pain of Charlie's loss.

"The threat? The one left on the front step?" she asked now.

Thomas lifted a shoulder. "She must have done that on her own."

"What about Kerns's house? Was that supposed to send a message, too?"

"No. She wanted to kill him. She hated him."

After so many excuses, the bald statement shocked her.

Edgar spoke up again, his voice sandpapery. His skin was gray and sagged loose from his cheekbones and chin. In the months since Lola had last seen him, his slender frame had gone gaunt. His fingers whitened as he pressed them to the glass. It was as though, Lola thought, he wanted to reach through the pane and wrap them around Thomas's neck. She felt the same way herself.

He took the receiver from her. "How do you know she wanted to kill him?" he asked. Still seeking the shred that would tell him it wasn't as bad as he'd thought, that the story Thomas sketched for authorities was somehow untrue. Or, even if only partly true, that there'd be some merciful detail that would spare Naomi from complete responsibility. Maybe Thomas had laid everything on Naomi to save his own skin. Yet here he sat in a federal prison for untold decades to come, put there largely by his own words. He'd admitted complicity immediately. Now something beseeching flitted across his face.

"She asked me about Kerns. Before, I mean. She wanted to know when he left the house in the morning, when he came home. She knew I'd know because my uncle works at the mine."

"Along with half the reservation," Edgar said. "She could have asked anyone."

"She didn't want to raise suspicions."

Lola pulled Edgar's hand from the glass and took the phone back. "And she knew you'd tell her. Even though you knew why she was asking."

Thomas dipped his chin. "Yes," he said simply. "At least, I was pretty sure. So I told her that every Tuesday he and his wife had a standing lunch date at the house. I made a little joke of it, something about their weekly nooner. Even though I knew that his wife and her friends went to Phoenix on that day."

"So when the house blew up, nobody was home," Lola said.

The half-nod. "I thought that was the end of it. She said she wanted to do something so big that the mine would shut down and never come back."

"How'd she get the bomb in their house? My husband was with her all the time at work. 'Providing security.' Damn shame you didn't tell him that he was the one needing security."

Thomas just looked at her.

"You put it there, didn't you? When?"

"I sneaked out of the house in the middle of the night and drove down there. I took the Prius. No engine noise. I used her car a lot when I needed to go somewhere at night." Lola remembered the night Charlie had thought he'd heard a car door. He'd been right.

292

"Who took Bub?" She couldn't look at Edgar. He'd lost his wife; she, her husband. She'd probably insulted both of them by her insistence upon including the dog's disappearance in the list of Naomi's crimes.

"I did that, too," Thomas said. "She told me to, and I did it. She wanted me to scare you off. But I didn't kill him." Again, the imploring look.

"I'll give you that much." Lola spoke past the bile rising in her throat. "And that night I was kidnapped—" She'd read about it once, in the charging documents, but had only skimmed it, tears blurring the words describing the actions that inevitably led to Charlie's death.

Down the row, a guard raised his voice. "Five more minutes." A choked sob came from the chair next to Lola, and she pushed away the bitter thought that at least that woman still had her man, behind bars though he was. She'd have taken Charlie in prison. In a hospital bed. At home in a wheelchair. She'd have taken him any way she could have kept him. And the man sitting on the other side of the glass was a large part of the reason he was gone.

"I just parked the car and left you in the trunk. She did it. She told everyone she was in the house making phone calls, trying to see if anyone had seen or heard anything, but she took my car and drove it to the ruins. She promised me she wouldn't kill you. She kept that promise. At least give her some credit for that."

Lola leapt to her feet, fists pounding the Plexiglas. Thomas jerked back so abruptly he nearly fell from his chair. Lola was dimly aware of Edgar's grasp. "Lola, Lola, stop!"

Footsteps pounded down the row. Guards shoved Edgar aside, took her arms, lifted her away from the window, dragged her down the row, oblivious to her screams. "She should have killed me! I'd have been better off. Goddammit, why didn't you just let her kill me?"

FORTY-EIGHT

THEY SAT, AS THEY had so many times before, in the shade house, their chairs pulled close to the outdoor fireplace, trying to catch the bits of warmth thrown off by the leaping flames.

Lola had followed Edgar back to Gaitero in her rental car. She'd wanted to return immediately to Montana, but Margaret had demanded she bring home a firsthand report on Juliana. Lola had hoped the six-hour drive from Tucson might calm her. Instead, she gave thanks for the car's solitude as she moaned in rage and pain at the sight of the places where she'd spent her last days with Charlie.

In the shade house, she huddled in a down vest. It would have made more sense to visit indoors, but the house felt too personal, too full of memories. There, Lola had fought with Charlie, made up with him, last slept in his arms. And there Edgar had spent all the years of his marriage with Naomi. He lifted his chin toward a bedroll to one side of the fireplace. "Can't sleep back in the house even yet," he said. "I go in, make my meals, shower, and get the hell out of it. Can't wait until somebody takes the damn place off my hands."

A *For Sale* sign, its metallic surface pitted by wind-driven grit, had greeted Lola at the end of the driveway. She wondered again, as she had the first time she'd seen it, how many people on the reservation could afford such a home. Edgar might end up sleeping on the ground all winter long. At least, she thought, the tarantulas would be deep in their hidey-holes throughout the colder months.

A shadow bisected the window's square of golden light. Betty Begay, moving about the kitchen, cleaning up after a simple dinner of mutton stew. She'd moved in after the bombing to help Edgar with Juliana. And her daughter, Edgar told Lola, had taken leave from her job in Salt Lake to join the cobbled-together household. "It was too much for Betty," he said. "She still has the sheep, after all. Her daughter—Loretta's her name—goes up and looks after them during the day, then comes down here in the afternoon when Juliana gets home from school. She stays up there some nights, though. That's where she is now."

"How is Juliana?" Lola chided herself for the stupidity of the question. How could she possibly be, her mother dead, her father a shell, her friend and protector Thomas in prison? The girl had emerged from the house and given Lola a polite bedtime hug before retreating without ever making eye contact. Lola noticed the key chain from Thomas's bookbag dangling from her pocket.

"That key chain is with her twenty-four/seven," Edgar said. "She's like a baby with a blanket. She doesn't know it, but Betty's made some duplicates in case this one—God forbid—gets lost. Betty's even scuffed them up so they don't look new. Think about it. Juliana was worried about Thomas from the beginning. She feels guilty, even though there's no way a nine-year-old could have foreseen how this would go. How's Margaret?"

Shattered, Lola thought. Just as she herself was. But at least she and Margaret weren't dealing both with loss and with the knowledge that the person they'd loved had destroyed so many other lives—not accidentally, like Thomas did, but with months of cold, deliberate planning. Lola tried, as she had so many times before, to imagine Naomi's thought process. Couldn't.

"Well?"

Lola hadn't considered that Edgar's question was anything more than rote. She dredged around for an answer. "She doesn't talk about it. Ever."

"Counseling?"

"You're kidding, right?" They shared a grimace of acknowledgment at the lack of luxuries like grief counselors in the vast rural stretches of western Indian reservations.

"Seriously," he persisted. "Great Falls isn't that far away. There's got to be somebody there. Under the circumstances, it's worth the drive."

"Seriously, we tried. It didn't take."

The counselor had admitted defeat after the insurance-allotted six sessions with Margaret, who responded to each question, each proffered coloring book or toy, with silence and a blank stare, showing enthusiasm only when the clock ticked past the final minute of the prescribed fifty, at which point she hurtled from her chair toward the door, flinging a "bye" over her shoulder.

"Bye," the counselor told Lola. "That's all she's ever said to me." She counted off on her fingers. "Bye. Bye. Bye. Bye. Bye. Bye. I hate to think what each of those words cost. What about you?" she'd asked. "How's it going with your own counseling?"

Lola lifted her hand. "Bye," she said.

She herself had endured only a single session, one that she'd entered braced for an unbearable conversation about Charlie, and fled when the counselor took the discussion well beyond that. "You're the walking definition of PTSD," he'd said after fifteen minutes of questions. "Your husband's death, your best friend's death, your own history for putting yourself in danger, your time in war zones…"

"They didn't die." Lola was on her feet, already edging toward the door.

"Excuse me?" The counselor rearranged his face, no doubt adjusting to the fact that his client appeared delusional as well as traumatized.

"They were murdered. And I don't 'put myself' in danger. I do stories. Sometimes they're in bad places. It's part of the job. Would you accuse a cop of putting himself in danger? A soldier? A high-rise window washer?"

"I didn't accuse—"

"Like hell you didn't." But she was already out the door. Maybe he heard "condescending prick" as she left. She didn't really care.

She threw the topic back at Edgar now. "You? There's got to be somebody in Phoenix."

He ran a hand through his pompadour. He'd let it go too long without a trim and it leaned this way and that in unruly bunches, making him look diminished, vulnerable.

"What's the point?" He turned his attention to the fire. Long pieces of silvery, twisted juniper lay near the fireplace, beside a thicker round with a hatchet sunk in it. Edgar extracted the hatchet, picked up a piece of juniper, lay it atop the round, and hacked it into manageable lengths, throwing a few on the fire. The heat released the wood's fragrance, one that Lola would forever associate with this part of the world, the same way the scent of sagebrush meant Montana. Edgar, too, seemed to be thinking of home.

"I thought it would be warmer here in the winter. It was one of the ways I convinced myself to move down here. And it is warmer, temperature-wise. It just doesn't feel that way. Something about all this naked rock. Back home, the snow covered up all the bareness. Made it easier, somehow."

Lola blew on her fingers and held them toward the fire. "Why'd you come here? I mean, beyond Juliana. You could have been like every other couple who shared custody. You didn't have to marry her." Edgar could have returned to his home reservation. And even though he and Naomi had worked out their differences, they hadn't wed until well after Juliana's birth, much like Lola and Charlie themselves. If she hadn't had Margaret, Lola thought—as she had every day, every hour since the explosion—there'd have been no reason to marry Charlie, and there'd be none of the agony that had dug its claws into her soul in the instant of his death and refused to release her.

"I married that woman because I loved her. I couldn't imagine life without her. Why'd you stay in Montana? The way Charlie tells it, you could have gone anywhere."

Margaret, Lola wanted to say. But Margaret's existence had been well in the future when, thanks to Charlie's persistence, she'd opted for life as a small-town newspaper reporter rather than stick with the Baltimore paper.

"I loved him. But I didn't love him enough," she said. "Look how things worked out here. When the bombings started ramping up, he had reservations about staying. But I wanted to know what was going on. I should have listened to him. Somebody else would have figured it out."

Edgar stabbed at the fire with another stick. Sparks rose up like stars. Some landed on Lola's jeans. She brushed at them, welcoming their pinprick stings.

Edgar dropped the stick with a clatter. "Or maybe even more people would have died. I loved Naomi enough not to say anything, and I lost her anyway."

The fire popped. Another starburst arose, shooting larger embers their way. One landed on Lola's knee, burning fast through fabric to bare flesh. She watched it wink out and die.

"Hey, Lola, hey! Careful!" Edgar knocked the bit of charcoal away. "You're going to want to clean that, put some salve in it. I'll ask Betty for some." He started to rise from his chair.

Lola put up her hand. "Wait. What did you say?"

His forehead creased. "That you'll need some salve."

"Before that." Lola could barely hear her own words over the triphammer thud in her chest. "About Naomi. You loved her enough not to say anything."

Edgar sank back into his seat and looked everywhere but at Lola.

"You knew," she said.

"I had an idea. She and Thomas had their heads together a lot. I thought maybe they were having an affair. And for all I know, they were. She's capable of that, especially if it meant she could get him to do whatever she wanted. Just like she got me to work for the coal company. Because it served her purposes."

Lola pulled the edges of blackened fabric away from the burn. A blister bubbled. "If you'd told someone. Anyone. Even if you didn't know for sure. You could have told Charlie. You could have told me." *And Charlie would still be alive.* She couldn't bring herself to say the words aloud. Naomi would still be alive, too. But she didn't give a damn about Naomi, beyond her fervent wish that the woman lay in an uneasy grave.

"From everything Charlie had told me about you, if I'd said something, you'd just have starting digging even harder. And even without saying anything, I was afraid she'd go after you. That day Kerns's place blew up? You'd left the house by yourself. And you'd been talking with Kerns. I was so worried that you'd made some arrangement to interview him at his house."

Lola remembered his look when she'd returned that day. So he'd been relieved. "That explains it."

"Explains what?"

"Never mind."

"I tried to save you. All of you. I was afraid something bad would happen—I never imagined it would be this bad—if you got mixed up in things. I tried to get you to leave."

"You mean—?" Lola thought of the cruel remarks about her marrying an Indian man, the insinuation that she'd never really be part of the family. The surliness, the glares.

He nodded. "Sorry."

"Sorry my ass. At least Thomas owned it." And would spend years of his life in prison. "You're still walking around free. You probably could have been prosecuted as an accessory."

"Free." His tone invested the word with the certainty that he felt anything but. "There was Juliana to think of. The last thing she needed was a dead mother and a father in prison. Besides, prison or not, I'm trapped here."

"You could bring Juliana to Montana," Lola said. "She's half Blackfeet, after all. Or close enough."

"Not nearly close enough."

Lola remembered that like so many Indian people, Charlie and Edgar had enough white ancestors to dilute the crucial blood quantum that dictated tribal enrollment. They qualified, as had their children—just—but Juliana was more Navajo than anything, and besides, except for the few short months the girl had spent with Charlie as a

300

toddler, she'd lived her whole life on the Navajo Nation. "I can't disrupt her life any more than it already has been," Edgar said.

An immense weariness settled upon Lola, pressing her back into the chair, defeating her impulse to scream at him, to point out the obvious—that he was still sleeping in his own bed, or at least a bedroll on his own property, and still able to go where he wanted, spew any old kind of bullshit that came into his mind, while still collecting his hefty paycheck.

Against all odds, the mine had revived. China had been the unlikely savior, its burgeoning middle class creating a voracious demand for coal. Conrad Coal would have to dig deeper for the last of the reserves beneath the mesa, but the astronomical prices being paid by the Chinese would make the cost worthwhile. The reservation's residents would keep their jobs. The mine would continue to suck the land dry, spew choking particulates into the air. Naomi's work—and Charlie's death, along with those of the elder and the truck driver—had been for naught.

Lola said as much.

"He saved me." Edgar's words came in a whisper. "You too."

Lola's throat loosened. Her words shot free. "Wish he hadn't. In both cases."

"But Juliana. Margaret."

There it was. Lola went to bed each night wishing she'd somehow die in her sleep, woke every morning pissed off that she hadn't. And every morning, after that first split-second of grief and resentment, she remembered Margaret. So she couldn't die. Couldn't kill herself, although she'd catalogued all the various opportunities lying so temptingly around the house—knives, ropes, Charlie's backup gun, untouched in its usual spot atop the refrigerator.

She thought of the house, the weathered boards and uneven front porch that belied the solidity of its structure, its imperviousness to the worst weather that Montana could throw at it. Charlie had insulated its walls and attic to bursting, had installed double-paned windows, had put his time and money into how things worked rather than how they looked. Same with the outbuildings and fences. There wasn't much he could do with the scrubby acres that surrounded it, but they were no better or worse than the rest of the nearby land. People ran cattle and the occasional band of sheep, and the money Charlie made from leasing his land to surrounding ranches supplemented his sheriff's salary, as it now would bolster Lola's considerably more slender earnings from the *Daily Express*.

The place was hers now—he'd taken care of that, writing a will the day after they'd married—and the fact that it was off the reservation kept it free of tribal entanglements. Margaret would continue to get the benefits due her as an enrolled member of the tribe. Charlie was, in his way, still taking care of them. He'd accounted for everything, Lola thought, except for the anguish that had left her this strange husk of herself.

"You're right," she said now to Edgar. "You stay here and take care of yourself. It's what you do best."

Edgar sucked in a breath. A rectangle of light fell across him, crushing whatever he was about to say. Juliana stood in the open door and gave Lola an excuse to turn her back on Edgar.

"I have something for Margaret." The girl held out her hand.

Lola cupped a palm beneath it. The key chain dropped into it, the two-inch square of wool soft and warm against her skin.

"But, Juliana." Wasn't giving away your most precious possessions some sort of danger sign? Lola might have disapproved of psychiatry when applied to herself, but she knew enough to be worried about Juliana.

"She needs it." The girl didn't smile, not exactly, but her expression softened. "Besides, I know that *Shimá* has made more for me."

Lola folded her hand around it and said, as much to herself as to Juliana and Edgar, "I need to get home and take care of my daughter."

And of Bub and Spot and even the chickens, a web of mandatory nurturing both burden and salvation.

Charlie may have met his death in Arizona, but he was buried in Montana within sight of Ninahstako, his beloved Chief Mountain, as requested, and there his spirit would surround her. She got in the car and pointed it north, sending her own battered spirit toward his.

THE END

ACKNOWLEDGMENTS

I'm so grateful to the Midnight Ink team—acquisitions editor Terri Bischoff, who ever so tactfully reins in Lola's excesses; production editor Sandy Sullivan; publicist Katie Mickschl; cover designer Ellen Lawson; production designer Bob Gaul; and copywriter Alisha Bjorklund—and to agent Barbara Braun.

Deepest thanks to University of Montana journalism professor Jason Begay for answering my many, many questions—at least, the ones I knew to ask—about the Navajo Nation. Thanks also to the intrepid Kileen Marshall for sharing her climbing knowledge, and to former Missoula Police Department evidence technician Barb Kelsch Fortunate for walking me through evidence collection. I owe a continuing debt to two critique groups: this year's Creel gathering—Bill Oram, Alex Sakariassen, Camilla Mortensen, Matthew LaPlante, and Steven Paul Dark; and the Badasses—Jamie Raintree, Aimie K. Runyan, Kate Moretti, Andrea Catalano, Orly Konig, Theresa Allen, and Ella Olsen.

My aunt and uncle, Dr. Peter and Anne Piper, who worked for a time at the hospital in Ganado, are owed posthumous thanks. Their stories inspired and informed my repeated trips to the Navajo Nation, both as a journalist and now as a novelist. While Antelope Canyon and Window Rock are among the real places mentioned in this book, others such as the Conrad Coal mine and the town of Gaitero are fictional.

Finally, always, gratitude beyond expression for Scott's unswerving support.

ABOUT THE AUTHOR

Veteran journalist Gwen Florio has covered stories ranging from the shootings at Columbine High School and the trial of Oklahoma City bomber Timothy McVeigh to the glitz of the Miss America pageant and the more practical Miss Navajo contest, whose participants slaughter a sheep. She's reported from Afghanistan, Iraq, and Somalia, as well as Lost Springs, Wyoming (population three). Her journalism has been nominated three times for the Pulitzer Prize and her short fiction for the Pushcart Prize. Learn more at http://gwenflorio.net/.